Acknowledgments

I am grateful to Kristina Anderson, San Francisco artist and bookbinder, for an introduction to the bookmaker's craft. Carol Dawson, writer, and Lenore Coral, librarian at Cornell, refreshed my memories of London in general and Sotheby's in particular. My daughter, Mona Helen Preuss, slogged through old auction catalogues at the library of the University of California and Berkeley. The staff of the rare-book room of the San Francisco Public Library were customarily, anonymously, efficient and helpful. Thanks to them all, and let them be reassured that my mistakes are my own.

—Paul Preuss

ARTHUR C. CLARKE'S

VENUS PRIME

Arthur C. Clarke is the world-renowned author of such science fiction classics as *2001: A Space Odyssey*, for which he shared an Oscar nomination with director Stanley Kubrick, and its popular sequels, *2010: Odyssey Two*, *2061: Odyssey Three*, and *3001: Final Odyssey*; the highly acclaimed *The Songs of Distant Earth*; the bestselling collection of original short stories, *The Sentinel*; and over two dozen other books of fiction and nonfiction. He received the Marconi International Fellowship in 1982. He resides in Sri Lanka, where he continues to write and consult on issues of science, technology, and the future.

PAUL PREUSS

Paul Preuss began his successful writing career after years of producing documentary and television films and writing screenplays. He is the author of thirteen novels, including *Secret Passages* and the near-future thrillers *Core* and *Starfire*. His nonfiction has appeared in *The Washington Post*, the *Los Angeles Times*, *New York Newsday*, and the *San Francisco Chronicle*. Besides writing, he has been a science consultant for several film companies. He lives near San Francisco, California.

ARTHUR C. CLARKE'S

VENUS PRIME

VOLUME I

PAUL PREUSS

ibooks
new york
www.ibooksinc.com

DISTRIBUTED BY SIMON & SCHUSTER, INC.

Introduction

by ARTHUR C. CLARKE

Unlike some authors, I have not generally been given to collaborative work in the science fiction area, especially in regard to my novels which, for the most part, have been written alone. There have been, however, some notable exceptions. In the 1960s, I worked with director Stanley Kubrick on the most realistic SF film done to that time, an ambitious little project called *2001: A Space Odyssey*. Over a decade and a half later, I had another close encounter with a Hollywood director named Peter Hyams, who produced and directed the visually impressive adaptation of my sequel, *2010*.

Both films were rewarding experiences, and I found myself both surprised and delighted by some of the results. Now I find myself once again involved in an intriguing collaborative venture that has evolved from my original story, *Breaking Strain*.

The novella (horrid word!) *Breaking Strain* was written in the summer of 1948, while I was taking my belated degree at King's College, London. My agent, Scott Meredith, then in his early twenties, promptly sold it to *Thrilling Wonder Stories*; it can be more conveniently located in my first collection of stories, *Expedition to Earth* (1954).

Soon after *Breaking Strain* appeared, some perceptive critic remarked that I apparently aspired to be the Kipling of the Spaceways. Even if I was not conscious of it, that was certainly a noble ambition—especially as I never imagined that the dawn of the Space Age was only nine years ahead.

And if I may be allowed to continue the immodest comparison, Kipling made two excellent attempts to being the Clarke of the Air Age; see "With the Night Mail" and "As Easy As ABC." The ABC, incidentally, stands for Aerial Board of Control.

Oh, yes, *Breaking Strain.* The original story is of course now slightly dated, though not as much as I had expected. In any case, that doesn't matter; the kind of situation it describes is one which must have occurred countless times in the past and will be with us—in ever more sophisticated forms—as long as the human race endures.

Indeed, the near-catastrophe of the 1970 Apollo 13 mission presents some very close parallels. I still have hanging up on my wall the first page of the mission summary, on which NASA Administrator Tom Paine has written: "Just as you always said it would be, Arthur."

But the planet Venus, alas, has gone; my friend Brian Aldiss neatly summed up our sense of loss in the title of his anthology *Farewell, Fantastic Venus . . .*

Where are the great rivers and seas, home of gigantic monsters that could provide a worthy challenge to heroes in the Edgar Rice Burroughs mold? (Yes, ERB made several visits there, when Mars got boring.) Gone with the thousand-degree-Farenheit wind of sulphuric acid vapor . . .

Yet all is not lost. Though no human beings may ever walk the surface of Venus as it is today, in a few centuries—or millennia—we may refashion the planet nearer to the heart's desire. The beautiful Evening Star may become the twin of Earth that we once thought it to be, and the remote successors of *Star Queen* will ply the spaceways between the worlds.

Paul Preuss, who knows about all these things, has cleverly updated my old tale and introduced some elements of which I never dreamed (though I'm amazed to see that *The Seven Pillars of Wisdom* was in the original; when I read the new text, I thought that was Paul's invention). Although I deplore the fact that crime stories have such a universal attraction, I suppose that somebody will still be trying to make a dishonest buck selling life insurance the day before the Universe collapses into the final Black Hole.

It is also an interesting challenge combining the two genres of crime and science fiction, especially as some experts have claimed that it's impossible. (My sole contribution here is "Trouble with Time"; and though I hate to say so, Isaac What's-His-Name managed it superbly in his *Caves of Steel* series.)

Now it's Paul's turn. I think he's done a pretty good job.

—Arthur C. Clarke
Columbo, Sri Lanka

PART ONE

THE FOX
AND THE HEDGEHOG

I

"Does the word Sparta mean anything to you?"

A young woman sat on a spoke-backed chair of varnished pine. Her face was turned to the tall window; her unmarked features were pale in the diffuse light that flooded the white room, reflected from the wintry landscape outside.

Her interrogator fussed with his trim salt-and-pepper beard and peered at her over the top of his spectacles as he waited for an answer. He sat behind a battered oak desk a hundred and fifty years old, a kindly fellow with all the time in the world.

"Of course." In her oval face her brows were wide ink strokes above eyes of liquid brown; beneath her upturned nose her mouth was full, her lips innocent in their delicate, natural pinkness. The unwashed brown hair that lay in lank strands against her cheeks, her shapeless dressing gown, these could not disguise her beauty.

"What does it mean to you?"

"What?"

"The word Sparta, what does that mean to you?"

"Sparta is my name." Still she did not look at him.

"What about the name Linda? Does that mean any-thing to you?"

She shook her head.

"Or how about Ellen?"

She did not respond.

"Do you know who I am?" he asked.

"I don't believe we've met, Doctor." She continued to stare out the window, studying something a great distance away.

"But you do know that I'm a doctor."

She shifted in her chair, glanced around the room, taking in the diplomas, the books, returning her gaze to him with a thin smile. The doctor smiled back. Though in fact they had met every week for the past year, her point was taken—again. Yes, any sane person would know she was in a doctor's office. Her smile faded and she turned back to the window.

"Do you know where you are?"

"No. They brought me here during the night. Usually I'm in . . . the program."

"Where is that?"

"In . . . Maryland."

"What is the name of the program?"

"I . . ." She hesitated. A frown creased her brow.

". . . I can't tell you that."

"Can you remember it?"

Her eyes flashed angrily. "It's not on the white side."

"You mean it's classified?"

"Yes. I can't tell anyone without a Q clearance."

"I have a Q clearance, Linda."

"That is not my name. How do I know you have a clearance? If my father tells me I can talk to you about the program, I will."

He had often told her that her parents were dead. Invariably she greeted the news with disbelief. If he did not repeat it within five or ten minutes, she promptly forgot; if, however, he persisted, trying to persuade her, she became wild with confusion and grief—only to recover her sad calm a few minutes after he relented. He had long since ceased to torture her with temporary horrors.

Of all his patients, she was the one who most excited his frustration and regret. He longed to restore her lost core and he believed he could do it, if her keepers would permit him to.

Frustrated, bored perhaps, he abandoned the script of the interview. "What do you see out there?" he asked.

"Trees. Mountains." Her voice was a longing whisper. "Snow on the ground."

If he were to continue the routine they had established, a routine he remembered but she did not, he would ask her to recount what had happened to her yesterday, and she would recite in great detail events that had occurred over three years ago. He rose abruptly—surprising himself, for he rarely varied his work schedule. "Would you like to go outside?"

She seemed as surprised as he.

The nurses grumbled and fussed over her, bundling her into wool trousers, flannel shirt, scarf, fur-lined leather boots, a thick overcoat of some shiny gray quilted material—a fabulously expensive wardrobe, which she took for granted. She was fully capable of dressing herself, but she often forgot to change her clothes. They found it easier to leave her in her robe and slippers then, pretending to themselves that she was helpless. They helped her now, and she allowed it.

The doctor waited for her outside on the icy steps of the stone veranda, studying the French doors with their peeling frames, the yellow paint pigment turning to powder in the dry, thin air. He was a tall and very round man, made rounder by the bulk of his black Chesterfield coat with its elegant velvet collar. The coat was worth the price of an average dwelling. It was a sign of the compromises he had made.

The girl emerged, urged forward by the nurses, gasping at the sharpness of the air. High on her cheeks two rosy patches bloomed beneath the transparent surface of her blue-white skin. She was neither tall nor unusually slender, but there was a quick unthinking certainty in her movements that reminded him she was a dancer. Among other things.

He and the girl walked on the grounds behind the main building. From this altitude they could see a hundred miles across the patchwork brown and white plains to the east, a desert of overgrazed, farmed-out grit. Not all the white was snow; some was salt. Afternoon sun glinted from the windows of a moving magneplane heading south, too far away to see; ice-welded blades of brown grass crunched under their feet where the sunlight had sublimed the snow cover.

The edge of the lawn was marked by bare cottonwoods planted close together, paralleling an ancient wall of brownstone. The ten-foot electrified fence beyond the wall was almost invisible against the mountainside, which rose abruptly into shadow; higher up, blue drifts of snow persisted beneath squat junipers.

They sat on a bench in sunlight. He brought a chess pad from the pocket of his coat and laid it flat between them. "Would you like to play?"

"Are you any good?" she asked simply.

"Fair. Not as good as you."

"How do you know?"

He hesitated—they had played often—but he was weary of challenging her with the truth. "It was in your file."

"I would like to see that file someday."

"I'm afraid I no longer have access to it," he lied. The file she had in mind was a different file.

The chess pad assigned her the white pieces and she opened swiftly with the Giuco Piano, throwing the doctor off balance with pawn to bishop-three on the fourth move. To give himself time to think he asked, "Is there anything else you would like?"

"Anything else?"

"Is there anything we can do for you?"

"I would like to see my mother and father."

He didn't answer, pondering the board instead. Like most amateurs, he struggled to think two or three moves deep but was unable to hold all the permutations in his mind. Like most masters, she thought in patterns; although at this moment she could no longer recall her opening moves, it didn't matter. Years ago, before her short-term memory had been destroyed, she had stored uncounted patterns.

He pushed the piece-keys and she replied instantly. On her next move one of his bishops was pinned. He smiled ruefully. Another rout in the making. Nevertheless he did his best to stay with her, to give her an interesting game. Until her keepers untied his hands he had little else to give her.

An hour passed—time was nothing to her—before she said "check" for the last time. His queen was long gone, his situation hopeless. "Your game," he said. She smiled, thanked him. He slipped the chess pad into his pocket.

With the pad out of sight, her longing stare returned.

They made a final tour of the wall. The shadows were long and their breath congealed before their faces; overhead the hazy blue sky was crisscrossed with a thousand icy contrails. A nurse met them at the door, but the doctor stayed outside. When he said good-bye the girl looked at him curiously, having forgotten who he was.

Some rekindled spark of rebellion inspired the doctor to key the phonelink. "I want to talk to Laird."

The face on the videoplate was bland and polite.

"Terribly sorry. I'm afraid the director cannot accept unscheduled calls."

"It's personal and urgent. Please tell him that. I'll wait."

"Doctor, believe me, there's simply no way . . ."

He was on the link a long time with one aide after another, finally wringing a promise from the last of them that the director would call him in the morning. These obstinate encounters fanned the rebellious spark, and the doctor was deeply angry when the last connection was cut.

His patient had asked to see her file—the file of which she had been the subject until a year before her arrival at the hospital. He had meant to wait for clearance, but why bother? Laird and the rest of them would be incredulous, but there was no way she could use, or abuse, what she would see: she would forget it almost instantly.

That, after all, was the point of this whole shameful exercise.

He knocked on the door of her upstairs room. She

opened it, still wearing the boots and shirt and trousers she had put on for her walk. "Yes?"

"You asked to see your file."

She studied him. "Did my father send you?"

"No. One of the M.I. staff."

"I'm not allowed to see my file. None of us are."

"An . . . exception has been made in your case. But it's at your discretion. Only if you're interested."

Wordlessly, she followed him down the echoing corridor, down flights of creaking stairs.

The basement room was bright and warm, thickly carpeted, quite unlike the drafty halls and wards of the old sanatorium above. The doctor showed her to a carrel. "I've entered the appropriate code already. I'll be right here if you have any questions." He sat across the narrow aisle, two carrels down, with his back turned to her. He wanted her to feel that she had some privacy, but not to forget that he was present.

She studied the flatscreen on the desk. Then her fingers expertly stroked the hemispheres of the manual input. Alphanumerics appeared on the screen: "WARNING: unauthorized access to this file is punishable by fine and/or imprisonment under the National Security Act." After a few seconds a stylized logo appeared, the image of a fox. That image disappeared, to be replaced by more words and numbers. "Case L. N. 30851005, Specified Aptitude Resource Training and Assessment project. Access by other than authorized Multiple Intelligence personnel is strictly forbidden."

She stroked the input again.

Across the aisle the doctor nervously smoked a cigarette—ancient and hideous vice—while he waited, seeing what she saw on the screen in front of him. The procedures and evaluations would be familiar to her, embedded in long-term memory, engrained there, because so much of what she had learned was not mere information, but was process, performance. . . .

She was reminded of what had become part of her. She had been taught languages—many of them, including her own—by conversing and reading aloud at far beyond the level of vocabulary considered appropriate to her age. She had been taught to perform on the violin and the piano since infancy, since long before the fingers of her hands could stretch to form chords, and in the same way she had been taught dance and gymnastics and horseback riding, by being made to practice incessantly, by having the most expected of her. She had manipulated space-filling images on a computer, and learned drawing and sculpture from masters; she had been immersed in a swirling social matrix in the schoolroom since before she could speak; she had been tutored in set theory, geometry, and algebra from the time she had been able to distinguish among her toes and demonstrate Piagetian conservation. "L. N." had a long number attached to her file name, but she was the first subject of SPARTA, which had been created by her father and mother.

Her parents had tried not to unduly influence the rating of their daughter's achievements. But even where double-blind scoring was impossible, her mastery was evident. Revealed here on the flatscreen, as she had never seen it confirmed before, her excellence was enough to make her weep.

The doctor was immediately at her side. "Is something wrong?" She wiped at her tears and shook her head, but he gently insisted. "It's my job to be of help."

"It's only—I wish *they* could tell me," she said. "Tell me themselves. That I'm doing all right."

He pulled a chair around and sat beside her. "They would if they could, you know. They really can't. Under the circumstances."

She nodded but did not answer. She advanced the file.

How would she respond to what came next? he wondered, and watched with what he hoped was strictly professional curiosity. Her memories terminated abruptly in her seventeenth year. The file did not. She was almost twenty-one now. . . .

She frowned at the screen. "What is that evaluation? 'Cellular programming.' I never studied that. I don't even know what it is."

"Oh?" The doctor leaned forward. "What's the date?"

"You're right." She laughed. "It must be what they're planning for next spring."

"But look, they've already assigned you scores. A whole group."

She laughed again, delighted. "They probably think that's what I *ought* to score."

For him, no surprises after all—and in her mind, no surprises would be permitted. Her immersion in the reality her brain had recreated for her could not be drained by a few numbers on a flatscreen. "They think they know you pretty well," the doctor said dryly.

"Perhaps I'll fool them." She was happy at the prospect.

The file ended abruptly at the conclusion of her standard training, three years ago. On the screen, only the logo of the Multiple Intelligence agency: the fox. The quick brown fox. The fox who knows many things . . .

The doctor observed that her cheerfulness persisted longer than usual, while she stared at that logo. Perhaps it maintained her in a present of some continuity with her past.

"Perhaps you will," he murmured.

Leaving her at the door of her room—she already forgetting him, having already forgotten what they both had seen—he moved his bulk ponderously down the old stairs to his office. The high-ceilinged, drafty brick building, built on the flanks of the Rocky Mountains in the late 19th century as a tuberculosis sanatorium, now two hundred years later well served its role as a private asylum for disturbed members of the families of the modestly well-to-do. The doctor did his best for those who were innocently committed here, but case L. N. 30851005 was quite different, and increasingly absorbed his attention.

On his own flatscreen he called up the clinical file the institution had kept since her arrival. An odd emotion took hold of him then—when decision overtakes a mind, even a normal one, it often happens so quickly it erases the track of its own processes—and the doctor was shaken by a shuddering warmth, the certainty of revealed truth.

He pressed his finger against his ear and keyed his commlink with the sanatorium staff. "I'm concerned that Linda has not been sleeping well this week."

"Really, Doctor?" The nurse was surprised. "Sorry. We haven't noticed anything unusual."

"Well, let's try sodium pentobarbital tonight, shall we? Two hundred milligrams."

The nurse hesitated, then acquiesced. "Certainly, Doctor."

*　　*　　*

He waited until everyone was asleep except the two night nurses. The man would be prowling the corridors, supposedly alert for trouble, actually nursing his own insomnia. The woman would be dozing in front of the videoplate monitors at her station on the main floor.

He nodded to her as he passed by, on his way up the stairs. "I'll just have a look around before I go home." She looked up, belatedly alert.

Everything he needed fitted easily inside his luxurious Chesterfield without appreciably adding to his bulk. He climbed the stairs and moved down the second floor corridor, conscientiously poking his head into every ward and private room.

He came to L. N. 30851005's room and entered. The photogram camera was watching from its invisible position high in the corner; he could keep his back to it, but someone passing in the hall would have a different angle of view, so he casually swung the door half closed behind him.

He bent over her unconscious form, then swiftly turned her head upright. Her respiration was steady and deep. First out of his pocket was a flat CT scope the size of a checkbook. He laid it across her closed eyes; its screen displayed a map of her skull and brain as if they had been sliced through. Digital coordinates appeared in one corner of the screen. He adjusted the CT scope's depth finder until the gray matter of the hippocampus was centered.

He was still bent over her. He drew a long hypodermic from his sleeve, a seemingly primitive instrument frightening in its undisguised purpose. But within the shank of the steel needle nested other needles, needles within needles, graduated in fineness until the slimmest of them was finer than a human hair, invisible. They were needles that possessed a mind of their own. He dipped the tip of the barrel in disinfectant in a small, clear vial. He felt the bridge of her nose, pressed his fingers down to widen her nostrils, then carefully, inexorably—watching its progress on the miniature screen—he shoved the long, telescoping shaft into her brain.

II

The olfactory lobes are perhaps the most atavistic portions of the brain, having evolved in the nervous systems of blind worms that felt their way through the opaque muck of Cambrian seas. To function they must be in close contact with the environment, and so, beneath the bridge of the nose, the brain is almost completely exposed to the outside world. It is a dangerous arrangement. The body's immune system is incompatible with the brain's processes, everywhere sealed out by the blood-brain barrier—except in the nasal passages, where mucous membranes are the brain's only defense, and every winter cold is an all-out struggle against brain disease.

When the defenses are breached, the brain itself feels nothing; the flower of the central nervous system is itself nerveless. The micro-needle that probed past L. N.'s olfactory lobes and into her hippocampus left no internal sensation. It did, however, leave an infection, spreading fast. . . .

*   *   *

Waking late, the woman who thought of herself as Sparta felt an itching sensation high in her nose, beside her right eye.

As recently as yesterday she had been in Maryland, at the project facilities north of the capital. She had gone to bed in the dormitory, wishing she could be in her own room at her parents' home in New York City but accepting the fact that that would be inappropriate under the current circumstances. Everyone had been very good to her here. She should have felt—she tried to feel—*honored* to be where she was.

This morning she was somewhere else. The room was high-ceilinged, layered with a century's accumulation of white enamel, and its tall windows, hung with dusty lace, were fitted with panes of imperfect glass whose pinhole bubbles refocused the sun into golden liquid galaxies. She didn't know where she was, exactly, but that was nothing new. They must have brought her here in the night. She would find her way around, as she had in many other strange places.

She sneezed twice and briefly wondered if she were catching a cold. The stale taste of her mouth unpleasantly grew to dominate her sensations; she could taste what must have been last night's dinner as vividly as if it were in front of her, except that all the flavors were here at once, green beans mingling with custard, a fragment of rice throbbing with odors of gunny sack, crumbs of ground beef stewing in saliva . . . Vaguely apprehended formulas of amines and esters and carbohydrates danced through her mind with a slippery, tickly quality that was familiar although she had no idea what they signified.

She rose quickly from the bed, put on gown and slippers—she merely assumed they were hers—and went off in search of someplace to scrub her teeth. The smell in the drafty hall was overwhelming, wax and urine and ammonia and bile and turpentine—insistent odors and their accompanying, ungraspable mathematical analogues summoning ghosts, the ghosts of vanished supplicants and benefactors, workers and inmates of this building, and their visitors and keepers, everyone who had passed this way for a century. She sneezed again and again, and finally the clamorous stench subsided.

She found the bathroom without any trouble. Peering at herself in the mirror on the wooden cabinet, she was suddenly thrust out of herself—her image appeared to enlarge—until she was staring at an immensely magnified view of her own eye. Dark brown, liquid at its surface, it was an eye of glassy perfection. At the same time she could still see her ordinary reflection in the glass; the giant eye was superimposed upon the familiar face. She closed one eye—she saw only her face. She closed the other—she was staring into the liquid depths of an immense open pupil. The blackness within was unfathomable.

Her right eye seemed to have something . . . wrong? . . . with it.

She blinked a couple of times and the double exposure vanished. Her face was itself. Again it occurred to her to brush her teeth. After several monotonous minutes the vibrating brush massaged her into dreaminess. . . .

The helicopter made a loud thrumming outside, soundly rattling the windows as it landed on the lawn. The staff scurried hurriedly about; the unexpected arrival of a helicopter generally meant an inspection.

When the doctor came upstairs from his apartment he

found one of the director's aides waiting in his office. The doctor was bothered but tried not to show it.

"We promised you the director would get back to you," said the aide. He was a small fellow and scrupulously polite, with bright orange hair curled tightly against his skull.

"I thought you were still at Fort Meade."

"The director asked me to deliver his message personally."

"Surely he could have called."

"The director requests that you leave with me and come to headquarters. Right away, I'm afraid."

"That's impossible." The doctor sat down, tensely upright in his old wooden armchair.

"Quite." The aide sighed. "Which is why the phone just wouldn't do, you see." The orange-haired fellow was still wearing his camel's hair overcoat and a Peruvian wool scarf around his neck, bright orange; his shoes were hightops of some shiny orange leather. All organics, flaunting his high salary. Carefully he opened the coat and removed a .38 caliber Colt Aetherweight with a four-inch suppressor from the open holster under his armpit. He was a symphony in orange. The pistol was of dull blue steel. He leveled it at the doctor's ample belly. "Do please come with me now."

On her way back to her room, Sparta felt a pain in her left ear, so fierce it made her stumble and lean against the plaster wall. *Buzz and moan of sixty-cycle current through lath and plaster walls, clatter of pots washing in the kitchen, groans of an old woman*—the old woman in 206, Sparta realized, without knowing how she knew there was an old woman in 206—*other rooms, other noises, two men talking somewhere, voices that seemed familiar*—

* * *

The doctor hesitated. He was not really surprised, but the game was moving faster than he had hoped. "Let's say . . ." He swallowed once, and went on, "that I don't come with you." He had the feeling that this was happening to someone else, and wished that were true.

"Doctor . . ." The orange man shook his head once, ruefully. "The staff here is utterly loyal. Whatever passes between you and me will never be discussed outside this room, I assure you."

The doctor stood then and moved slowly to the door. The orange man stood at the same time, never taking his eyes from the doctor, managing to seem deferential even while he kept the long barrel of the Colt, hardly wavering, aimed at the fork of the doctor's wishbone.

The doctor took his Chesterfield from the coat rack and, hauling it on, got himself tangled with his scarf.

The orange man smiled sympathetically and said, "Sorry," indicating that had circumstances permitted he would have lent a hand. Finally the doctor pulled himself into the coat. He glanced backward; his eyes were wet and he was trembling, his face contorted with fear.

"After you, please," said the orange man, amiably.

The doctor plucked at the doorknob, jerked the door open, stepped into the hall—stumbling against the sill in what seemed imminent panic. As he went to one knee the orange man came forward with his left hand outstretched, contempt curling his smile. "Really, there's nothing to be so upset . . ."

But as the hand came toward him the doctor erupted from his crouch, pinned the dapper orange man against the door frame with a massive shoulder, thrust the fist with the gun in it high to the side. The doctor's right hand came up swiftly with brutal force, brushing aside the man's flailing left, pushing up hard under his breastbone.

"Aaahhh . . . ?" It was no scream, but a surprised gasp, rising on a note of anxiety. The orange man lowered his startled eyes to his midriff. The barrel of an outsized hypodermic needle, still gripped in the doctor's fist, protruded from the camel's hair coat at the level of his diaphragm.

No blood showed. The bleeding was internal.

The orange man was not dead yet, not nearly dead. His coat was thick and the shaft of the hypodermic too short to reach his heart. The telescoping shafts within it were still thrusting, seeking his heart muscle when he twisted his right wrist and brought the barrel of the Colt to bear, pulled the trigger spasmodically—

The *phttt, phttt, phttt, phttt* of the silenced weapon howled like a rocket launcher in Sparta's painfully sensitive ear. She recoiled and stumbled down the hall toward her room, her head ringing with the screams and agonized gasps, the tremor of running feet on the floor below shaking her like an earthquake.

Into her mind like a slide flashed on a screen came an image to match one of the voices she'd heard—that of a little man who always dressed in expensive clothes that were too loud, a man with curly orange hair, a man she knew she disliked and feared. With the conscious formation of that image, the amplified sounds vanished.

By now the other inmates were wandering bewildered in the hall, clinging to the walls, for even ordinary hearing was enough to apprehend the commotion downstairs. In her room Sparta tore off her nightgown and quickly dressed in the warmest clothes she could find in the unfamiliar closet, clothes she didn't really recognize but that were obviously her own. For reasons her memory would not reveal, she knew she must flee.

The doctor's body lay face up across the sill, blood pooling under his head. Next to him the orange man was writhing on the floor, plucking at the thing in his midriff. "Help me, help me!" he gasped to the nurses who were already trying their fumbling best to help him. A woman in a pilot's uniform thrust the nurses aside and bent to catch his words, but a sudden hooting of sirens filled the air. "After her! Take her..." he gasped at the pilot, then tried to shove her out of the way. He screeched in pain—the hypodermic had come out in his hand, but not all of it—"Take her to the director!" Then his voice rose in a terrified howl—"Oh, help me, help me"—as the questing hair-fine remnant of the needle pierced and paralyzed his heart.

A nurse slammed into L. N.'s room and found it deserted. One side of the bed had collapsed on the floor. The window sash had been thrust up and the yellowing lace curtains were stirring in the frigid outside air—an iron bar was thrust like a spear through the screen of heavy wire that covered the outside of the window, twisting it aside. The iron bar in the screen had been part of the bed frame.

The nurse rushed to the window as the rising pitch of twin turbine engines reached a near-supersonic shriek. Black against the frozen brown grass of the lawn below, a sleek shape ascended and hovered, a viperlike snout quested this way and that under the *thump, thump* of counter-rotating rotors.

The pilot stumbled into the room, holding a drawn pistol; she shoved the nurse away from the window. Below, the black tactical helicopter rose another couple of meters, leaned forward, and skimmed off over the fence between two poplars, hugging the ground.

"Damm it!" The pilot watched in disbelief, not bothering to waste any rounds on the armored machine. "Who the hell is in that thing?"

"She is," said the nurse.

"Who the hell is *she*?"

"The one we were hiding here. The one he wanted you to take to the director."

The pilot stared after the helicopter until it dropped into an arroyo beyond the highway and failed to reappear. She swore and turned away.

Sparta had no clear idea what she was doing. The irregular frozen ground was racing past a meter or two beneath the skids, the arroyo's low mud and gravel walls swaying too close to the whirling tips of the blades as she played with the stick and pedals. She dug up gravel with a skid: the machine lurched, declined to flip over, flew on.

A moving map of the terrain was displayed in space in front of Sparta, holographically superimposed upon the reality she saw through the windscreen. Just now she was flying uphill—the interstate magneplane tracks she had crossed before finding the arroyo now reappeared in front of her, carried on a steel trestle, barring her path. She flew under the trestle. The howl of the aircraft's engines echoed for a split second, and one rotor rang sharp and clear from nicking a steel pylon.

The arroyo narrowed and its walls grew higher; it had been cut—languidly, over centuries—into an alluvial fan from the uplifted mountains ahead, and there ahead the gorge through which the eroding waters flowed loomed abruptly, a gash in the red rock as acute as a gun sight.

She was still flying by hand, and she felt more confident with every passing second she stayed in the air. She contemplated her ability to handle a piece of complicated machinery she could not remember ever having seen before—knowing what it was for without thinking about it, knowing the logic of it, knowing the particular layout of its controls and instruments and the capabilities of its brainy subsystems.

She reasoned that she had practiced in it. Knowing this, she reasoned that there was some weighty cause for her memory lapse.

She further reasoned that there was cause for her fear of the orange man, the fear that had made her run. She reasoned—because she remembered the entire day (why did that in itself seem strange?) from the moment she had awakened with an urgent desire to brush her teeth, and the accumulated anomalies of that day could not be ignored—that a chunk of her life had been deliberately taken from her and that she was in danger precisely because of that, and that the orange man had had something to do with her missing years and with her present danger.

Sparta—not her real name, it occurred to her, but an identity she had assumed for a sufficient yet still hidden reason—spoke to the helicopter. "Snark, this is L. N. 30851005, do you acknowledge?"

After a momentary pause the helicopter said, "I acknowledge your command."

"Westerly heading, minimum altitude and maximum ground speed consistent with evasion protocols. On auto, please."

"Auto confirmed."

Flatiron walls of red Jurassic sandstone loomed and flashed by on either side of the ship. A streambed of tumbled granite boulders mounted in irregular stairsteps up the rapidly ascending gorge—dry now but for patches of snow, it would be an intermittent torrent during the storms of late summer. One moment the ship was brushing the bare pink branches of tangled willows in the streambed, the next it was flying almost straight up the mountainside, dodging leaning ponderosas and overhangs of basaltic cliff, until suddenly the gorge narrowed to a shallow ravine in a forest of pines, and the mountain flattened into meadowland dotted with stands of aspen.

Sparta had adjusted the scale of the terrain-matching projection that unscrolled in front of her and now studied it, searching the image until she found the topography she needed. "Snark, proceed to forty degrees north, one hundred and five degrees, forty minutes, twenty seconds west."

"Forty north, one-oh-five, forty, twenty west confirmed." The helicopter slowed suddenly and hesitated at the edge of the aspen woods, its snout quivering as if sniffing for a trail.

A moment later the ship streaked across the open, snowy flat, toward the range of distant, much higher peaks that glistened in the sun.

"We have visual acquisition."

On a videoplate screen in a basement room fifteen hundred miles to the east, a small group of men and women watched the helicopter racing over the ground, its sharp, highly magnified image observed from a satellite four hundred miles above it.

"Why isn't she using evasion protocols?"

"Maybe she doesn't know how."

"She knows how to *fly* the thing." The speaker was a man in his fifties with silver-gray hair clipped close to his scalp. He wore a dark-gray wool suit and patternless gray silk tie over a light-gray cotton shirt; it was business attire, but it might as well have been a military uniform.

The man's outburst was an unanswerable accusation; he got no reply but a nervous shifting of feet.

A woman touched his sleeve, caught his eye, jerked her chin. They stepped into the shadows of the control room, away from the others. "What is it?" he rasped.

"If McPhee actually did restore her short-term memory using synthetic-cellular implant, she may be accessing skills she acquired before intervention," she whispered. She was a handsome woman, as clipped and gray and rigid as he was, her dark eyes pools of shadow in the dim room.

"You led me to believe she'd already forgotten every-thing she saw or did for the last three years," he said petulantly, straining to keep his voice down.

"The permanence—that is, the degree—of retroactive amnesia due to loss of short-term memory is often unpre-dictable . . ."

"Why am I learning this *now?*" he snarled, loud enough to make heads turn.

". . . except that, as ever, we can be completely confi-dent that she will never remember anything that occurred *after* the intervention." The gray woman paused. "Until the reintervention. Before today, that is."

The two of them fell silent, and for a moment no one in the dark room spoke. They all studied the helicopter, which was fleeing its own shadow over snowy hummocks, over frozen ponds, among pines and aspens, down steep defiles, a darting dragonfly with its twin interlocking rotors fluttering like membranous wings in the crosshairs of the tracking satellite, but with a more evident purpose to its flight.

The image stuttered momentarily, then steadied at a slightly different angle, as a new satellite took over the tracking task.

"Mr. Laird," said the tracking operator, "I don't know if this is significant. . . ."

"Let's have it," said the gray man.

"The target has been gradually turning counterclockwise for the past two minutes. It is now on a southeasterly heading."

"She's lost," someone—an enthusiastic aide—volunteered. "She's flying blind and she doesn't know which way she's going."

The gray man ignored him. "Give me the whole sector."

The image on the screen immediately widened to show the Great Plains surging like a frozen ocean against the Front Range, the cities beached there like flotsam: Cheyenne, Denver, Colorado Springs, fused by their suburbs into a single threadlike agglomeration. The helicopter was microscopic, invisible at this scale, although its position was still clearly marked by the centered crosshairs.

"The target appears to be holding steady on course," said the operator.

"Dammit, she's heading straight for Space Command," said the gray man. He stared bitterly at the gray woman.

"Seeking sanctuary?" she said mildly.

"We've got to shoot it down," blurted the same enthusiastic aide, whose enthusiasm had been converted to panic.

"With what?" the gray man inquired. "The only armed

vehicle we own within five hundred miles of her position is the one she's flying." He turned to the woman, hissing the words but hardly bothering to keep them inaudible. "If only I'd never listened to your clever explanations . . ." He bit off the sentence, snapping his teeth in his fury, and bent over the console. "She's not using evasion protocols. What's the chance of jamming her?"

"We can't jam the target's navigation and control circuits, sir. They're shielded against everything."

"Outgoing transmissions?"

"We'd have a good chance there."

"Do it right away."

"Sir, that's not exactly a surgically precise operation. Air Defense Command will pop a gasket."

"Do it now. I'll take care of ADC." He turned to an aide. "A blackline to Commander in Chief, NORAD. Let me see the profile before you put it through."

The aide handed him a phonelink. "CINCNORAD is a General Lime, sir. His profile's coming on screen B."

The gray man spoke into the phonelink and waited, quickly reading the general's psychological profile off the little flatscreen, planning his spiel as he shifted his attention to the big screen.

The spy satellite's crosshairs moved inexorably toward Air Force Space Command headquarters east of Colorado Springs. A curt voice came on the line, and the gray man quickly replied. "General, Bill Laird here"—his voice was warm, confiding, deferential—"I'm very sorry to disturb you, but I have a serious problem and I'm afraid I've let it get out of hand—so much so, in fact, I confess it's become your problem too. Which will explain the EM interference your people are experiencing on combat channels . . ."

*   *   *

The phone conversation drew heavily upon the director's resources of amiability and persuasion. It was not the last call he had to make; General Lime refused to commit to action without confirmation from Laird's superior.

More earnest lies went through the aether, and when the director finally put the phone down he was trembling behind his tight smile. He yanked at the gray woman's sleeve and propelled her back into the shadows. "This program is about to be ended, thanks to you," he said angrily. "And we will have lost years of work. Do you think I can hold my post after this debacle? We'll be lucky to escape prosecution."

"I certainly doubt that the president would . . ."

"*You!* Keep her alive, you said."

"She was magnificent, William. In the early stages. She was a natural adept."

"She *never* committed herself to the Knowledge."

"She's still a child!"

He gave her an angry cough for a reply. He paced about, brooding, then halted, shaking his head. "Right. Time we dissolve our band, disperse into the common herd."

"William . . ."

"Oh, we'll be in touch," he said bitterly. "There will be places in government for both us, I'm sure. But a great deal of reconstruction lies ahead." He knitted his fingers, flexed his arms in his jacket, cracked his knuckles. "That sanatorium will have to go. All of them will have to go. Right now's the time to do it."

The gray woman knew better than to object.

*   *   *

"This bogie's a drone?" The sergeant was incredulous. Efficiently she tapped the coordinates of the approaching helicopter into AARGGS, the anti-aircraft railgun guidance system.

"Story is, it's some kind of experimental ECM ship that went nuts," replied the captain. "Ops says the people who let it loose think it's homing on our ground stations."

Out on the perimeter of the Space Command headquarters base, batteries of TEUCER railguns bobbed and swung on their pedestals.

"Interceptors can't catch it?"

"Sure they could catch it. An F-41 could climb right on top of it, look down, shoot down. You seen any of these new army choppers in action, Sergeant? They can fly about three feet off the ground at six hundred klicks. And what's on the ground between here and the mountains?"

"Oh."

"That's right. Houses, schools, that sort of thing. So it's up to us in perimeter defense."

The sergeant looked at the radar scope. "Well, in about twenty seconds we'll know. It's still coming." She ordered AARGGS to arm even before the captain told her to do so.

The Snark howled across suburban ranch-house rooftops and backyard swimming pools and rock gardens, across wide boulevards and artificial lagoons, lifting loose shingles, shaking the last dead leaves from ornamental aspens, terrifying pedestrians, raising dust, and leaving muddy recirculated lagoon water surging in its wake. The helicopter's antennas were continually broadcasting on all restricted and unrestricted channels as it closed on the base, but it received no reply to its urgent communications. The bare flat ground of the base perimeter swiftly approached. . . .

As the helicopter screamed in over the fences, over the waiting fire trucks and ambulances and police vehicles, some observers noted—and later testified—that the craft did not appear to be aiming for the forest of space-directed radio antennas that were HQ Space Command's most distinctive feature, but instead was headed for the Operations Building, in front of which there was a helipad. It was a fine distinction—much too fine upon which to base a split-second decision.

Three TEUCER hypervelocity missiles leaped into the air as the Snark crossed the perimeter. They were no more than shaped steel rods, dead rounds carrying no explosives, but they impacted with the momentum of meteoroids, of flying bulldozers. Two-tenths of a second after they left the launcher they ripped through the armored helicopter. There was no explosion. The disintegrated aircraft simply scattered itself over the parade ground like a handful of burning confetti. The larger bits of smoking metal rolled away like charred wads of newspaper.

III

Sparta waited among the bare aspens on the edge of the frozen field, waited until the buttery light had faded from the cloud-clotted western sky. Her toes and fingers and earlobes and the tip of her nose were numb, and her stomach was growling. Walking, she hadn't minded the cold, but when she finally had to stand and wait for darkness she'd begun to shiver. Now that darkness had come, she could move in.

She'd garnered valuable information from the Snark before—in that split second when it had paused, hovering motionless inches above the ground, computing new coordinates—she'd jumped clear and sent it on its unprotected way. Precisely where she was. Precisely what day, month, and year it was. That last had come as a shock. Memories had been swarming more thickly with every passing minute, but now she knew that even the most recent of them was more than a year old. And in the hours since she'd jumped, while she'd been trudging through the snow, she'd contemplated the burgeoning strangeness of her sense of herself.

She grasped, viscerally, that in the past hour—even had she not been indulging in self-inspection—her wild and surging sensibilities had started to bring themselves partially under her conscious control; she'd even managed to remember what some of those sensibilities were for . . . and thus she could better modulate the insistent vividness of her senses—taste, smell, hearing, touch. And her remarkably flexible vision.

But those senses were still getting away from her—only sporadically, but then overwhelmingly. The acid sweetness of pine needles fallen upon snow threatened more than once to overcome her with swooning ecstasy. The melting mother-of-pearl of the setting sun more than once sent the visible world a-spinning kaleidoscopically, inside her throbbing brain, in an epiphany of light. She waited out those intoxicating moments, knowing that in the scheme of things they must recur, knowing that when they did she could, with effort, suppress them. Then she pressed on.

She had a much better understanding of the nature of her predicament. She knew it could be fatal if anyone learned of her peculiarities, and equally fatal to put herself in the hands of the authorities, any authorities.

At last it was dark enough to cover her approach. She trudged across the snowy field toward a far cluster of lights where two narrow asphalt roads, recently plowed, formed a T intersection. One of the weather-bleached wooden buildings had a sign hanging from its rusted iron eaves, lit by a single yellow bulb: "BEER. FOOD."

Half a dozen cars were parked in front of the rustic

tavern, sporty cars and all-terrain-vehicles with ski racks on top. She stopped outside and *listened.* . . .

She heard the clink and thump of bottles, a cat whining for its dinner, the creak of wooden chairs and floorboards, a toilet flushing in the back, and over all a surround-sound system cranked up just shy of pain level. Under the music—hoarse energetic anger of a male singer, rolling thunder of a bass line, twined sinuous howls of a synthe-kord doing harmony and three kinds of percussion—she picked out some conversations.

"Rocks and straw," a girl was saying, *"they got a nerve even selling a lift ticket,"* and elsewhere a boy was trying to wheedle college class notes out of his companion. At another location—the bar, she estimated—someone was talking about a remodeling job on a nearby ranch. She listened a moment and tuned in on that one; it sounded the most promising—

". . . and this other dolly, blond hair down to *there,* just standing there staring through me, wearin' nothin' but this little pink piece of transparent silk like you see in those department store ads. But like I wasn't even in the same room."

"Prob'ly on somethin'. They're all on somethin' up there, man. You know that big sensie-mixer they got, that's supposed to be payin' for the place? That guy that runs it's so Z-based all the time, I don't know how he feels *any*thin' . . ."

"But the dollies," said the first voice. "That's what impressed me. I mean, we're walkin' back and forth carryin' about one plank of knotty pine panel per trip, right? And these blond and brunette and red-headed dollies are just sittin' and standin' and lyin' around there. . . ."

"Most of the people who come through here, claim they're goin' up to rent the studio facilities? They're just dealin', man," the second voice confided. "Just buyin' and sellin'..."

Sparta listened until she had what she needed. She let the cacophony fade and turned her attention to the vehicles in the parking lot.

She tuned her vision toward the infrared until she could see warm handprints glowing on the doorhandles, the brightest of them only a few minutes old. She inspected the more recent arrivals. Their occupants were less likely to be leaving soon. She peered into the interior of a mud-spattered two-seater; bright outlines of human bottoms glowed like valentines in both bucket seats. A lap robe bundled on the floor in front of the passenger seat hid another warm object. Sparta hoped it was what she was looking for.

Sparta pulled off her right glove. Chitinous spines slid from beneath her fingernails; gingerly, she worked the probes extending from her index and middle fingers into the sliverport in the door on the passenger side. She sensed the minute tingle of electrons along her conducting polymers: images of numerical patterns danced at the threshold of consciousness; the surface molecules of her probes reprogrammed themselves—all so quickly that only the intention was conscious, not the process. As she withdrew her fingertips the probes retracted. The car door swung open, its lock-and-alarm disarmed.

She pulled her glove on and lifted the lap rug. The object under it, recently handled, was a purse. She removed the registration sliver, then left it as it had been— exactly as it had been, with the lap robe folded precisely as it was folded before, according to the image of it temporarily stored in her memory. She nudged the door closed.

Sparta stomped the snow off her boots on the covered porch and pushed through the ramshackle double doors, to be greeted by a blast of smoky air and badly amplified surround-sound. Most of the small crowd were couples, college kids on the way back from skiing. A few local males, wearing tattered jeans and threadbare plaid flannel shirts over red long-johns, were hanging out at the end of the long mahogany bar. Their eyes fixed on her as she walked boldly toward them.

The carpenter she'd overheard was easy to identify; he was the one wearing a laser-rule in a worn leather holster on his hip. She hitched herself onto the stool beside him and gave him a long, contemptuous stare, her eyes focused slightly behind his head, before turning her eyes to the bartender.

The bartender's curly orange hair startled her. That passed quickly—he also wore a frizzy beard. "What'll it be, lady?"

"Glass of red. You got anything decent to eat? I'm starved."

"Usual autochef stuff."

"Hell . . . cheeseburger, then. Medium. Everything on it. Fries."

The bartender went to the grease-streaked stainless steel console behind the bar and shoved four buttons. He took a glass from the overhead rack and stuck a hose into it, filling it with fizzy wine the color of cranberry juice. On the way back he took the burger and fries from the maw of the steel autochef, holding both plates in his wide right hand, and slid everything onto the bartop in front of Sparta. "Forty-three bucks. Servee-compree."

She handed him the sliver. He recorded the transaction and laid the sliver in front of her. She let it sit there, wondering which of the women in the tavern was buying her dinner.

The bartender, the carpenter, and the other men at the bar had apparently run out of conversation; they all stared at Sparta wordlessly while she ate.

The sensations of smelling, tasting, chewing, swallowing nearly overloaded her eager internal systems. The curdled fat, the carbonized sugar, already half-digested proteins were at once desperately craved and nauseating in their richness. For a few minutes hunger suppressed revulsion.

Then she was done. But she didn't look up until she had licked the last drop of grease from her fingers.

She peered at the carpenter again, giving him the same cold, lingering stare, ignoring the black-bearded man behind him, who stared at her in pop-eyed fascination.

"I know you from somewhere," the carpenter said.

"I never laid eyes on you before in my life," she said.

"No, I know you. Wasn't you one of them up at Cloud Ranch this mornin'?"

"Don't mention that place to me. I never want to hear that place mentioned in my presence as long as I live."

"So you was up there." He nodded in satisfaction, giving the bartender a significant glance. His bearded buddy also gave the bartender a significant glance, but what it signified was a mystery to them all. The carpenter turned back to Sparta, looking her slowly up and down. "I knew it was you, just from the way you stared at me. 'Course you don't much look the same as you did."

"How good would you look if you'd been walking in

the snow half the day?" She tugged at a strand of her matted brown hair, as if he'd hurt her feelings.

"Nobody willin' to give you a ride out?"

Sparta shrugged and stared straight ahead, pretending to sip the glass of foul wine.

He persisted. "Get in over your head?"

"What are you, a stinking shrink?" she snarled. "I play the fiddle. When somebody hires me to play the fiddle, I expect to play the fiddle, period. How come the only people who make money in this business are creeps?"

"Lady, don't get me wrong." The carpenter ran a hand through his matted blond hair. "I thought everybody around here knew they made a lot more than just *music* sensies up there."

"I'm not from around here."

"Yeah." He sipped thoughtfully at his beer. So did his buddy. "Well . . . sorry." For a while they all stared at their drinks, a school of philosophers deep in contemplation. The bartender absently swiped at the bartop with his rag.

"Where *are* you from?" the carpenter resumed, hopefully.

"Back east," she replied. "And I wish I was back there now. Tell me there's a bus out of here in ten minutes and you'll make my day."

The bearded guy behind the carpenter laughed at that, but the carpenter didn't. "There's no buses through here," he said.

"No surprise."

"Don't get me wrong, but I'm driving down to Boulder tonight. You could get a bus from there."

"Don't get *me* wrong." she said. "I said you'd make my day."

"Sure, lady."

He seemed humble enough, but he was male and naturally he was playing the odds. That was fine with her, as long as she got within reach of civilization.

The carpenter ended up having his van drive them both all the way to the Denver shuttleport, almost a hundred miles away. He gave her no trouble during the seventy-minute ride. He seemed grateful for what little conversation she was willing to give him, and parted from her cheerfully with a firm handshake.

Sparta went into the terminal and threw herself joyfully into the nearest contoured, chrome-and-black-plastic chair in the busy lobby. To her, the noise and the winking neon ads and glaring videoplate billboards, the diffuse green light that bounced off every reflective surface, were sooth.ng. She pulled her quilted coat tight around her, hugging herself, letting fatigue and relief wash over her— she was back, back among crowds of people, with access to transportation and communication and financial services, the whole vast neural network of electronics that knit the country, the world, the colonies of space together. She could get what she wanted without making herself memorable. And for a few minutes she could sit right here in the open and rest, not bothering to hide, confident that nothing about her nondescript appearance would attract the slightest attention.

Her eyes opened to find an airport cop looking down at her suspiciously, his finger poised at his right ear, about to key his commlink. "You been out for half an hour, lady. You need sleep, use the hive in Five." He tapped his ear. "Or you want me to call work-shelter?"

"Goodness, officer. I'm terribly sorry, I didn't realize." She looked past him, startled, in the direction of the flight announcement screen. "Oh, don't tell me I'm going to miss *this* one *too!*" She stood up and dashed for the nearest people-mover headed for the launch pads.

She didn't look back until she was surrounded by other passengers. There was a certain air of glumness about the belt riders, huddled in their festive plastic-and-foil vacation clothes, probably because for most of them the vacation was over; they were headed back to the reservation. She made a discreet show of searching her pockets in distress before stepping off the rolling walkway at the first interchange and heading back toward the waiting area.

She walked straight into the women's room and peered into the mirror. She got a shock. Nondescript wasn't the word for her; she was bedraggled. Her drab brown hair hung in greasy snakes; there were dark circles under her eyes; her boots and pants and the skirts of her coat were splashed with dried red mud to the knee.

No wonder the cop had suspected her of being non-R. He was right, of course—only one agency held her registration—but right for the wrong reasons, and she'd have to do something about those reasons quickly.

She washed her face, splashing it repeatedly with icy water until she was wide awake. Then she left to find the nearest information booth.

She slipped into the booth and peered at the blank flatscreen. Here, on this little flat plate and mounded keyboard, was light-speed access to anyone on Earth or in space who wished to be accessible (access to persons who didn't want to be accessible took a bit longer). Here was access to vast libraries of data (access to protected data took a bit longer). Here were the means of making or securing loans, paying debts, investing, wagering, buying every imaginable kind of legal goods or services, or just giving money away (other kinds of goods, services, and transactions took a bit longer). All that was required of the client was a valid I.D. sliver and sufficient credit in a registered account.

Sparta no longer had the sliver she had stolen, having deliberately dropped it in the snow outside the door of the mountain tavern, for she had no intention of leaving a trail of illicit transactions behind her. But in the intimate privacy of an information booth—the sort of privacy only a place surrounded by crowds could provide—her lack of a sliver was not an immediate concern.

Like the long struggle between people who design armor and people who design armor-piercing projectiles, the long struggle between people who design software and people who want to penetrate it was an endless evolutionary spiral. In these days of the late 21st century, fiddling with open-access programs wasn't easy, even for those with inside knowledge.

Yet it was another of the things Sparta was sure she had been trained for—to what purpose, she could not remember. With fingerprobes thrust deep into the sliverport she was able to bypass the keyboard and taste the flavor of the system directly. . . .

Alas, there are no glittering informationscapes, no pretty crystal structures of data, no glowing nodes of inference and signification. There are no pictures in the electricity—nor in the light—except as encoded, and such pictures as there are must be filtered through crude external analogue devices, steerable beams, glowing phosphors, excited diodes, writhing liquid magnetized suspensions, the raster. But although there are no pictures in the electricity, there are relationships. There are patterns, harmonics, conformations.

Datastreams are numbers, huge numbers of huge numbers, huger numbers of lesser numbers, a virtual infinity of bits. To attempt to visualize even part of the stream is beyond the capacity of any general-purpose system ever evolved. Smell and taste are different. Feel is different. The sense of harmony is different. All are acutely sensitive to pattern, and because there are higher-process analogues of these patterns, it is possible for some people to savor numbers. Calculating prodigies—geniuses, and more frequently *idiots savants*—occur naturally in every age; to create one purposely requires a prodigious grasp of the peculiar neurology of the numerically gifted. So far the task had been accomplished just once.

Sparta didn't even know it. Sparta, like natural calculators, had a particular fascination and facility with prime numbers; unlike natural calculators, her right brain housed artificial neural structures that vastly expanded the range and size of the primes she could manipulate, structures of which she was yet unaware, even as she used them. It was not wholly by coincidence that data encryption systems often depend on keys that are large primes.

Sitting quietly in the Denver information booth, watching the flatscreen, Sparta appeared to be studying the dance of the alphanumerics; the blurring symbols on the screen had no significance, however, for she was questing far beyond the interface, following the sharp tang of a familiar key through the communication networks like a salmon following the trace of its home brook through the labyrinth of ocean—except that Sparta was immobile, and the informational ocean surged through her mind. Sitting still, she swam ever closer to home.

The budgets of the most secret agencies of government are not labeled in public print but are broken up and scattered through the budgets of many other agencies, disguised as insignificant line items, with the funds frequently channeled through transactions with cooperative contractors and commercial bankers. Occasionally the ploy backfires—as when a legate whose colleagues have kept him in the dark inquires loudly and publicly why the defense forces, for example, have paid millions for "helicopter replacement parts" and have only a handful of cheap nuts and bolts to show for it—but generally only a few people know or care what the money is really for, or where it really goes.

The money is electronic, of course, spreadsheet numbers of constantly changing magnitude, transactions tagged in electronic code. Sparta was tracking the routes of one code in particular. Sliding into the memory of the First Tradesmen's Bank of Manhattan through a coded trap door, Sparta's awareness uncovered the golden thread she had been seeking.

The people who had created her had not imagined the playful uses to which she would put her talents.

Here in the information booth it was a simple matter to transfer a modest and reasonable amount, a few hundreds of thousands, from an insignificant line item in her target's budget ("office maintenance and custodial") to a real contractor, to that contractor's real subcontractor, to a well-known phony consultant firm, and now into a cutout loop through the black side of another agency—who would not miss what they had held for only a microsecond flip-flop, but would stop any inquiries cold—and finally through a random cascade of addresses to another, much smaller New York institution, the Great Hook Savings and

Loan, which appealed to her for the naiveté of its pseudo-prime key and whose Manhattan branch thus acquired a new customer without even knowing it—a young woman whose name was . . .

She needed a name, fast, not her real name, not Linda, not L. N., but *Ellen*, and now a last name, *Ellen, Ellen* . . . before the flatscreen dumped her she keyed in the first word that popped into her mind. Her name was Ellen Troy.

Sparta needed the information booth only a few seconds longer, to reserve a seat for Ellen Troy on the next hypersonic ramjet flight from Denver to JFK. The voucher and gate pass slid soundlessly from the printer slot. She withdrew her newly programmed fingernail PIN spines from the sliverport.

Her flight was not until morning. She would walk to the hive in Terminal Building Five, take a cubicle for the rest of the night, wash up, clean her clothes, get some rest. It would have been nice to shop for new clothes, but with the economy as it was, robots doing all the technical stuff and people competing for the rest, the shops in heavily used public places were overcrowded with sales people on duty around the clock. She couldn't buy from machines just yet; she would have to wait until she had managed to secure an ID sliver of her own before she could buy anything, right out in public.

She was confident that the Great Hook Savings and Loan would be more than happy to replace the sliver Ellen Troy had "lost." Their records would show that Miss Troy had been a loyal customer for the past three years.

IV

The plan seemed a good one at first. She wanted to find her parents, or find out what had become of them. Meanwhile she had to survive. She needed an occupation that would help her do both, and before long she found one.

The old United Nations buildings on Manhattan's East River now housed the U.N.'s successor, the Council of Worlds. Beside Earth, the worlds in question were the orbiting space stations and colonized moons and planets of the inner solar system, dominated by shifting coalitions of Earthly nations. The historic U.N. treaties against territorial claims in space were still honored in letter, if not in spirit; like Earth's open oceans, space knew no borders, but its resources went to those who could exploit them.

Among the Council of Worlds' largest bureaucracies was, therefore, the Board of Space Control, formulating and enforcing safety regulations, shipping rates and schedules, customs and passport restrictions, and interplanetary treaties and law. The Space Board had huge data banks, sophisticated forensic laboratories, its own gleaming-white fast ships emblazoned with a diagonal blue band and gold star, and an elite corps of trained and motivated inspectors.

The Space Board also employed thousands of non-elite—technicians and clerks and administrators—scattered among offices on every space station and inhabited body of the solar system but particularly concentrated at Earth Central, near the Council of Worlds headquarters in Manhattan.

Central as it was on the interplanetary scale, the Board's administrative functions were widely dispersed throughout the city. Twenty-one-year-old "Ellen Troy" had no difficulty getting a job with the Space Board, for her credentials were excellent—electronic transcripts from her Queens high school and the Flushing Meadow College of Business, from which she had graduated at age twenty, showed that she had excellent word-and data-processing skills. References from the employer she had worked for the year after her graduation, the now unfortunately defunct Manhattan Air Rights Development Corporation, showed that she had been a model employee. Ellen breezed through the Space Board's qualifying exam and found herself placed exactly where she wanted to be, with access to the largest interlinked computer network in the solar system, protected in her anonymity by a new name and a new appearance (Sparta's hair was no longer brown, her face was no longer gaunt in its beauty, her teeth were no longer hidden by perpetually closed thin lips; instead her full lips were always slightly parted), and further camouflaged by an enormous bureaucracy in which she figured only as another cipher.

Sparta's plan was at once bold and cautious, simple and intricate. She would learn what she could from the Board's vast stores of information. Later, whatever effort it took, she would earn the badge of a Space Board inspector; having achieved that, she would have gained the freedom to act. . . .

In this plan there were only a few minor hitches. She knew now that sometime during her eighteenth year, the first of the three years she could not recall, she had been altered significantly, beyond what was obvious—altered, that is, beyond her enhanced senses of taste, smell, hearing and sight, beyond even the PIN spines under her fingers, the polymer inserts which were already coming into fashion among the more avant-garde rich. (She did what she could to conceal hers, for Ellen Troy was a daughter of the working class.)

These alterations had left their marks inside her body, some of which showed up on routine medical scans. She devised a cover story, not too difficult a task . . . but she further had to learn to control certain extraordinary abilities, some of them obvious, some unexpected, and some that manifested themselves at inconvenient moments. For the most part she no longer tasted what she did not want to taste, heard what she did not want to hear, saw what she did not want to see—at least while she was conscious—but now and then strange sensations overcame her, and she felt urgencies she could not fully bring to awareness.

Meanwhile, life and work went on; a year passed, then two. On a hot and humid August morning Sparta bent close over the papers on her desk, hardcopies of documents and articles she had pored over many times before, none of them secret, all easily available to the public, documenting the innocent beginnings of the SPARTA project. One of them began:

A PROPOSAL submitted to the United States Office of Education for a demonstration project in the development of multiple intelligences.

Introduction

It has frequently been suggested that the brain of the average human being has unrealized potential for growth and learning—potential which is unrealized, that is, in all but a tiny, haphazard minority of individuals we recognize as "geniuses." From time to time educational programs have been suggested which would have as their goal the maximization of this unused intellectual capacity in the developing child. At no time before the present, however, have actual methods of stimulating intellectual growth been precisely identifiable, much less subject to conscious control and application. Claims to the contrary have proven at worst false, at best difficult to verify.

Moreover, the mistaken view persists that intelligence is a single, quantifiable trait, a heritable or even a genetic trait—a view perpetuated by the continued widespread use of long-discredited Intelligence Quotient (IQ) tests by schools and other institutions. This continued use can only be understood as an attempt by administrators to find a convenient (and most probably a self-fulfilling) predictor upon which to base the allocation of resources perceived as scarce. The continued use of the IQ has had a chilling effect on the testing of alternate theories.

The authors of this proposal intend to demonstrate that there are no unidimensional geniuses,
that each individual human being possesses many
intelligences, and that several, perhaps all, of these
intelligences may be nurtured and encouraged to
grow by simple, mindful intervention on the part
of appropriately trained teachers and educational
technicians. . . .

Shaved of its academic fuzz, this document—a draft,
rejected by the government to which it had been submitted, and dating from some years before Sparta herself had
been born—was a fair statement of what Sparta's parents
had set out to do.

They were cognitive scientists, Hungarian immigrants
with a special interest in human development. In their
view an IQ number, lacking inherent meaning, was a label
that blessed some, damned many, and gave easy comfort
to racists. Most pernicious was the peculiar notion that
some mysterious something, reified as IQ, was not only
heritable but fixed, that not even the most beneficial intervention in the growth of the child could increase the
quantity of this magical mental substance, at least not
more than a few insignificant percentage points.

Sparta's parents intended to prove the opposite. But
despite their revolutionary rhetoric, the public and the
granting agencies perceived something old-fashioned
about their up-by-your-bootstraps ideas, and it was several years before support materialized, in the form of a
modest grant from an anonymous donor. Their first subject, as their convictions demanded, was their own young
daughter. Her name was still Linda, then.

Not long after, New York State and then the Ford

Foundation chipped in grants of their own. The SPARTA project got its acronymous name, plus a small staff and several new students. After it had been officially underway for two years, the Science section of the *New York Times* carried a notice:

> Bullish on Fox, Bearish on Hedgehog
>
> Psychologists at the New School for Social Research hope to resolve an argument that goes back at least as far as the 8th century B.C., when the Greek poet Archilochus made the enigmatic statement, "The fox knows many things, but the hedgehog knows one big thing." In recent times the poet's remark has symbolized the debate between those who think intelligences are many—linguistic, bodily, mathematical, social, and so forth—and those who believe intelligence comes as a lump sum, symbolized by an IQ score, which is resistant to change and can probably be blamed on one's genes.
>
> Now comes new evidence from the New School, favoring the fox. . . .

Other articles and stories, in a widening circle of media, glamorized the SPARTA project. The little girl who was its first and for a while its only subject became a star—a mysterious star, whose parents insisted she be kept out of public view; there were no pictures of herself among the chips and clippings on Ellen Troy's desk. Then at last the U.S. territorial government showed interest in the project. . . .

"Ellen, you're hiding something."

Sparta looked up at the broad brown face in front of her. The big woman wasn't smiling, exactly, but her accusatory expression hid mischief. "What are you talking about, boss?" Sparta asked.

The woman settled her considerable weight into the chair facing Sparta's desk, Ellen Troy's desk. "Taking first things first, honey, you applied to get out from under my thumb, *again*. You think Sister Arlene doesn't know what goes on in her own department?"

Sparta shook her head once, sharply. "I'm not hiding anything. I've been trying to get out from behind this desk for the past two years. As often as the regs let me apply." The desk in question was one of fifty just like it in the information-processing department of the Board of Space Control's Investigatory Services Division, housed in a pink brick and blue glass building overlooking Manhattan's Union Square.

The boss, Arlene Diaz, was the IP department manager. "You and me both know, anybody's had the surgery you've had doesn't stand a prayer of getting out of the office and onto the beat. So how come you keep doin' it, Ellen? Tryin' to get out there?"

"Because I keep hoping somebody upstairs has some common sense, that's why. I want to be judged by what I can do, Arlene. Not by what's on my scans."

Arlene sighed heavily. "Truth is, field supervisors are mighty partial to perfect physical specimens."

"There's nothing wrong with me, Arlene." She let the color come into her cheeks. "When I was sixteen some drunk squashed me and my scooter against a light pole. Okay, the scooter was a total loss. But *me* they patched up—it's all on file for anybody who wants to look."

"You got to admit it was a pretty weird fix, honey. All those *lumps* and *wires* and *hollow* places..." Arlene paused. "I'm sorry. You wouldn't know it, but it's policy that when a person wants to transfer, their supervisor sits on the review panel. I've pondered your scans, dear. More than a couple of times."

"The docs who patched me up did the best they could." Sparta seemed embarrassed, as if she were apologizing for them. "They were local talent."

"They did fine," Arlene said. "Mayo Clinic it wasn't, but what they did works."

"You think so"—Sparta studied her boss from under arched brows, and became suspicious—"what do the others on the panel think?"

When Arlene didn't say anything, Sparta smiled. "Faker," she said. "*You're* the one who's hiding something."

Arlene grinned back at her. "Congratulations, honey. We're gonna miss you around here."

It wasn't quite that easy.

There were the physicals to do all over again, the lies to rehearse and keep straight, the phony electronic documents to plant instantly, backing up the new stories.

And then the work. The six-month basic training for a Space Board Investigator was as rigorous as any astronaut's. Sparta was smart, quick, coordinated, and she could store far more knowledge than the academy's instructors had to give (a capacity she did not reveal), but she was not physically strong, and some of the things that had been done to her for reasons she was still trying to understand had left her highly sensitive to pain and vulnerable to fatigue. It was clear from day one that Sparta was in danger of washing out.

The investigator-trainees did not live in barracks; the Space Board regarded them as adults who would show up for classes if they wanted to and meanwhile keep their noses out of trouble, being responsible for themselves. Sparta reported daily to the training division's facilities in the New Jersey marshes and each night boarded the magneplane back to Manhattan, wondering if she would have the courage to return the next morning. It was a long ride, not long in minutes so much as in the repeated lesson of what sort of world she lived in. Sweet Manhattan was a jewel nestled in a swamp, cinched in by seaweed and algae farms that filled the once flowing rivers that made it an island, ringed by hideous shacks and crumbled slums beyond the river shores, wholly walled about by smoking refineries that transformed human waste and garbage into hydrocarbons and salvageable metals.

She barely survived early cut on the shock tests—electrical, thermal, chemical, light, noise, high gees on the centrifuge, spatial disorientation in the bird cage—extreme stresses that consumed all her energy in her silent, secret defense of her delicate neural structures. She struggled through the obstacle courses, the heavy weapons courses, the team contact sports where the brute strength of the other players often overwhelmed her grace and quickness. Exhausted, bruised, her muscles afire and her nerves ragged, she would stumble into the magneplane, glide smoothly through the fires and smoke of Purgatory, arrive late at her NoHo home and climb into her bed in the condo-apt she shared with three strangers she rarely saw.

Her loneliness and discouragement would get the better of her sometimes, and then she would cry herself to sleep—wondering why she was doing it, how long she could keep doing it. The second question was dependent on the first. If she wavered in her belief that earning credentials as a Space Board investigator would give her the access, the freedom she needed to know what she needed to, her re-solve would quickly crumble.

At night there were the dreams. In a year she had not found a sure way to control them. They would begin in-nocently enough with some fragment of the distant past, her mother's face—or with the immediate past, some boy she'd met that very day, or a classroom lecture she'd not been prepared for, or been overprepared for—and then they'd segué into the dark corridors of an endless building, a vague goal to be achieved if only she could find her way through the maze, the sense that her friends were with her but that she was utterly alone, that it made no difference whether or not she found what she needed but that if she didn't she would die—and then the colored lights came wheeling in, gently, from the edges, and the riot of smells overcame her.

Trainees had Sundays off. Sparta habitually spent hers walking Manhattan, from one side to the other, from the Battery to the Bronx, even in rain, snow, sleet, and wind. Although she was not strong, she was tough. Twenty-five miles in a day was not unusual for her. She walked to free her mind of focused thought, of the need to detect and plan and store data. Periodic mental rest was essential to avoid overload and breakdown.

As originally conceived, the SPARTA project would never have used artificial brain implants. But when gov-ernment agencies came in, the project changed; suddenly there were many more students, and new and larger fa-cilities. Sparta was a teenager then, and it didn't seem strange at first that she saw less of her busy parents, and less of the others, most of them younger children, of whom only one or two were near her own age. One day her father called her into his office and explained that she was to be sent away to Maryland for a series of government evaluations. He promised that he and her mother would visit as often as they could manage. Her father seemed under great strain; before she left the room he hugged her tightly, almost desperately, but he said nothing beyond a murmured "Good-bye" and "We love you." A man with orange hair had been there in the office the entire time, watching.

Of what came next her memory was still fragmented. Down in Maryland they had done far more than test her, but much of what they had done to her brain she had only recently deduced. What they had done to her body she was still learning.

Sparta walked up the airy length of Park Avenue, toward the Grand Central Conservatory. It was early spring; the day was sunny and warm. Along the avenue the rows of decorative cherry trees were in full bloom, their fragrant pink petals drifting like perfumed confetti onto the glittering esplanade. Shining glass and steel, scrubbed concrete and polished granite rose all about her; helicopters threshed the lanes of air among their tops. Omnibuses and an occasional police cruiser whispered past on the smooth pavement. Magneplanes hummed in swift assurance along thin steel tracks held aloft on high pylons, while quaint old electric subway cars, painted in cheerful colors, clattered and screeched beneath Sparta's feet, visible through blocks of glass paving.

Early in the century, when the mid-Atlantic states had been merged for administrative convenience, Manhattan had been designated a federal demonstration center—"Skyscraper National Park," as cynics would have it. Although the island was ringed with stinking industries and fetid suburbs, the streets of the model city were crowded, and most people in the crowd were sleek, colorfully and expensively dressed, happy-faced. In federal demonstration centers poverty was a crime, punishable by resettlement.

Sparta was not among the cheerful. Pass/fail in her training program was two months away. After that the physical stress would lift a bit and the academic side would take over, but just now she trembled on the brink of quitting. Sixty exhausting days to go. At this moment she felt she couldn't make it.

As she approached the formal gardens of the 42nd Street mall she noticed a man following her. She wondered how long he'd been at it; she'd been deliberately tuned out, walking in a semi-trance, or she would have seen him instantly. He could be someone in the training division checking up on her. He could be someone else.

She roused herself to maximum alertness. Stopping at a flower stand, she raised a bunch of yellow daffodils to her nose. The flowers had no perfume, but their heady vegetable odor exploded in her brain. She peered through them, closing one eye, her macrozoom gaze zeroing in . . .

He was young, with thick auburn hair chopped in the fashion of the day, and he wore a stylish, shiny black polymer jacket. He was a handsome young man of obvious Chinese and Black Irish ancestry, with high cheekbones, soft dark eyes, and a sprinkle of freckles; at present he seemed oddly uncomfortable and uncertain.

As soon as she'd stopped at the flower stand he had hesitated, and for a moment she thought he was going to come forward, say something. Instead he turned and pretended to study a display in the nearest store window. To his evident dismay, it was a clothing store displaying expensive women's underwear. When he realized what he was looking at, his skin brightened under his freckles.

She had identified him instantly, although the last time she'd seen him he'd looked quite different; he'd only been sixteen years old. He'd had even more freckles then, and his crewcut hair had been redder. His name was Blake Redfield. He was a year younger than she was, and he was the closest to her age of all the other students in the original SPARTA.

But she could see that he wasn't yet sure he recognized her. Unlike the girl she reminded him of, whose hair had been long and brown, Ellen Troy was a dishwater blond; she wore her unremarkable medium light hair in a practical cut, straight and short. Her eyes were blue and her lips were full. But despite these superficial alterations, Ellen's facial bone structure had not been altered, could not have been safely altered, so to a great extent Ellen still resembled the girl whose name had been Linda.

Luckily Blake Redfield was as bashful as ever, too shy to walk up to a strange woman on the street.

Sparta handed the flower vendor her sliver, took the daffodils, and walked on. She tuned her hearing to Blake's footsteps, selectively amplifying the distinctive *click, click* of his heels from the hundreds of other slaps and taps and shuffles that rolled around her. It was essential that she lose him, but in a way that kept him from realizing he'd been seen. Strolling as aimlessly as before, she passed under the arches of the Grand Central Conservatory.

The last time she'd visited the conservatory the scenery was sand and rocks and spiny things, with twisted desert peaks rising in the distance, but the theme this month was tropical. On every side palms and hardwoods reached for the lofty ceiling and lacy draperies of vines and orchids descended. Eastman Kodak's panoramic hologram extended the jungle view to a distant landscape of mist and waterfalls.

There were a lot of people in the conservatory, but most of them were on the mezzanine looking into the forest galleries from above, or strolling the broad paths that surrounded the central forest. She paused, then walked casually into the trees. The thick mat of leaves on the floor muffled the hoots of monkeys and the screeches of parrots overhead. She'd gone a few steps into the green shadows and then, even without amplification, she could plainly hear Blake's footsteps on the path behind her.

Another casual turn here, into a narrow path behind a screen of vines as fat and tangled as the tentacles of a giant squid . . . Blake's footsteps hesitated, but he made the turn and stayed on her trail.

Another turn, behind glossy dark leaves as big as the elephant ears they were named for, but stiffer, like dead, dried leather. Yet another turn among the knees of a sprawling banyan, its roots like veils of pale wood as smooth and thin as travertine stone. Suddenly she came upon the awesome waterfall, which descended in soundless torrents into the glistening gorge below. Behind her, Blake was still coming—but hesitantly now.

The true thunder of the waterfall was muted, but realistic mist drifted from sprinklers high in the walls, invisible behind the holographic projection. A vista point with a rustic bamboo railing, presently deserted, was perched on the edge of the vast, illusory gorge into which the water careened.

Sparta crouched against a tree trunk, wondering what

to do. She had hoped to leave Blake Redfield behind her in the movie-set rain forest, but he was not to be shaken so easily. She took the risk of losing track of his whereabouts in order to tune her hearing to the high-frequency hum of the Kodak hologram's projection system. The depth-of-focus circuitry was mounted somewhere on the wall a few feet in front of her. The shape of the electric pulses gave her a crude approximation of its program, but she had no physical access to the control center—

—then an unsettling sensation came over her, spreading from her midsection up through her chest to her arms. Her belly began to burn. The sensation was strange and familiar at the same time. When studying her own scans, months ago, she had seen the sheetlike structures under her diaphragm and suspected she knew what they were, powerful polymer batteries, but she could not remember how to utilize them, or even what they were for. Suddenly, responding to her unconscious demand, that memory returned.

She stretched out her arms and hands and curved them into the arc of a microwave-length antenna. Her facial mask set in concentration. Data cascaded through her frontal lobes; she beamed a single burst of instructions into the heart of the projection control processor.

The hologram leaped forward. Tons of water descended upon her—

—and she was staring at the old railroad station's polished marble wall. She lowered her arms and relaxed her trance. She walked to the fake bamboo railing of the vista point, which stood on the floor less than three feet from the wall. Above her an array of hologram projectors twinkled yellow, cyan, and magenta. She turned back and looked at the jungle trees. She could see nothing of the animated hologram from inside the projection, but if her beamed instructions had worked, the apparent edge of that deep gorge should now be at the end of the path, just in front of the trees. . . .

Blake emerged from the jungle, took two steps toward her and stopped, staring past her head at torrents of cascading water. His eyes followed the water down into the gorge.

Her back was to the railing. In a step she could have reached out and touched his handsome, friendly, freckled face. A crumpled chewing gum pack lay on the floor between them, where he saw canyons of mist. The light on him was just that which the conservatory's skylights and the projected whitewater of the hologram spilled on him. There was nothing at all between them except the chewing gum pack and that insubstantial light.

She was reminded how much she had liked him, once, although at that age she wasn't much interested in younger kids—she was a sophisticated seventeen and he was only a gawky sixteen, after all—and she probably hadn't been much good at communicating simple feelings anyway.

Now, simply by knowing that she existed, he could destroy her. Blake ran a hand through his auburn hair, then turned away, bemused, into the jungle. Sparta ducked under the rail. She walked along the smooth marble wall, emerged from behind the waterfall, and disappeared into a crowded passage that led toward Madison Avenue.

Blake Redfield paused in the trees and looked back at the tumbling water. He was a product of the early SPARTA, the pure SPARTA, before it had been disbanded. There had been no tinkering with his physical nature, only with the conditions of his education. He had no zoom-lens eyes or tunable ears, no enhanced RAM in his skull or PIN spines under his fingernails, no batteries in his belly or antennas wrapped around his bones.

But he was multiply intelligent too, bright enough to have recognized Linda immediately, bright enough to have realized immediately that she did not wish to be recognized. And he was curious enough to wonder why. After all, he'd half-suspected she was dead. . . .

So he'd followed her until she disappeared. He wasn't quite sure how she'd managed that, but he knew it was deliberate.

He had long wondered what became of her. Now he wondered just how hard it would be to find out.

PART TWO

THE SEVEN PILLARS
OF WISDOM

V

In the last part of the 21st century the sky had grown ever more crowded, from ground level right on up into space, until little Earth was ringed like giant Saturn—with machines and vehicles, not with innocent snowballs. There were bright power stations collecting sunlight and beaming microwaves to antenna farms in Arabia and Mongolia and Angola and Brazil. There were refineries, using sunlight to smelt metal from moon sand and captured asteroids, distilling hydrocarbons from carbonaceous chondrites and mining diamonds from meteoroids. There were factories that used these materials to cast the perfect ball bearing, to brew the perfect antibiotic, to extrude the perfect polymer. There were luxury terminals to serve the great interplanetary liners and entertain their wealthy passengers, and there were orbiting dockyards for the working freighters. There were a dozen shipyards, two dozen scientific stations, a hundred weather satellites, five hundred communications satellites, a thousand spy-eyes twinkling among the night stars, measuring the Earth, seeking out the last of its resources, gauging the flow of its precious and dwindling fresh water, watching and listening to the constantly shifting alliances, the occasional flare-ups of battle on the surface of the world below—like the vicious tank and helicopter engagement presently raging in south central Asia. By intricate international treaty, all weapons with a range of over one kilometer were barred from space, including rockets, railguns, beam projectors, every sort of directed-energy device, and even exploding satellites, whose debris would spread unchecked, but excluding satellites themselves. So another few thousand objects orbiting the Earth were essentially inert, little more than bags of moon rocks, mischievous threats by one power bloc against another to destroy orbiting facilities by simple collision, although implicit was the ability to destroy whole cities on Earth by guided artificial meteorite.

Yet most of the whirling planet, wondrously, maintained an awkward peace. The North Continental Treaty Alliance, consisting of the Russians, Europeans, Canadians, and Americans, usually called the Euro-Americans, had been on good terms for many years with the Azure Dragon Mutual Prosperity Sphere, usually known as the Nippon-Sino-Arabs. Together the industrial conglomerates had cooperated to build stations on or around the inner planets and in the Mainbelt. The Latin-Africans and the Indo-Asians had stations of their own, and had founded tenuous settlements on two of Jupiter's moons. The lure of solar system colonization had both sharpened and, paradoxically, attenuated Earthly rivalries: the rivalry was real, but no group wanted to risk its lines of communication.

Space travel had never been inexpensive, but early in

the century an economic watershed had been crossed, like a saddle in low hills that nevertheless marks a continental divide. Nuclear technology moved into its most appropriate sphere, outer space; the principles were sufficiently simple and the techniques sufficiently easy to master that private companies could afford to enter the interplanetary shipping market. With the shippers came the yards, the drydocks, the outfitters.

The Falaron shipyards, one of the originals, orbited Earth two hundred and fifty miles up. Presently the only vessel in the yards was an old atomic freighter, getting an overhaul and a face lift—a new reactor core, new main engine nozzles, refurbished life-support systems, new paint inside and out. When all the work was done the ship was to be recommissioned and given a new, rather grand, name: *Star Queen.*

The huge atomic engines had been mounted and tested. Spacesuited workers wielding plasma torches were fitting new holds, big cylinders that fastened to the thin central shaft of the ship below the spherical crew module.

The flicker and glare of the torches cast planes of shadow through the windows of the outfitter's office. In the odd light young Nikos Pavlakis's bristling mustache sprouted horns of black shadow, rendering his appearance demonic. "Curse you for a liar and a thief, Dimitrios. Repeatedly you assured us everything was on schedule, everything was under control. No problem, no problem, you told me! Now you say we will be a month late unless I am prepared to bear the cost of overtime!"

"My boy, I am terribly sorry, but we are helpless in the hands of the workers' consortium." Dimitrios spread his own hands to demonstrate helplessness, although it was hard to find remorse on his broad, wrinkled face. "You cannot expect me to absorb the entire cost of the extortion by myself."

"How much are you getting back from them? Ten percent? Fifteen? What is your commission for helping to rob your friends and relatives?"

"How do you find the hardness to say such things to me, Nikos?"

"Easily, old thief."

"I have dandled you on my knee as if you were my own godson!" the old man objected.

"Dimitrios, I have known you for what you were since I was ten years old. I am not blind, like my father."

"Your father is hardly blind. Do not doubt that I will report these slanders to him. Perhaps you had better leave—before I lose my patience and dandle you into the vacuum."

"I'll wait while you make the call, Dimitrios. I would like to hear what you have to say to him."

"You think I won't?" Dimitrios shouted, his face darkening. But he made no move to reach for the radiolink. A magnificent scowl gathered on his brow, worthy of Pan. "My hair is gray, my son. Your hair is brown. For forty years I have . . ."

"Other shipyards hold to their contracts," Pavlakis impatiently interrupted. "Why is my father's own cousin an incompetent? Or is it more than mere incompetence?"

Dimitrios stopped emoting. His face froze. "There is more to business than what is written in contracts, little Nikos."

"Dimitrios, you are right—you *are* an old man, and the world has changed. These days the Pavlakis family runs a shipping line. We are no longer smugglers. We are not pirates."

"You insult your own fa—"

"We stand to make more money from this *contract* with Ishtar Mining Corporation than you have dreamed of in all your years of petty larceny," Pavlakis shouted angrily. "But the *Star Queen* must be ready on time."

What hung in the close artificial air between them, known to them both but unmentionable, was the desperate situation of the once powerful Pavlakis Lines, reduced from the four interplanetary freighters it had owned to the single, aging vessel now in the yards. Dimitrios had intimated that he had creative solutions to such problems, but young Pavlakis would not hear of them.

"Instruct me, young master," the old man said poisonously, his voice trembling. "How does one, in this new world of yours, persuade workers to finish their jobs without the inducement of their accustomed overtime?"

"It's too late, isn't it? You've seen to that." Pavlakis drifted to the window and watched the flashing of the plasma torches. He spoke without facing the old man. "Very well, keep them at it, and meanwhile take as many bribes as you can, gray-hair. It will be the last job you do for us. And who else will deal with you then?"

Dimitrios thrust his chin up, dismissing him.

Nikos Pavlakis took a convenient shuttle to London that same afternoon. He sat cursing himself for losing his temper. As the craft descended, screaming through the atmosphere toward Heathrow, Pavlakis kept a string of amber worry beads moving across his knuckles. He was not at all certain his father would support him against Dimitrios; the two cousins went back a long way, and Nikos did not even want to think about what they might have gotten up to together in the early, loosely regulated days of commercial space shipping. Perhaps his father could not disentangle himself from Dimitrios if he wanted to. All that would change when Nikos took over the firm, of course ... if the firm did not collapse before it happened. Meanwhile, no one must know the true state of the Company's affairs, or everything would collapse immediately.

The worry beads clicked as Nikos muttered a prayer that his father would enjoy a long life. In retirement.

It had been a mistake to confront Dimitrios before Pavlakis was sure of his own position, but there could be no backing down now. He would have to put people he could trust on the site to see to the completion of the work. And—this was a more delicate matter—he would have to do what he could about extending the launch deadline.

Freighters, blessedly, did not leave for the planets every month; it was not a simple matter to find room for a shipment as massive as this consignment of robots from the Ishtar Mining Corporation. A delay in *Star Queen's* departure for Venus was not the most auspicious beginning to a new contract, but with luck it would not be fatal. Perhaps he could arrange an informal discussion with Sondra Sylvester, the Ishtar Mining Corporation's chief executive, before talking the situation over with his father.

Rehearsing his arguments, Pavlakis descended toward London.

At the same moment Mrs. Sondra Sylvester was flying through the dark overcast sky west of London in a Rolls-Royce executive helicopter, accompanied by a ruddy, tweedy fellow, Arthur Gordon by name, who having failed to press a cup of Scotch whiskey upon her was helping himself from a Sterling Silver decanter from the recessed bulkhead bar. Gordon was head of Defence Manufactures at Rolls-Royce, and he was much taken with his tall, dark-eyed passenger in her elegant black silks and boots. His helicopter flew itself, with just the two of them in it, toward the army proving grounds on the Salisbury Plain.

"Lucky for us the army were eager to help," Gordon said expansively. "Frankly your machine is of great interest to them—they've been pestering us for details ever since we undertook development. Haven't given them anything proprietary, of course," Gordon said, fixing her with a round brown eye over the lip of the silver cup. "And they've declined to go all official on us, so there's been no unpleasantness."

"I can't imagine the army is planning maneuvers on the surface of Venus," Sylvester remarked.

"Bless me, neither can I, ha ha." Gordon took another sip of the whiskey. "But I imagine they're thinking that a machine which can operate in that sort of hell can easily do so in the mundane terrestrial variety as well."

Two days earlier Sylvester had arrived at the plant to inspect the new machines, designed to Ishtar Mining Corporation's specifications and virtually handmade by Rolls-Royce. They were lined up at attention, waiting for her on the spotless factory floor, six of them squatting like immense horned and winged beetles. Sylvester had peered at each in turn, looking at her slim reflection in their polished titanium-alloy skins, while Gordon and his managers stood by beaming. Sylvester had turned to the men and briskly announced that before taking delivery she wished to see one of the robots in action. See for herself. No use hauling all that mass to Venus if it wouldn't do the job.

The Rolls-Royce people had traded shrewd glances and confident smiles. No difficulty there. It had taken them very little time to make the arrangements.

The helicopter banked and descended. "Looks like we're just about there," Gordon said. "If you look out the window to your left you can catch a glimpse of Stonehenge." Without undue haste he screwed the top back on the silver flask of Scotch; instead of returning it to the bar he tucked it into the pocket of his overcoat.

The helicopter came down on a wind-blasted moor, where a squad of soldiers in battle fatigues stood to attention, their camouflage trousers flapping about their knees like flags in a stiff breeze. Gordon and Sylvester dismounted from the helicopter. A group of officers approached.

A lieutenant colonel, the highest ranking among them, stepped forward smartly and inclined his head in a sharp bow. "Lieutenant Colonel Guy Witherspoon, madame, at your service." He pronounced it "lef-tenant."

She held out her hand and he shook it stiffly. She had the impression he would rather have saluted. The colonel turned and shook Gordon's hand. "Marvelous beast you've constructed here. Awfully good of you folks to let us look on. May I introduce my adjutant, Captain Reed?"

More handshakes. "Are you making records of these tests, Colonel?" Sylvester asked him.

"We had planned to do, Mrs. Sylvester."

"I have no objection to the army's knowing, as long as the information is kept strictly confidential. Ishtar is not the only mining company on Venus, Colonel Witherspoon."

"Quite. The Arabs and Ni . . . hmm, that is, the Japanese—need no help from us."

"I'm glad you understand." Sylvester hooked a loose

strand of her long black hair away from her red lips. She had one of those faces that was impossible to place—Castilian? Magyar?—and equally impossible to overlook or forget. She gave the belted young officer with the gingery mustache a warm smile. "We are grateful for your cooperation, Colonel. Please proceed whenever you're ready."

The colonel's flat-fingered right hand sprang to the bill of his peaked cap, his urge to salute having proved irrepressible. He instantly turned away and barked orders at the waiting soldiers.

The machine to be tested, one chosen at random by Sylvester from among the six on the factory floor, had been airlifted to the proving ground yesterday; it was now crouched at the edge of the raw earth landing pad. Six jointed legs held its belly only inches from the ground, but it was a fat beast, its back as high as a man's head. Two soldiers in white suits with hoods and faceplates stood at ease beside the machine; their overalls bore bright yellow radiation warning signs. Silhouetted against a sky of scudding black clouds, the robot's diamond-studded eye ports and spiny electromagnetic sensors gave it the visage of a samurai crab or beetle. No wonder the very sight of it had fired the military imagination.

"Captain Reed, when you're ready." The whitesuited team double-timed to a truck plastered with yellow radiation warnings and opened its rear doors. They removed a three-foot metal cylinder, which they carried slowly and carefully to the robot, then proceeded to load it into the metal insect's abdomen.

Meanwhile Colonel Witherspoon led Sylvester and Gordon to a bank of seats erected on the lip of the landing pad, shielded from the blustery wind by plastic windscreens. The little observation post looked northward from a low ridge into a wide, shallow valley. The ridge crests on both sides were pocked with pillboxes, and the ground around had been torn up by generations of horses' hooves, gun-carriage wheels, cleated tires, tank treads, and countless booted feet.

While they waited Sylvester once more declined Gordon's urgings to sip from his flask.

Within a few seconds the robot was fueled and critical. The soldiers stood well back. Witherspoon gave the signal and Captain Reed manipulated the sticks and knobs on the tiny control unit he held in his left hand.

On the control unit's screen Reed could see what the robot saw, a view of the world that encompassed almost two hundred radial degrees but was oddly distorted, like an anamorphic lens—a distortion programmed to compensate for the glassy atmosphere of Venus.

Within moments, the carbon-carbon cooling fins on the back of the robot began to glow—first dull orange, soon a bright cherry, finally a pearly white. The robot was powered by a high-temperature nuclear reactor cooled by liquid lithium. The extreme temperature of the cooling fins was excessive on Earth, but essential to create a sufficient gradient for radiative cooling in the eight-hundred degree surface temperatures on Venus.

The smell of hot metal reached them across the flat, windy ground. Witherspoon turned to his guests. "The robot is now fully powered, Mrs. Sylvester."

She cocked her head. "Possibly you have a demonstration of your own in mind, Colonel?"

He nodded. "With your permission, ma'am—first, unguided terrain navigation according to stored satellite maps. Objective, the crest of that far ridge."

"Carry on," Sylvester said, her lips curving in an anticipatory smile.

Witherspoon signaled his adjutant. With a chorus of whining motors the robot came to life. It raised its radiator-crested, antennaed head. Its chassis was of heat-resistant molybdenum steel and titanium-alloy, mounted on six titanium-alloy legs for traversing terrain more wildly irregular than any that could be found in England or anywhere else on Earth. It moved its legs with intricate and startling rapidity, and as it scuttled forward, turned, then plunged down the hillside, a novel set of tracks was left in the earth of Salisbury Plain.

The gigantic metal beast scurried along, raising a plume of dust behind it that blew strongly to the east, like a dust devil racing across the desert.

For some forgotten exercise in siegecraft, moats had been dug across the breadth of the valley and berms piled behind them; the robot scurried into trenches and over the rises without pause, thundering straight up the valley like the entire Light Brigade at Balaklava. Now outcroppings of gray rock blocked it from its goal at valley's end. The robot ran around the sheerer cliffs, but where the slope was not too steep, it simply scrambled over them, scrabbling for purchase among cracks and ledges of stone. Within a few moments it had reached its objective, a row of concrete pillboxes on the scudding heights. There it stopped.

"Those emplacements were constructed in the 19th century, Mrs. Sylvester," Witherspoon informed her. "Four feet of steel-reinforced concrete. The army have declared them surplus."

"I would be delighted for you to proceed with the second part of your demonstration," Sylvester said. "I only wish I had a better view."

"Captain Reed? Over here, if you will," Witherspoon called sharply. Reed brought his control unit close enough for Sylvester and the others to see the robot's-eye view on its videoplate. "And please take these, ma'am." Witherspoon handed her a pair of heavy binoculars, sheathed in sticky black plastic.

The binoculars were electromagnetically stabilized oil-lens viewers with selective radiation filtration and image enhancement. When she held them to her eyes she saw the robot so close and sharp she could have been standing ten feet away, although the perspective was markedly flat and graphic. There it crouched, a firebug, implacable, facing the squat bunker.

The robot needed to do more than move about on the surface of Venus. It was a prospector and a miner; it was equipped to seek out and analyze mineral samples and, when it came upon ore of commercial value, to dig out and partially process the ore, preparing it for further processing by other machines and eventual transportation off-planet.

"Go ahead, Colonel," Sylvester said.

Witherspoon gave the signal; Reed manipulated the controls. The robot's diamond-edge proboscis and claws slashed into the old bunker. Rust and gray dust flew up in a cloud. The robot ate into the bunker, ate around the walls, and when the roof collapsed on top of it, ate through that. It ate into the floor; slab-iron gun mounts and railings went into its maw, and rubber and steel and copper cables, and even the contents of the drains, choked with ancient grease. Soon there was nothing left of the bunker except a cavity in the hillside. The robot ceased working. Behind itself it had deposited neat molten piles—gleaming iron, ruddy copper, baked calcium.

"Excellent," said Sylvester, handing the binoculars to Witherspoon. "What's next?"

"We thought possibly, remote control navigation?" the officer suggested.

"Fine. Any problem if I do the controlling?" she asked.

"Our pleasure." Witherspoon waved Reed over; he handed her the control unit. She studied it a moment, and Gordon leaned his head to hers and judiciously murmured something about forward and back, but by the time he'd finished her fingers were already conjuring with the controls. The robot, a glowing dot in the naked-eye distance, scuttled backward, away from the ex-bunker. It turned and headed downslope, toward them.

She deliberately tried to run it over one of the steep outcrops. At the very edge of the cliff, it refused to go. She would not countermand her order, so the robot took rudimentary thought and found a solution: it began to eat the outcrop away from under itself. Sylvester laughed to see it chew its own switchbacks to the bottom of the cliff.

She ran it at full speed toward their position. It scrambled over the red ground, growing impressively larger as it came, leaving dust and wavering plumes of heat in its wake.

She turned to Witherspoon, her eyes gleaming. "Heat!"

He blinked at her fervor. "Why, yes . . . we had thought—" He pointed to a long open bunker lying to the north, halfway up the ridge. "Phosphorus," Witherspoon said. "Close as we could come on short notice. If you'll just steer the machine in there."

She bent to the controls again. The robot swerved toward the open bunker. As it rushed close, the bunker suddenly erupted with a glaring white light. Coruscating fountains of whistling, hissing flame leaped high into the air. Without pausing, the robot charged into the midst of the inferno. There it stopped.

It rested there, its own radiators gleaming through the fire. After several long seconds the pyre subsided. At Sylvester's gentle urging on the controls, the robot turned, quite unperturbed, and climbed straight up to the crest of the ridge. The soldiers stolidly kept their positions as the metal juggernaut rose above the ridge and bore down upon them. When the fiery beetle was a few yards away Sylvester lifted her hands from the control unit. The robot halted, radiant.

"Well done, Colonel," said Sylvester, handing the controls to Witherspoon. Again she hooked her long hair out of her eyes. "Mr. Gordon, my congratulations to Rolls-Royce."

When Sylvester reached her hotel that evening the desk clerk informed her that a Mr. Nikos Pavlakis was waiting for her in the lounge. She marched straight in and surprised him hunched over the bar, his big shoulders straining the tight jacket of his suit, a tumbler of water and a shot glass of cloudy ouzo in front of him, deep into what looked like his second bowl of peanuts. She smiled when he mumbled something she took to be an invitation to have a drink.

"I'm terribly sorry, Mr. Pavlakis, but I've had a busy day and I'm facing a full evening. If you'd called earlier . . ."

"Apologies, dear lady"—he choked as he downed a peanut—"on my way to Victoria, unexpected stopover. I thought I would take a minute to catch you up. But some other time..."

"So long as there is no delay in the schedule we discussed, you don't need to trouble yourself to report to me," she said. He had a very expressive face; she could have sworn that his mustache drooped, that his hair had just lost some of its curl. Her own expression hardened. "What's the problem, Mr. Pavlakis?"

"There is no problem, I assure you. We will be ready on time. No problem. Some additional costs we must absorb..."

"There is a problem, then."

"Our problem, dear lady. Not yours." He smiled, displaying fine white teeth, but his eyes were not smiling with them.

Sylvester contemplated him. "All right then. If in fact there's no problem please wire me tomorrow, here at the hotel, reconfirming your intention to begin loading cargo within two weeks, as agreed." When he nodded glumly she added, "Until then, we won't need to talk again."

Pavlakis muttered, "Good night, dear lady," but she was already marching away.

VI

London had not fared as well as Manhattan in the new century; it was as cramped and soot-blackened as ever, as severely Balkanized by differences of accent, skin color, class. In a moment one's square black taxicab passed from elegant brick townhouses and clever converted carriage houses on quaint mews into steaming, crumbling slums. The weather was as foul as ever, too, with gray-bellied clouds excreting thin drizzle and the occasional riverbottom fog bringing equal parts romance and respiratory disease. Nevertheless Sondra Sylvester liked the place—if not as much as she liked Paris or Florence, which were even less changed from what they had been, still rather better than she liked New York, which was no longer real. Living on Port Hesperus, Sylvester got her fill of artificial luxury ten months out of the year; when she took her annual trip to Earth she wanted the thing itself, the dirt with the polish, the noise with the music, the sour with the sweet.

The taxi stopped in New Bond Street. Sylvester pushed

her sliver into the taxi's meter slot, then opened the door and stepped to the damp pavement; while she waited for the machine to record the transaction she adjusted the line of her silk skirt and pulled her chinchilla coat closer against the clinging fog. The sliver rebounded and the cab's robot voice said, "Much obliged, m'um."

She pushed through hungry-looking crowds on the sidewalk and walked briskly into the building, nodding to a rosy-cheeked young staffer at the door who smiled back in recognition. She entered the cramped auction room where the book and manuscript sales were held. She'd been here often, as recently as yesterday afternoon, when she'd come to preview today's offerings. Up for sale were bits and pieces of two private collections, one of them from the estate of the recently deceased Lord Lancelot Quayle, the other anonymous. The two collections had been broken into a hundred lots—most of them of little interest to Sylvester.

Although she was early the room had begun to fill. She took a folding chair in the middle of the room and sat down to wait. It was like being early to church. There was a little transeptlike wing to her right, difficult to see into from her position; bidders who preferred anonymity often seated themselves there. The oldest booksellers, Magg's, Blackwell's, Quaritch, the rest, were already at their traditional places around the table in front of the podium. The first rows of folding chairs had been grabbed by out-landishly dressed viddie people whose demeanor was less than dignified. All that preening and squawking! Surely they would be asked to leave if they continued making so much noise. . . .

Two items drew the entertainers and the rest of the unusually large crowd. One of them was a distinct oddity.

As a result of Lord Quayle's lifelong Romish mania, his library had tossed up, among the miscellany, what purported to be an eyewitness account—scrawled in squid ink on fragmented parchment in execrable Greek by a fellow named Flavius Peticius, an undereducated, obviously gullible Roman centurion (or perhaps written by his nearly illiterate scribe)—of the crucifixion of one Joshua of Nazareth and two other malefactors outside the Jerusalem wall, early in the first century A.D.

Here was spectacle, the very stuff of epic! Not to mention timely publicity—and this is what drew the movie folk—for the BBC had recently mounted a lavish production of Desiree Gilfoley's "While Rome Burns," featuring the lissome former model, Lady Adastra Malypense, in an acting debut made memorable by the fact that in only one of her many scenes had Lady Malypense appeared wearing any clothes at all, and those in the Egyptian mode of pleated linen, which is to say transparent. Perhaps Lady Malypense herself was among the noisemakers in the front row; Sylvester would not have recognized her, clothed or otherwise.

As far as Sylvester was concerned they could have been auctioning a piece of the True Cross—so much for the intrinsic value of the parchment. Sonya Sylvester and most of the serious collectors had been attracted by lot 61, a single, thick volume; ironically, had its text not formed the basis of a classic British film of the previous century, the news media might have overlooked it, which Sylvester would have preferred.

She had inspected it yesterday on the plain bookshelf behind the podium, where it was guarded by burly porters in their dust coats and discreetly watched over by the business-suited young men and women of the staff. The book rested open to reveal a scrap of paper lying on its title page, written in an irregular vertical hand: "To Jonathan . . ."

Using this pseudonymous address, the last of the truly great, truly mad English adventurers—who was also the first of the great, mad philosophers of modern war—had conveyed his book into the hands of a close friend. Who could trace its travels since? Not Sotheby's.

Valuable books—fortunately or unfortunately, depending upon one's point of view—had never been as valuable as, for example, valuable paintings. Even the rarest printed book was understood to be one of a set of duplicates, not a unique original. Conversely, the rarest painting, while unique, could easily be reproduced in a hundred billion copies, its likeness distributed throughout the inhabited worlds in hardcopy texts and magazines and stored electronic images, thus becoming widely known—while no book, rare or common, could be so casually copied or so casually apprehended. Printed books were not unique, thus subtracting from their value. But printed books could not be easily reproduced, thus subtracting from their fame—and so again subtracting from their speculative market value.

Rarely there came upon the auction block a book both famous and unique. Lot 61 was such a book, *The Seven Pillars of Wisdom* in its first, private, and very limited edition—different from subsequent editions not only in its printing and binding but by almost a third of its text. Before today's auction only one copy had been known to exist, all others having disappeared or been destroyed; the survivor resided in the Library of Congress in Washington,

D.C. Not even the Gutenberg Bible could combine fame with such rarity; this was the only available original copy of an acknowledged masterwork of 20th century literature.

Sylvester's hopes of acquiring the book were not unreasonable, although every major collector and library on this and the colonized planets would be represented at the sale. Quaritch would be acting for the University of Texas, who were surely frantic to add this missing and most precious piece to their extensive collection of the author's works and memorabilia. Sotheby's staff held orders from other bidders, and some of them flanking the auctioneer's podium already had their heads cocked to the phone-links in their ears, receiving last minute instructions from far places. But all the bidders would have their top limits, and Sylvester's was very high.

Promptly at eleven the auctioneer stepped to the podium. "Good morning, ladies and gentlemen. Welcome to Sotheby and Company." He was a tall man, striving to overcome the East End and to achieve Oxbridge in his speech and demeanor, and he got the sale moving without delay. Although there were flurries of interest over 16th century English translations of Caesar's *Commentaries* and Plutarch's *Lives,* most of Quayle's library was disposed of rapidly.

Then the crucifixion parchment came up, and the mediahounds zeroed in with their photogram cameras. The viddie denizens of the front row cooed and fluttered. Sure enough, someone addressed the blond woman who made the first bid as "Adastra, darling," in a stage whisper loud enough to be heard at the back of the room. After a few quick rounds only Lady Malypense and two other serious bidders remained. A Sotheby's staffer was representing one of them, and Sylvester suspected that the bidder was

Harvard, perhaps hoping to acquire a crucifixion account to match the one Yale already possessed. The third bidder was behind her, a man with the accent of an Alabama preacher. It became a two-way contest when Harvard dropped out; the Southern churchman was implacable.

At last Lady Malypense failed to respond to the last "do I hear . . . ?" As if the gavel were a cue, the actress and her claque abruptly marched out, looking daggers at the portly victor.

The anonymous collection, "the property of a gentleman," was now offered in lots. Most were items of military history, in which Sylvester took no special interest; her field was early 20th century literature, particularly English—that is, British.

Eventually lot 60, a first edition account of Patrick Leigh Fermor's exploits during the Cretan resistance of World War II, went under the gavel. Sylvester would have liked to have had that book, and she bid on it—not that she cared about Crete or a half-forgotten war, but Leigh Fermor was a fine describer of places—but its price rose swiftly higher than she was willing to go. Soon the auctioneer said "sold" and the room immediately fell silent.

"Lot 61. Lawrence, T. E., *The Seven Pillars of Wisdom*"—as the director spoke, a solemn young man bore the heavy book forward and held it aloft, turning it slowly from side to side. "Printed in linotype on Bible paper, recto only, double columns. Bound in full tan morocco, edges gilt, in marbled slipcase. Inserted loose in the front, two leaves, handwritten, one a note in dedication 'to Jonathan' and signed by the author 'at Farnborough, 18 November 1922,' the other being comments written in pencil, in a hand thought to be that of Robert Graves. This very rare book is one of eight printed by the Oxford Times Press in

1922 at the author's behest, three of which were destroyed by him, and three others presumed lost. The reserve is five hundred thousand pounds."

He had hardly concluded his description when the bidding commenced. A little rustle of excitement rippled through the room as the auctioneer recited increasingly greater numbers, almost without pausing: "Six hundred thousand, I am bid six hundred thousand . . . six hundred and fifty thousand . . . seven hundred thousand." No one spoke, but fingers were flickering and heads were nodding, at the dealers' table and elsewhere in the room, so rapidly that the auctioneer did not even have time to acknowledge those who had made the bids.

"Eight hundred and seventy-five thousand pounds," said the auctioneer. For the first time there was a momentary pause before he got a response. It was clear that many bidders were approaching their limits. By the rules of the game, the higher the price, the higher the minimum advance; the price was now so high that the minimum advance was five thousand pounds. "Am I bid eight hundred and eighty thousand pounds?" the auctioneer asked matter-of-factly.

Quaritch and a single other bookseller responded. The auctioneer's gaze flickered to the transept on his left; evidently whoever was seated there, out of sight, had also bid.

"Am I bid eight hundred and eighty-five thousand?"

"Nine hundred thousand pounds," Sondra Sylvester said, speaking for the first time. Her voice in the crowded room was new, rich, darkly colored, a voice—it was obvious to everyone—accustomed to giving orders. The auctioneer nodded at her, smiling in recognition.

At the front table the gentleman from Quaritch, who

was in fact representing the University of Texas, seemed unperturbed—the humanities department of Texas had an extensive Lawrence collection and was no doubt prepared to go to extreme lengths to acquire the prize—but the remaining rival bookseller leaned back in resignation, dropping his pencil.

"I am bid nine hundred thousand pounds. Am I bid nine hundred and five?" The auctioneer glanced to his left once, twice, then announced, "One million pounds."

An appreciative groan rumbled through the audience. The man from Quaritch glanced curiously over his shoulder, made a note on the pad in front of him—and declined to bid further, having reached his client's top. The minimum advance was now ten thousand pounds.

"One million ten thousand pounds," Sylvester said. She sounded confident, more confident than in fact she felt. Who was in the transept? Who was bidding against her?

The auctioneer nodded. "I am bid . . ." He hesitated as he glanced to his left, then momentarily fixed his gaze there. He turned to look straight at Sondra Sylvester and almost shyly indicated the transept with a spasm of his hand. "I am bid one million, five hundred thousand pounds," he said, his voice carrying to her with peculiar intimacy.

A collective hiss whiffled through the audience. Sylvester felt her face grow stiff and cold. For a moment she did not move, but there was little point in calculating her resources; she was soundly beaten.

"I am bid one million and five hundred thousand. Am I bid one million five hundred thousand and ten?" The auctioneer was still looking at her. Still she did not move. He averted his gaze then, politely, looking without seeing into the bright eyes of his delighted audience. "I am bid one million five hundred thousand." The gavel hovered over the block. "For the last time . . . I have a bid of one million five hundred thousand." The gavel descended. *"Sold."*

The audience burst into applause, spiced with little cries of delight. Who was being applauded, Sylvester wondered bitterly—a deceased author, or a spendthrift acquisitor?

Porters ceremoniously removed the printed relic from public view. A few people leaped up, scuttling for the door as the auctioneer cleared his throat and announced. "Lot 62, miscellaneous autographs . . ."

Sylvester sat where she was, not moving, feeling the eyes of the curious burning into her. In the depths of her disappointment she was curious, too, to know who had outbid her. She rose slowly and moved as quietly as she could toward the aisle. Inching toward the transept wing, standing beside it, waiting there patiently as the sale continued . . . more and more people leaving throughout the final routine minutes . . . and then it was over. Sylvester stepped in front of the transept wing.

She confronted a young man with chopped auburn hair, wearing a lapel button in his conservative suit that identified him as a member of the staff. "You were the one?"

"On behalf of a client, of course." His accent was mid-Atlantic—American, cultured, East Coast. His face was handsome in an odd way, soft-eyed and freckled.

"Are you free to divulge . . . ?"

"I'm very sorry, Mrs. Sylvester, I'm under strict instructions."

"You know me." She scrutinized him: very handsome,

rather appealing. "Are you free to tell me your own name?"

He smiled. "My name's Blake Redfield, ma'am."

"That's some progress. Perhaps you would like to join me for lunch, Mr. Redfield?"

He inclined his head in the merest sketch of a bow.

"You are very gracious. Unhappily..."

She watched him a moment. He seemed in no hurry to leave; he was watching her as closely as she was watching him. She said, "Too bad. Another time?"

"That would be delightful."

"Another time, then." Sylvester walked briskly out of the room. At the entrance she paused, then asked the girl to call a taxi; while she waited she asked, "How long has Mr. Redfield been with the firm?"

"Let me see"—the red-cheeked girl twisted her little rosebud mouth charmingly as she made the effort to re-call—"perhaps a year, Mrs. Sylvester. He's not a regular employee, really."

"No?"

"More like a consultant," said the girl. "Books and manuscripts, 19th and 20th centuries."

"So young?"

"He is rather, isn't he? But quite the genius, to hear the assessors speak of him. Here's your taxi now."

"I'm sorry I troubled you." Sylvester hardly glanced at the square black shape humming driverless at the curb. "I think, after all, that I'll walk a bit."

Her pace was determined, not meditative; she needed to let her angry blood circulate. She strode rapidly down the street toward Piccadilly, turning east through the maze of all the little Burlingtons and across the end of Saville

Row, her destination a shop near Charing Cross Road, an ancient and, in the past, sometimes disreputable place presently wearing a veneer of renewed respectability.

She reached it in no time. Gold letters on a plate glass window announced "Hermione Scrutton, Bookseller." While she was still half a block from the shop she saw Scrutton herself at the green-enameled door, twisting a decorative iron key in a decorative iron lock while putting her eye to the eye of a bronze lion head that served as a doorknocker, but which also contained the retina-reader that triggered the door's real lock.

By the time Scrutton got the door open, Sylvester was close enough to hear the spring-mounted brass bell clamor as she entered.

Moments later the same bell announced Sylvester's arrival; from an aisle of crumbling yellow volumes Scrutton emerged, having seen to the alarm system. She was a stocky, bushy-browed imp in brown tweeds, a gold ascot at her throat, a bald patch visible through her thin graying hair, the color high on her cheeks—which were incongruously tan to begin with—and a smile playing on her mobile red lips. "My dear Syl. Can't say. Ah, really. Mm, simply devastated . . ."

"Oh, Hermione, you're not bothered in the least. I couldn't have afforded to spend a penny on you for the next five years."

"Mm, I confess the thought had occurred to me. And certainly I would have missed your, ah, most elegant presence in my humble, ah establishment." Scrutton smirked. "But then one has no difficulty placing the really rare items, does one? Mm?"

"Who outbid me? Do you know?"

She shook her head, once, her dewlaps flapping. "No

one whose agent I recognized. I was seated behind you. 'Fraid I couldn't see the bidder."

"*Anon* was the bidder," she informed her. "Represented by a young man named Blake Redfield."

Scrutton's eyebrows fluttered up and down rapidly. "Ahh, Redfield. Mm, I say." She turned away to fuss with the nearest shelf of books. "Redfield, eh? Indeed. Oh, yes."

"Hermione, you're toying with me"—the words came out of the back of her throat, a panther's warning growl—"and I'll have your artificially tanned hide for it."

"That so?" The bookseller half turned, cocking a cantilevered eyebrow. "What's it worth to you?"

"Lunch." Sylvester said immediately.

"Not your local pub fare," she warned.

"Wherever you choose. The Ritz, for God's sake."

"Done," said Scrutton, rubbing her palms. "Mm. Haven't eaten since breakfast, at least."

Somewhere between the butter lettuce and the prawns, encouraged by half a bottle of *Moët et Chandon*, Scrutton revealed her suspicion that Redfield was representing none other than Vincent Darlington—at which Sylvester dropped her fork.

Scrutton, her eyebrows oscillating with alarm, gaped at her. In all the years she had known Sylvester she had never seen her like this: her beautiful face was darkening quite alarmingly, and Scrutton was not at all certain that she had not suffered a stroke. She glanced around, but to her relief no one in the airy dining room seemed to have noticed anything amiss, with the possible exception of a poised and anxious waiter.

Sylvester's color improved. "What a surprise," she whispered.

"Syl, dearest, I had no idea..."

"This is vendetta, of course. Never mind the language, never mind the period, sweet Vincent has not the least interest in literature. I doubt he could distinguish *The Seven Pillars of Wisdom* from *Lady Chatterly's Lover*."

"Hm, yes"—Scrutton's cheek quivered, but she could not resist—"they are rather close in date..."

"Hermione," Sylvester warned, fixing a cool eye upon her; chastened, Scrutton subsided. "Hermione, Vincent Darlington does not *read*. He did not buy that book because he knows its worth; he bought it to shame me, because I shamed him—in quite another arena." Sylvester leaned back in her chair, dabbing at her lips with a heavy linen napkin.

"Really, my dear girl," Scrutton murmured. "Understand perfectly."

"No, *not* really, Hermione." Sylvester said sharply. "But you mean well, I think. Therefore I am about to put my life, or at least my reputation, into your hands. If you ever need to blackmail me, remember this moment—the moment I swore I would revenge myself upon that worm Darlington. If it costs me my fortune."

"Mm, ah." Scrutton sipped her champagne, then set it down carefully upon the linen. "Well, Syl, let us hope it doesn't come to that."

One ships an object worth a million and a half pounds discreetly, and with due regard for its physical well-being. Fortunately *The Seven Pillars of Wisdom* had been printed in those long gone days when it was assumed as a matter of course that printed pages ought to last. Blake Redfield had only to place the book into a padded gray Styrene briefcase and find a shipper who could provide temperature-and humidity-controlled storage.

Lloyd's register listed two suitable ships that would arrive at Port Hesperus within twenty-four hours of each other. Neither would get to Venus in much less than two months, but no one else would arrive sooner, and no other ships were scheduled for several more weeks; that was the nature of interplanetary travel. One of the two was a freighter, *Star Queen*, due to depart Earth orbit in three weeks. The other ship was a liner, *Helios*, scheduled to leave later on a faster crossing. Prudence suggested that Blake reserve space on both; the asterisk beside *Star Queen's* name warned that the ship was undergoing repairs and had yet to be cleared for commerce by the Board of Space Control.

Blake was sealing the magnetic lock on the Styrene case when the door of Sotheby's back room exploded with a loud bang.

A young woman was silhouetted against the brick hallway. "Heavens, Blake, what have you been up to?" she inquired, waving a hand to dispel the acrid smoke.

"I've been up to a few grains of potassium chlorate and sulfur, actually. If you hadn't been *you*, dear, this rather expensive object before me would have been whisked out of your sight and into the vault before you'd cleared the air in front of your cute nose."

"Couldn't you have used a little buzzer or something? Did you have to destroy the doorknob?"

"I didn't destroy the doorknob. More noise than punch. Might have blistered the venerable paint. Regrets."

The apple-cheeked young woman was modestly uniformed in a conservative metal skirt. She came to the desk and watched Blake lock the plastic case. "Didn't you think it was too bad she lost the bidding? She had such good taste."

"She?"

"She came up to you after the sale," she said. "Very beautiful for someone her age. She asked you something that made you blush."

"Blush? You have *quite* a vivid imagination."

"You're no good at pretending, Blake. Blame your Irish grandfather for your freckles."

"Mrs. Sylvester is an attractive woman. . . ."

"She asked about you afterwards. I told her you were a genius."

"I doubt she has any personal interest in me. And I certainly have no interest in her."

"Oh? Do you have an interest in Vincent Darlington?"

"Oh yes, pure lust." He laughed. "For his money."

She leaned a mesh-covered hip against the back of his chair; he could feel her heat on his cheek. "Darlington's an illiterate pig," she announced. "He doesn't deserve that thing."

" ' 'Tis a thing, devised by the enemy,' " he murmured, and he rose abruptly, moving away from her, to put the locked case into the vault. "Right." He turned to face her across the cluttered yellow office. "Did you bring me the pamphlet?"

She smiled, her rosy cheeks and sparkling eyes signaling her frank interest. "I found a shelf full, but they're still at my flat. Come home with me and I will introduce you to the secrets of the *prophetae*."

He eyed her, a bit askance, then shrugged. "Sure." After all, it was a subject that had long intrigued him.

VII

A discreet knocking at the door, repeated at intervals ...
Sondra Sylvester came striding out of the bathroom, her
blue silk nightgown clinging heavily to her long body. She
unchained the door.

"Your tea, mu'm."

"By the window, that will be fine."

The uniformed young man picked his way through
feminine litter and laid the heavy silver tray of tea things
on the table. The windows of the spacious suite had a fine
view of Hyde Park, but this morning they were heavily
curtained against the light. Sylvester searched the dim
room and spotted her velvet clutch purse on the floor beside a clothes-draped armchair. She found paper money
inside and dug out a bill in time to thrust it into the young
man's hand.

"Thank *you*, mu'm."

"You've been very good," she said, slightly flustered.

She closed the door behind him. "God, how much did I give him?" she muttered. "I'm hardly awake."

A rounded form stirred under the bedsheets. Nancybeth's tousled dark hair and violet eyes peered from the sheets.

Sylvester watched as the rest of Nancybeth rose into view, graceful neck, slender shoulders, heavy breasts darkly nippled. "How becoming of you to wait until he left. And how novel."

"What are you bitching about?" Nancybeth yawned, displaying perfect little teeth, a darting pink tongue.

Sylvester crossed to the videoplate on the wall and fiddled with the controls hidden in its carved and gilded frame. "You said you were awake. I asked you to turn on the news."

"I went back to sleep."

"You were into my purse again."

Nancybeth glared at her with pale eyes that tended to cross when she was concentrating. "Syl, sometimes you act more like a mother..." She sprang from the bed and strode to the bathroom.

"Than like what?"

But Nancybeth ignored her, walking through the dressing room, leaving the door open, on into the shower stall.

Sylvester's heart was thudding—God, that shelf, those majestic flanks, those vibrant calves. Part Italian, part Polynesian, she was a bronzed Galatea, sculpture made flesh. Irritably Sylvester punched the controls of the video picture until the plastic mask of a BBC announcer appeared.

She set the volume just loud enough to hear the announcer talk about rising tensions in south central Asia as she went about picking clothes off the floor and hurling them onto the bed. From the bathroom came the hiss and dribble of the shower and Nancybeth's husky, off-tune voice singing something torchy and unintelligible. Sylvester looked at the heavy silver teapot and the china cups with distaste. She went into the dressing room and pulled a bottle of *Moët et Chandon* from the refrigerator under the counter. The videoplate mumbled words that caught her attention: "A secret unveiled: develops that the winning bid in yesterday's spectacular auction at Sotheby's . . ." Sylvester darted to the wall screen and boosted the volume. ". . . first-edition *Seven Pillars of Wisdom* by T. E Lawrence—the legendary Lawrence of Arabia—was placed by Mr. Vincent Darlington, director of the Hesperian Museum. Reached by radio-link, Mr. Darlington at first refused comment but later admitted that he had bought the extremely rare book on behalf of the Port Hesperus museum, an institution of which he is the proprietor—not, it might be said, an institution hitherto known for its collection of written works. In other news of the art world . . ."

Sylvester punched off the video. She ripped the foil off the bottle and untangled its wire cage. She began twisting the bulging champagne cork with a strong, steady grip.

Nancybeth emerged from the shower. Steam rose from her skin, backlit in the glow from the dressing room light. She was perfectly unconcerned about the water she was dripping onto the rug. "Was that something about Vince? On the news?"

"Seems he was the one who outbid me for the Lawrence." The champagne cork came out with a satisfying *thud*.

"Vince? He doesn't care about books."

Sylvester watched her, a heavy dark Venus deliberately manifesting herself naked, deliberately letting her wet skin chill, letting her nipples rise. "He cared about you," Sylvester said.

"Oh." Nancybeth smiled complacently, her violet eyes half-lidded. "I guess it cost you."

"On the contrary, you've saved me a great deal of money I might otherwise have thrown away on a mere book. Fetch some glasses, will you? In the refrigerator."

Still naked, still wet, Nancybeth brought the tulip glasses to the table and settled herself on the plush chair. "Are we celebrating something?"

"Hardly," Sylvester said, pouring out the cold, seething liquid. "I'm consoling myself."

She handed a tulip to Nancybeth. They bent toward each other. The rims touched and chimed. "Still mad at me?" Nancybeth mewed.

Sylvester was fascinated, watching Nancybeth's nostrils widen as she lowered her upturned nose into the mouth of the tulip. "For being who you are?"

The tip of the pink tongue tasted sharp carbonic acid from dissolving bubbles. "Well, you don't have to *console* yourself, Syl." The violet eyes under the long, wet lashes lifted to transfix her.

"I don't?"

"Let me console you."

The magneplane whirred through the genteel greenery of London's southwestern suburbs, pausing now and again to drop off and take on passengers, depositing Nikos Pavlakis a mile from his Richmond destination. Pavlakis hired an autotaxi at the stand and as it drove away from the station he rolled down the windows to let the wet spring air invade the cab. Beyond the slate roofs of the passing semi-detached villas, pearly cloud puffs in the soft blue sky kept pace with the cab as it rolled past spruce lawns and hedges.

Lawrence Wycherly's house was a trim brick Georgian. Pavlakis put his sliver in the port, paying the cab to wait, then walked to the door of the house, feeling heavy in a black plastic suit that, like all his suits, was too tight for his massive shoulders. Mrs. Wycherly opened the door before he could reach for the bell. "Good morning, Mr. Pavlakis. Larry's in the sitting room."

She did not seem overjoyed to see him. She was a pale, smooth-skinned woman with fine blond hair, pretty once, now on the verge of fading into invisibility, leaving only her regret.

Pavlakis found Wycherly sitting in his pajamas, his feet up on a hassock, a plaid lap robe tucked under his thighs and an arsenal of plastic-back space thrillers and patent medicines littering the lamp table beside him. Wycherly lifted a thin hand. "Sorry, Nick. Would get up, but I've been a bit wobbly for the past day or two."

"I'm sorry to have to give you this trouble, Larry."

"Nothing of it. Sit down, will you? Be comfortable. Get you anything? Tea?"

Mrs. Wycherly was still in the room, somewhat to Pavlakis's surprise, temporarily reemerging from the shadows of the arch. "Mr. Pavlakis might prefer coffee."

"That would be very nice," he said gratefully. The English repeatedly amazed him with their sensitivity to such things.

"Right, then," Wycherly said, staring at her until she dissolved again. He cocked a canny eyebrow at Pavlakis, who was perching his muscular bulk delicately on an Empire settee. "All right, Nick. Something too special for the phone?"

"Larry, my friend..." Pavlakis leaned forward, hands primly on his knees, "Falaron Shipyards is cheating us— my father and me. Dimitrios is encouraging the worker consortiums to bribe us, and then taking kickbacks from them. For all of which we must pay. If we are to meet the launch window for *Star Queen*."

Wycherly said nothing, but a sour smile played over his lips. "Frankly, most of us who've worked with the firm over the years have accepted that that was always part of the arrangement between Dimitrios and your dad." Wycherly paused, then coughed repeatedly, making a humming sound like a balky two-cycle engine deep in his chest. For a moment Pavlakis was afraid he was choking, but he was merely clearing his throat. He recovered himself. "Standard practice, so to say."

"We can't afford this *standard practice* anymore," Pavlakis said. "These days we face worse than just the old competition..."

Wycherly grinned. "Besides which, you're no longer allowed to get rid of them by something as simple as, say, slitting a few throats."

"Yes." Pavlakis jerked his head forward, solemnly. "Because we are regulated. So many regulations. Set fees per kilo of mass..."

"...divided by time of transport, multiplied by mini-max distance between ports," Wycherly said wearily. "Right, Nick."

"So to attract business one must abide by the strictest adherence to launch windows."

"I *have* been with the firm awhile." Again Wycherly made that lawnmower sound in the back of his throat, struggling for breath.

"These calculations—I keep making them in my head,"

Pavlakis said. He was thinking that Wycherly did not look well; the whites of his eyes were rimmed in bright red and his gingery hair was standing up in tufts, like the feathers of a wet bird.

"Sorry for you, old man," Wycherly said wryly.

"We are so close to doing well. I have negotiated a long-term contract with the Ishtar Mining Corporation. The first shipment is six mining robots, nearly forty tonnes. That will pay for the trip, even give us a profit. But if we miss the launch window . . ."

"You lose the contract," Wycherly said, keeping it matter of fact.

Pavlakis shrugged. "Worse, we pay a penalty. Assuming we have not declared bankruptcy first."

"What else have you got for cargo?"

"Silly things. A pornography chip. A box of cigars. Yesterday we got a provisory reservation for a damned book."

"One book?" Pavlakis jerked his head again, yes, and Wycherly's eyebrow shot up. "Why 'damned'?"

"The entire package weighs four kilos, Larry." Pavlakis laughed, snorting like a bull. "Its freight will not pay your wages to the moon. But it is to be accompanied by a certificate of insurance in the amount of two million pounds! I would rather have the insurance."

"Maybe you could load it and then arrange a little accident." Wycherly started to laugh, but was taken by a spasm of coughing. Pavlakis looked away, pretending to be interested in the horse prints on the cream walls of the sitting room, the bookcases of unread leatherbound classics.

At last Wycherly recovered. "Well, of course you must know what book that is."

"Should I know?"

"Really, Nick, it was all the news yesterday. That book's *The Seven Pillars of Wisdom*. Must be. Lawrence of Arabia and all that." Wycherly's wasted face twisted in a grin. "Another of the old empire's treasures carried off to the colonies. And this time the colony's another planet."

"Very sad." Pavlakis's commiseration was brief. "Larry, without the Ishtar contract . . ."

But Wycherly was musing, staring past Pavlakis into the shadows of the hall. "That's a rather odd coincidence, isn't it?"

"What's odd?"

"Or maybe not, really. Port Hesperus, of course."

"I'm sorry, I fail to . . ."

Wycherly focused on him. "Sorry, Nick. Mrs. Sylvester, she's the chief exec at Ishtar Mining, isn't that right?"

His head bobbed forward. "Oh, yes."

"She was the other bidder for *The Seven Pillars of Wisdom*, you see. Went to over a million pounds and lost out."

"Ah." Pavlakis's eyelids drooped at the thought of that much personal wealth. "How sad for her."

"Port Hesperus is quite the center of wealth these days."

"Well . . . you see why we must retain the Ishtar contract. No room for Dimitrios and his . . . 'standard practices.' " Pavlakis struggled to get the conversation back on track. "Larry, I am not certain that my own father fully understands these matters—"

"But *you've* had no trouble making it all clear to Dimitrios." Wycherly studied Pavlakis and saw what he expected. "And he is not at all happy with you."

"I was foolish." Pavlakis fished for his worry beads.

"Could be so. He'll know this is his last chance to steal.

And still plenty of opportunities for the old crook to buy cheap and charge dear on the specs."

"I found no sign of cheating on the specifications when I inspected the work two days ago . . ."

"I won't be wanting to captain any substandard ship, Nick," Wycherly said sharply. "Whatever else has been going on between Dimitrios and your dad—and I suspect plenty—your dad never asked me to risk my neck in a craft that was unspaceworthy."

"I would not ask you that either, my friend . . ." Pavlakis was startled by Mrs. Wycherly, silently materializing at his elbow with a saucer. On it was balanced a cup filled with something brown. He looked up at her and smiled uncertainly. "You are very gracious, dear lady." He took it and sipped the liquid cautiously; normally he took Turkish coffee with double sugar, but this was coffee in the American style, plain and bitter. He smiled, hiding his chagrin. "Mmm."

His polite charade was wasted on Mrs. Wycherly, who was looking at her husband. "Please don't let yourself become exhausted, Larry." Wycherly shook his head impatiently.

When Pavlakis looked up from his cup, he discovered that she had gone. He set the coffee carefully aside. "What I had hoped was that you could help insure that *Star Queen* would not fail recertification by the board, Larry."

"How would I do that?" Wycherly muttered.

"I would be happy to put you on flight pay immediately, with bonuses, if you would consent to go up to Falaron and live there for the next month—as soon as you feel fit, of course—to act as my personal agent. To inspect the work daily, until the ship is ready."

Wycherly's dull eyes brightened. He hummed and sputtered a moment. "You're a clever fellow, Nick. Hiring a man to see to his own safety . . ." His gravelly voice broke into grinding coughs, and Pavlakis was aware that Mrs. Wycherly was nervously regaining solidity in the shadows. Wycherly's spasms subsided, and he glared at his wife with eyes full of pain. "An offer I can hardly refuse"—his eyes fell back to Pavlakis—"unless I'm unable."

"You'll do it?"

"I'll do it if I can."

Pavlakis stood up with unseemly haste, his dark bulk looming in the nebulous room. "Thank you, Larry. I'll let you be by yourself, now. I hope your recovery is swift."

As he hurried to the waiting autocab his amber beads were swirling and clicking. He muttered a prayer to Saint George for Wycherly's health, while voices were raised in anger in the house behind him.

Fifteen minutes on the swift magneplane brought Pavlakis back to the Heathrow Shuttleport and the local freight office of Pavlakis Lines. It was a cramped shed tacked onto the end of a spaceplane hangar, an enormous steel barn full of discarded, egglike fuel tanks and scavenged sections of booster fuselages. A smell of odorized methane and Gunk had worked its way into the paneling. When neither of the Pavlakises, Senior or Junior, was in England, the place was deserted except for the underemployed mechanics who hung around trying to make time with the secretary-receptionist, one of Nikos's cousins' sisters-in-law. Her name was Sofia, she was a wiry-yellow blond from the Peloponnese, heavier than her years, and she brooded. When Pavlakis walked into the office she had an open carton of yogurt on her desk, which she appeared to be ignoring in favor of the noonday news on her desktop videoplate.

"For those of you who may have needed an excuse, here's a good reason to plan a trip to Port Hesperus," the announcer was simpering. "Early this morning it was revealed that the buyer of that first-edition *Seven Pillars of Wisdom* . . ."

Sofia lifted smoldering eyes to Pavlakis when he came in, but no other part of her body moved. "A woman has been calling you."

"What woman?"

"I could not say what woman. She says you were to write her a letter. Or send her a wire. I forget." The smoldering eyes strayed back to the flatscreen.

"Mrs. Sylvester?"

Sofia's eyes stayed fixed on the screen, but her palms opened: maybe.

Cursing the very concept of cousins and in-laws, Pavlakis went past a paste-board divider into the inner sanctum. The desk that everybody used whenever they felt like it was piled high with greasy flimsies. A pink slip sat on top, scratched out in Sofia's degraded demotic, conveying the gist of Sondra Sylvester's last communication: "Imperative you reaffirm contract in writing this date. If Pavlakis Lines cannot guarantee launch window, Ishtar Mining Corporation must immediately terminate proposed contract."

Proposed contract . . . ?

The worry beads clicked. "Sofia," Pavlakis shouted. "Reach Mrs. Sylvester immediately."

"Where to reach the lady?" came the delayed reply.

"At the Battenberg." Idiot. By what folly did her father

name her Sofia, Wisdom? Pavlakis scuffled through the flimsies, searching for anything new and hopeful. His hand fell on yesterday's query from Sotheby's. "Can you guarantee shipment of one book, four kilograms gross mass in case, to arrive Port Hesperus . . . ?"

"I've reached the woman," Sofia announced.

"Mr. Pavlakis? Are you there?"

Pavlakis snatched at the phonelink. "Yes, dear lady, I hope you will accept my personal apologies. Many unexpected matters . . ."

Sylvester's image coalesced on the little videoplate. "I don't need an apology. I need a confirmation. My business in England was to have been finished yesterday. Before I can leave London I must be persuaded that my equipment will arrive at Venus on time."

"Just at this very moment I have been sitting down to write a letter." Pavlakis resisted the urge to twist his beads in view of the videoplate.

"I'm not talking about a recording or a piece of paper, Mr. Pavlakis," said the cool, beautiful face on the screen. How was her face so alluring? Something disarranged about the hair, the heightened color around the cheeks, the lips—Pavlakis forced himself to concentrate on her words. "Frankly, your behavior has not been reassuring. I sense that I should look for another carrier."

Her words galvanized him. "You may have faith, dear lady! Indeed, you must. Even the Hesperian Museum has honored us to carry its recent and most valuable acquisition . . ." He hesitated, confused. Why had he said such a thing? To be . . . to be friendly, of course, to reassure her. "In which you yourself have had much interest, if I am correct?"

Great Christ, the woman had turned to metal. Her eyes

flashed like spinning drillpoints, her mouth was steel shutters, slammed shut. Pavlakis turned away, desperately swiped away the sweat that was pouring from his hairline. "Mrs. Sylvester, please, you must forgive me, I have been . . . under much strain lately."

"Don't trouble yourself so much, Mr. Pavlakis." To his surprise, her tone was as smooth and warm as her words . . . warmer, even. He half turned, looked at the screen. She was smiling! "Write me that letter you promised. And I will talk to you again when I return to London."

"You will trust in Pavlakis Lines? Oh, we will not fail you, dear lady!"

"Let us trust in one another."

Sylvester cut the phonelink and leaned back in the bed. Nancybeth was sprawled face down on top of the sheets, eyeing her from the slit of a heavy-lidded eye. "Will you be awfully unhappy if we delay the island for a day or two, sweet?" Sylvester whispered.

"Oh, God, Syl." Nancybeth rolled onto her back. "You mean I'm stuck in this soot pile for two *more* days?"

"I have unexpected work to do. If you want to go ahead without me . . ."

Nancybeth writhed in indecision, her round knees falling open. "I suppose I can find something . . ."

Suddenly Sylvester felt a touch of nausea. "Never mind. Once you're settled I may have to come back for a day or two."

Nancybeth smiled. "Just get me to the beach."

Sylvester picked up the phonelink and tapped out a code. Hermione Scrutton's ruddy face came on the screen with surprising quickness. "You, Syl?"

"Hermione, I find that my vacation plans have

changed. I require your advice. And possibly your assistance."

"Mm, ah," the bookseller replied, her eyes sparkling.
"And what will *that* be worth to you?"

"More than lunch, I assure you."

VIII

Captain Lawrence Wycherly made a remarkably rapid recovery from his chest ailment and took up residence at the Falaron Shipyards, where he ably represented the Pavlakis Lines as clerk of the works. The gaunt, determined Englishman bore down hard on the frustrated Peloponnesian, inspecting the ship daily without warning and hectoring the workers, and despite Dimitrios's surliness and frequent tantrums the job was finished on time. It was with a certain grim satisfaction that Nikos Pavlakis watched spacesuited workers electrobonding the name *Star Queen* across the equator of the crew module. He praised Wycherly lavishly and added a bonus to his already handsome pay before leaving to make the final arrangements at Pavlakis Lines headquarters in Athens.

Star Queen, though of a standard freighter design, was a spacecraft quite unlike anything that had been imagined at the dawn of modern rocketry—which is to say it looked nothing like an artillery shell with fins or the hood ornament of a gasoline-burning automobile. The basic configuration was two clusters of spheres and cylinders separated from each other by a cylindrical strut a hundred meters long. The whole thing somewhat resembled a Tinkertoy model of a simple molecule.

The forward cluster included the crew module, a sphere over five meters in diameter. A hemispherical cage of superconducting wires looped over the crew module, partially shielding the crew against cosmic rays and other charged particles in the interplanetary medium—which included the exhaust of other atomic ships. Snugged against the crew module's base were the four cylindrical holds, each seven meters across and twenty meters long, grouped around the central strut. Like the sea-land cargo containers of the previous century, the holds were detachable and could be parked in orbit or picked up as needed; each was attached to *Star Queen's* central shaft by its own airlock and was also accessible through outside pressure hatches. Each hold was divided into compartments which could be pressurized or left in vacuum, depending on the nature of the cargo.

At the other end of the ship's central strut were bulbous tanks of liquid hydrogen, surrounding the bulky cylinder of the atomic motor's reactor core. Despite massive radiation shielding, the aft of the ship was not a place for casual visits by living creatures—robot systems did what work needed to be done there.

For all its ad hoc practicality, *Star Queen* had an air of elegance, the elegance of form following function. Apart from the occasional horn of a maneuvering rocket or the spike or dish of a communications antenna, the shapes from which she had been assembled shared a geometric purity, and all alike shone dazzling white under their fresh coats of electrobonded paint.

For three days, Board of Space Control inspectors went over the refurbished ship, at last pronouncing it fully spaceworthy. *Star Queen* was duly recertified. Her launch date was confirmed. Heavy-lift shuttles brought up cargo from Earth; other, smaller parcels were delivered by bonded courier.

Captain Lawrence Wycherly, however, did not pass the Board's inspection. With one week to go before launch, flight surgeons discovered what Wycherly had disguised until now with illegal neural-enhancement preparations he had obtained from sources in Chile: he was dying from an incurable degeneration of the cerebellum. The viral infections and other minor illnesses that had plagued him were symptoms of a general failure of homeostasis. Never mind that the drugs might have accelerated his disease; Wycherly figured he was a dead man, and he was desperate for the money this last assignment was to have brought, for without it—the tale of his feckless investments and frantic spiral into debt was a cautionary tale of the age—his soon-to-be widow would lose their home, would lose everything.

The Board of Space Control notified the Pavlakis Lines home office in Athens that *Star Queen* was short a captain and that her launch permit had been withdrawn pending a qualified replacement. At the same time the Board routinely notified the ship's insurors and every firm and individual who had placed cargo on the ship.

Delayed by "technical difficulties" on his way from Athens to Heathrow (stewards were staging a slow-down in protest against the government-owned airline), Nikos

Pavlakis did not learn the devastating news until he stepped off the supersonic ramjet jitney at Heathrow. Miss Wisdom was glowering at him from behind the passport control screens, her paint-blackened eyes the very eyes of Nemesis beneath her helmet of wiry yellow hair. "*This* from your father," she spat at him, when he came within reach, thrusting into his hands the flimsy from Athens.

Temporarily, but only temporarily, it appeared that Saint George had let Nikos Pavlakis down. Pavlakis spent the next twenty-four hours on the radio and phonelinks, sustained by a kilo or so of sugar dissolved in several liters of boiled Turkish coffee, and at the end of that time a miracle occurred.

Neither God nor Saint George had provided a new pilot. No such luck, for Pavlakis could find no qualified pilots who would be free of their commitments or current assignments in time for *Star Queen*'s Venus window. And the miracle was not wholly unqualified, for no saint had prevented the prompt defection of a few of the shippers on the manifest—those for whom the arrival of their cargo at Port Hesperus was not time-critical, or whose cargo could easily be sold elsewhere. Bilbao Atmospherics was even now off-loading its tonne of liquid nitrogen from Hold B, and a valuable shipment of pine seedlings, the bulk of the cargo that was to have travelled in Hold A, had already been reclaimed by Silvawerke of Stuttgart.

Pavlakis's miracle was the intervention of Sondra Sylvester.

He did not call her, she called him, from her rented villa on the Isle du Levant. She informed him that after their last conversation she had made it her business to check up on him and the members of *Star Queen*'s crew. She praised Pavlakis for his measures to safeguard the integrity of *Star Queen* during the refitting; he could hardly be blamed for Wycherly's private difficulties. Her London solicitors had given her very full briefs on pilot Peter Grant and engineer Angus McNeil. In view of what she had learned, she had personally contacted the Board of Space Control and submitted an *amicus* brief on behalf of Pavlakis Lines's application for a waiver of the crew-of-three rule, citing her faith in the integrity of the firm and overriding economic considerations. She had also contacted Lloyd's, urging that insurance not be withdrawn. According to Sylvester's best information, the waiver was sure to be granted. *Star Queen* would launch with two men aboard, carrying sufficient cargo for a profitable voyage.

When Pavlakis signed off the phonelink he was giddy with elation.

Sylvester's best information proved correct, and Peter Grant was promoted to commander of a two-man crew. Two days later heavy tugs moved *Star Queen* into launch orbit, beyond the Van Allen belts. The atomic motor erupted in a stream of white light. Under steady acceleration the ship began a five-week hyperbolic dive toward Venus.

PART THREE

BREAKING STRAIN

IX

Peter Grant rather enjoyed command. He was as relaxed as a working man can be—lying weightless, loosely strapped into the command pilot's couch on *Star Queen*'s flight deck, dictating the ship's log between puffs of a rich Turkish cigarette—when a skullcracker slammed into the hull.

For the second or two that it took Grant to crush his cigarette and reset the switches, red lights glared and sirens hooted hysterically. "Assess and report!" he barked. He yanked an emergency air mask from the console and jammed it over his nose and mouth, and abruptly all was silent again. He waited an eternity as the console graphics rapidly shifted shape and color—thirty more seconds at least—while the computer assessed the damage.

"We have experienced severe overpressure in the southeast quadrant of the life support deck," the computer announced in its matter-of-fact contralto. "Number two fuel cell has been ruptured. Automatic switchover to number one and number three fuel cells has occurred. Gas lines from oxygen supply one and two have been sheared. Emergency air supply valves have been opened"—Grant knew that; he was breathing the stuff now. But what the hell *happened?*—"Sensors have recorded supersonic airflows at exterior hull panel L-43. Loss of pressure on the life support deck was total within twenty-three seconds. The deck has been sealed and is now in vacuum. There has been no further systemic or structural damage. There has been no further loss of atmospheric pressure in the connecting passages or in any other part of the crew module"—hearing which, Grant took the mask from his face and let it withdraw into the console panel. "This concludes damage assessment. Are there further queries?" the computer asked.

Yes, damn it all, what the hell *happened?* The computer didn't answer questions like that unless it knew the answer, unambiguously. "No further queries," Grant said, and keyed the comm: "McNeil, are you all right?"

No answer.

He tried the hi-band. "McNeil, Grant here. I want you on the flight deck."

No answer. McNeil was out of touch, possibly hurt. After a moment's thought Grant decided to steal just a couple of seconds more in an attempt to learn the cause of their predicament. With a few flicks of his fingertips he sent one of the external monitor eyes scurrying over the command module hull toward panel L-43, on the lowest part of the sphere.

The image on the videoplate was a racing blur until the robot eye halted over the designated panel. Then there it was, fixed and plain on Grant's screen: a black dot in the upper right quadrant of the white-painted steel panel as neat as a pellet hole in a paper target. "Meteoroid," Grant whispered. He flicked grids over the monitor image and read the hole at just under a millimeter in diameter. "Big one."

Where the devil was McNeil? He'd been down in the pressurized hold checking the humidifiers. Simple enough, so what was the problem?—the meteoroid hadn't penetrated the holds.... Grant slipped out of his straps and dived into the central corridor.

His feet had hardly cleared the deck when he grabbed a ladder rung and yanked himself to a halt. Immediately below the flight deck was the house-keeping deck. Unlike the curtains of the other two cabins, the curtain that partitioned McNeil's private cabin from the common areas stood open. And inside was McNeil, doubled up and turned toward the bulkhead, his face hidden, his fists knotted around the bulkhead grips.

"What's the matter, McNeil? Are you sick?"

The engineer shook his head. Grant noticed the little beads of moisture that broke away from his head and went glittering across the room. He took them for sweat, until he realized that McNeil was sobbing. Tears.

The sight repulsed him. Indeed. Grant was surprised at the strength of his own emotion; immediately he suppressed his reaction as unworthy. "Angus, pull out of it," he urged. "We've got to put our heads together." But McNeil didn't move, nor did Grant move to comfort him, or even touch him.

After a moment's hesitation Grant viciously yanked the curtain closed, veiling his mate's display of cowardice.

In a quick tour of the lower decks and the hold access corridor, Grant assured himself that whatever the damage to the life support deck the integrity of the crew's living and working quarters was not threatened. With a single bound he leaped through the center of the ship back to the flight deck, not even glancing at McNeil's cabin as he passed, and hooked himself into the command couch. He studied the graphics.

Oxygen supply one: flat. Oxygen supply two: flat. Grant gazed at the silent graphs as a man in ancient London, returning home one evening at the time of the plague, might have stared at a rough cross newly scrawled on his door. He tapped keys and the graphs bounced, but the fundamental equation that produced a flat curve did not yield to his coaxing. Grant could hardly doubt the message: news that is sufficiently bad somehow carries its own guarantee of truth, and only good reports need confirmation.

"Grant, I'm sorry."

Grant swung around to see McNeil floating by the ladder, his face flushed, the pouches under his eyes swollen from weeping. Even at a range of over a meter Grant could smell the "medicinal" brandy on his breath.

"What was it, a meteoroid?" McNeil seemed determined to be cheerful, to make up for the lapse, and when Grant nodded yes, McNeil even assayed a faint attempt at humor. "They say a ship this size could get hit once a century. We seem to have jumped the gun with ninety-nine point nine years still to go."

"Worse luck. Look at this"—Grant waved at the video-plate showing the damaged panel. "Where we were holed, the damned thing had to be coming in at practically right angles to us. Any other approach and it couldn't have hit anything vital." Grant swung around, facing the console and the wide flight deck windows that looked out on the starry night. For a moment he was silent, collecting his thoughts. What had happened was serious—deadly serious—but it need not be fatal. After all, the voyage was forty percent over. "You up to helping out?" he asked. "We should run some numbers."

"That I am." McNeil made for the engineer's work station.

"Then give me figures for total reserves, best and worst cases. Air in Hold A. Emergency reserves. Don't forget what's in the suit tanks and portable O-two packs."

"Right," said McNeil.

"I'll work on the mass ratios. See if we can gain anything by jettisoning the holds and making a run for it."

McNeil hesitated and muttered, "Uh . . ."

Grant paused. But whatever McNeil had been about to say, he thought better of it. Grant took a deep breath. He was in command here, and he already understood the obvious—that dumping the cargo would put the owners out of business, even with insurance, and put the insurance underwriters into the poor house, most likely. But after all, if it came to a matter of two human lives versus a few tonnes of dead weight, there really wasn't much question about it.

Grant's command of the ship at this moment was somewhat firmer than his command of himself. He was as much angry as he was frightened—angry with McNeil for breaking down, angry with the designers of the ship for assuming that a billion-to-one chance meant the same as impossible and therefore failing to provide additional meteor shielding in the soft underbelly of the command module. But the deadline for oxygen reserves was at least a couple of weeks away, and a lot could happen before then. The thought helped, for a moment anyway, to keep his fears at arm's length.

This was an emergency beyond doubt—but it was one of those peculiarly protracted emergencies, once characteristic of the sea, these days more typical of space—one of those emergencies where there was plenty of time to think. Perhaps too much time.

Grant was reminded of an old Cretan sailor he had met at the Pavlakis hangar in Heathrow, some ancient relative-of-a-relative of the old man's, there on a courtesy invitation, who had held an audience of clerks and mechanics in thrall as he recited the tale of a disastrous voyage he had worked as a young man, on a tramp steamer through the Red Sea. The captain of the vessel had inexplicably failed to provide his ship with sufficient fresh water against emergencies. The radio broke down, and then the engines. The ship drifted for weeks before attracting the attention of passing traffic, by which time the crew had been reduced to stretching the fresh water with salt. The old Cretan was among the survivors who merely spent a few weeks in hospital. Others were not so lucky; they had already died horribly of thirst and salt poisoning.

Slow disasters are like that: one unlikely thing happens, and that's complicated by a second unlikely event, and a third puts paid to somebody's life.

McNeil had grossly oversimplified matters when he said that the *Star Queen* might expect to be hit by a meteoroid once in a century. The answer depended on so many factors that three generations of statisticians and their computers had done little but lay down rules so vague that the insurance companies still shivered with apprehension when the great meteoroid swarms went sweeping like gales through the orbits of the inner worlds. Otherwise desirable interplanetary trajectories were put out of bounds by the insurors if they required a ship to intersect the orbit of the Leonids, say, at the peak of a shower—although even then the real chance of a ship and a meteoroid intersecting was, at worst, remote.

Much depends on one's subjective notion of what the words meteor and meteorite and meteoroid mean, of course. Each lump of cosmic slag that reaches the surface of the Earth—thus earning the moniker "meteorite"—has a million smaller brethren that perish utterly in the no-man's-land where the atmosphere has not quite ended and space has yet to begin, that ghostly region where Aurora walks by night. These are meteors—manifestations of the upper air, the original meaning of the word—the familiar shooting stars, which are seldom larger than a pin's head. And these in turn are outnumbered a millionfold again by particles too small to leave any visible trace of their dying as they drift down from the sky. All of them, the countless specks of dust, the rare boulders and even the wandering mountains that Earth encounters perhaps every dozen million years—all of them, flying free in space, are meteoroids.

For the purposes of space flight a meteoroid is only of interest if, on striking the hull, the resulting explosion interdicts vital functions, or produces destructive overpressures, or puts a hole in a pressurized compartment too big to prevent the rapid loss of atmosphere. These are matters both of size and relative speed. The efforts of the statisticians had resulted in tables showing approximate collision probabilities at various radiuses from the sun for meteoroids down to masses of a few milligrams. At the radius of Earth's orbit, for example, one might expect any given cubic kilometer of space to be traversed by a one-gram meteoroid, travelling toward the sun at perhaps forty kilometers per second, just once every three days. The likelihood of a spacecraft occupying the same cubic kilometer of space (except very near Earth itself) was much lower, and so was the calculated incidence of larger meteoroids—so that McNeil's "once in a century" collision estimate was in fact absurdly high.

The meteoroid which had struck *Star Queen* was big—likely a gram's worth of concreted dust and ice the size of a ball bearing. And it had somehow managed to avoid striking either the upper hemisphere of the crew module or the large cylindrical cargo holds below, in its nearly perpendicular angle of attack on the life support deck. The virtual certainty that such an occurrence would not happen again in the course of human history gave Grant and McNeil very little consolation.

Still, things might have been worse. *Star Queen* was fourteen days into her trajectory and had twenty-one days still to go to reach Port Hesperus. Thanks to her upgraded engines she was travelling much faster than the slow freighters, the tramp steamers of the space-ways who were restricted to Hohmann ellipses, those long tangential flight paths that expended minimum energy by just kissing the orbits of Earth and Venus on opposite sides of the sun. Passenger ships equipped with even more powerful gaseous-core reactors, or fast cutters using the still-new fusion drives, could slice across from planet to planet in as little as a fortnight, given favorable planetary alignments—and given a profit margin that allowed them to spend an order of magnitude more on fuel—but *Star Queen* was stuck in the middle of the equation. Her optimal acceleration and deceleration determined both her launch window and her time of arrival.

Surprising how long it takes to execute a simple computer program when your life depends on the outcome.

Grant entered the pertinent numbers a dozen different ways before he gave up hoping that the bottom line would change.

He turned to McNeil, still hunched over the engineering console across the circular room. "Looks like we can shave the ETA by almost half a day," he said. "Assuming we blow all the holds within the next hour or so."

For a second or two McNeil didn't reply. When at last he straightened and turned to face Grant his expression was calm and sober. "It appears the oxygen will last us eighteen days in the best case—fifteen in the worst. Seems we're a few days short."

The men regarded each other with a trancelike calmness that would have been remarkable had it not been obvious what was racing through their minds: there *must* be a way out!

Make oxygen!

Grow plants, for example—but there was nothing green aboard, not even a packet of grass seeds—and even if there were, despite the tall tales, when the entire energy cycle is taken into account, land plants are not efficient oxygen producers on much less than the scale of a small world. The only good it would have done them to have those pine seedlings aboard would have been the greater volume of air in the pressurized hold.

Electrolyze water then, reversing the fuel-cell cycle, getting from it elemental hydrogen and oxygen—but there was not enough water in the undamaged fuel cells or in the water tanks, or even in the two men's bodies, to keep them breathing for an additional seven days. At least not past their deaths from dehydration.

Extra oxygen was not to be had. Which left that last standby of space opera, the *deus ex machina* of a passing

spaceship—one that conveniently happened to be match-
ing one's course and velocity exactly.

There were no such ships, of course. Almost by defi-
nition, the spaceship that "happened to be passing" was
impossible. Even if other freighters already were skidding
toward Venus on the same trajectory—and Grant and
McNeil would have known if there were—then by the laws
that governed their movements, the very laws propounded
by Newton, they must keep their original separations without a heroic sacrifice of mass and a possibly fatal squandering of fuel. Any ship passing at a significantly greater
velocity—a passing liner, say—would be pursuing its own
hyperbolic trajectory and would likely be as inaccessible
as Pluto. But a fully provisioned cutter, if it started *now*
from Venus . . .

"What's docked at Port Hesperus?" McNeil inquired, as
if his thoughts had been on the same trajectory as Grant's.

Grant waited a moment, consulting the computer, before he replied. "A couple of old Hohmann freighters, according to Lloyd's Register—and the usual litter of
launches and tugs." He laughed abruptly. "Couple of solar
yachts. No help there."

"Seems we're drawing a blank," McNeil observed.
"P'raps we should have a word with the controllers on
Earth and Venus."

"I was about to do just that," Grant said irritably, "as
soon as I've decided how to phrase the query." He took a
swift breath. "Look, you've been a great help here. You
could do us another favor and do a personal check on
possible air leaks in the system. All right with you, then?"

"Certainly, that's all right." McNeil's voice was quiet.

Grant watched McNeil sidelong as he unbuckled his
loose straps and swam down, off the flight deck. The en-

gineer was probably going to give him trouble in the days that lay ahead, Grant mused. That shameful business, breaking down like a child . . . Until now they had got on well enough—like most men of substantial girth, McNeil was good-natured and easy-going—but now Grant realized that McNeil lacked fiber. Obviously he had become flabby, physically and mentally, through living too long in space.

X

The parabolic antenna on the communications boom was aimed at the gleaming arc lamp of Venus, less than twenty million kilometers away and moving on a converging path with the ship. A tone sounded on the console, indicating that a signal from Port Hesperus had been acquired.

The physical convergence would not occur for a month, but the three-millimeter waves from the ship's transmitter would make the trip in under a minute. How nice, at this moment, to be a radio wave.

Grant acknowledged the "go ahead" and began to talk steadily and, he hoped, quite dispassionately. He gave a careful analysis of the situation, appending pertinent data in telemetry, ending his speech with a request for advice. His fears concerning McNeil he left unspoken; the engineer was doubtless monitoring the transmission.

And on Port Hesperus—the Venus orbital station—the bombshell was about to burst, triggering trains of sympathetic ripples on all the inhabited worlds, as video and faxsheets took up the refrain: STAR QUEEN IN PERIL. An accident in space has a dramatic quality that tends to crowd all other items from the newsheads. At least until the corpses have been counted.

The actual reply from Port Hesperus, less dramatic, was as swift as the speed of light allowed: "Port Hesperus control to *Star Queen*, acknowledging your emergency status. We will shortly forward a detailed questionnaire. Please stand by."

They stood by. Or rather they floated by.

When the questions arrived Grant put them on printout. The message took nearly an hour to run through the printer and the questionnaire was so detailed, so extremely detailed—so extraordinarily detailed, in fact—that Grant wondered morosely if he and McNeil would live long enough to answer it. Two weeks, more or less.

Most of the queries were technical, concerning the status of the ship. Grant had no doubt the experts on Earth and Venus station were wracking their brains in an attempt to save *Star Queen* and her cargo. Perhaps especially her cargo.

"What do you think?" Grant asked McNeil, when the engineer had finished running through the message. He was studying McNeil carefully now, watching him for any signs of strain.

After a long, rigid silence, McNeil shrugged. His first words echoed Grant's thoughts. "It will certainly keep us busy. I doubt we'll get through this in a day. And I've got to admit I think half of these questions are crazy."

Grant nodded but said nothing. He let McNeil continue.

" 'Rate of leakage from the crew areas'—sensible enough, but we've already told them that. And what do they want with the efficiency of the radiation shields?"

"Could have something to do with seal erosion, I suppose," Grant murmured.

McNeil eyed him. "If you were to ask me, I'd say they were tryin' to keep our spirits up, pretendin' they have a bright idea or two. And meanwhile we're to keep ourselves too busy to worry about it."

Grant peered at McNeil with a queer mixture of relief and annoyance—relief because the Scot hadn't thrown another tantrum and, conversely, annoyance because he was now so damned calm, refusing to fit neatly into the mental category Grant had prepared for him. Had that momentary lapse after the meteoroid struck been typical of the man? Or might it have happened to anyone? Grant, to whom the world was very much a place of blacks and whites, felt angry at being unable to decide whether McNeil was cowardly or courageous. That he might be both never occurred to him.

In space, in flight, time is timeless. On Earth there is the great clock of the spinning globe itself, marking the hours with whole continents for hands. Even on the moon the shadows creep sluggishly from crag to crag as the sun makes its slow march across the sky. But in space the stars are fixed, or might as well be; the sun moves only if the pilot chooses to move the ship, and the chronometers tick off numbers that say days and hours but as far as sensation goes are meaningless.

Grant and McNeil had long since learned to regulate their lives accordingly; while in deep space they moved and thought with a kind of leisure—which vanished quickly enough when a voyage was nearing its end and the time for braking maneuvers arrived—and though they were now under sentence of death, they continued along the well-worn grooves of habit. Every day Grant carefully dictated the log, confirmed the ship's position, carried out his routine maintenance duties. McNeil was also behaving normally, as far as Grant could tell, although he suspected that some of the technical maintenance was being carried out with a very light hand, and he'd had a few sharp words with the engineer about the accumulation of dirty food trays following McNeil's turns in the galley.

It was now three days since the meteoroid had struck. Grant kept getting "buck up" messages from traffic control on Port Hesperus along the lines of "Sorry for the delay, fellows, we'll have something for you just as soon as we can"—and he waited for the results of the high-level review panel convened by the Board of Space Control, with its raft of specialists on two planets, which was running simulations of wild schemes to rescue *Star Queen*. He had waited impatiently at first, but his eagerness had slowly ebbed. He doubted that the finest technical brains in the solar system could save them now—though it was hard to abandon hope when everything still seemed so normal and the air was still clean and fresh.

On the fourth day Venus spoke. "Okay, fellows, here's what we've got for you. We're going to take this one system at a time, and some of this gets involved, so you be sure and ask for clarification if you need it. Okay, first we'll go into the cabin atmosphere system file, locus two-three-nine point four. Now I'll just give you a moment to find that locus. . . ."

Shorn of jargon, the long message was a funeral oration; the thrust of the instructions was to insure that *Star Queen* could arrive at Port Hesperus under remote control with its cargo intact, even if there were two dead bodies in the command module. Grant and McNeil had been written off.

One comfort: Grant already knew from his training in high-altitude chambers that death from hypoxia, near the end, anyway, would be a positively giddy affair.

McNeil vanished below soon after the message concluded, without a word of comment. Grant did not see him again for hours. He was frankly relieved, at first. He didn't feel like talking, either, and if McNeil wanted to look after himself that was his affair. Besides, there were various letters to write, loose ends to see to—though the last-will-and-testament business could come later. There were a couple of weeks left.

At supper time Grant went down to the common area, expecting to find McNeil at work at the galley. McNeil was a good cook, within the limitations of spacecraft cuisine, and he usually enjoyed his turn in the kitchen. He certainly took good enough care of his own stomach.

But there was no one in the common area. The curtain in front of McNeil's cabin was pulled shut.

Grant yanked the curtain aside and found McNeil lying in midair near his bunk, very much at peace with the universe. Hanging there beside him was a large plastic crate whose magnetic lock had somehow been jimmied. Grant had no need to examine it to know its contents; a glance at McNeil was enough.

"Ay, and it's a dirty shame," said the engineer without a trace of embarrassment, "to suck this stuff up through a tube." He cocked an eye at Grant. "Tell you what, cap'n—whyn't you put a little spin on the vessel so's we can drink 'er properly?" Grant glared at him contemptuously, but McNeil returned his gaze unabashed. "Oh, don't be a sourpuss, man—have some yourself! For what does it matter?"

He batted a bottle at Grant, who fielded it deftly. It was

a Cabernet Sauvignon from the Napa Valley of California—
fabulously valuable, Grant knew the consignment—and the
contents of that plastic case were worth thousands.

"I don't think there's any need," Grant said severely,
"to behave like a pig—even under these circumstances."

McNeil wasn't drunk yet. He had only reached the
brightly lit anteroom of intoxication and had not lost all
contact with the drab outer world. "I am prepared," he
announced with great solemnity, "to listen to any good
argument against my present course of action. A course
which seems eminently sensible to me." He blessed Grant
with a cherubic smile. "But you'd better convince me
quickly, while I'm still amenable to reason."

With that he squeezed the plastic bulb into which he'd
off-loaded a third of the bottle's contents, and shot a
ruddy purple jet into his open mouth.

"You're stealing company property—scheduled for sal-
vage," Grant announced, unaware of the absurdity but
conscious as he said it that his voice had taken on the
nasality, the constriction, of a young schoolmaster, "and
. . . and besides, you can hardly stay drunk for two weeks."

"That," said McNeil thoughtfully, "remains to be seen."

"I don't think so," retorted Grant. With his right hand
he secured himself to the bulkhead, with his left he swiped
at the crate and gave it a vicious shove that sent it soaring
through the open curtain.

As he wheeled and dived after it he heard McNeil's
pained yelp: "Why you constipated bastard! Of all the
dirty tricks!"

It would take McNeil some time in his present condition to organize a pursuit. Grant steered the crate down
to the hold airlock and into the pressurized, temperature-
controlled compartment it had come from. He sealed the

case and replaced it on its rack, strapping it securely into place. No point in trying to lock the case; McNeil had made a mess of the lock.

But Grant could make sure McNeil wouldn't get in here again—he would reset the combination on the hold airlock and keep the new combination to himself. As it happened, he had plenty of time to do it. McNeil hadn't bothered to follow him.

As Grant swam back toward the flight deck he passed the open curtain to McNeil's cabin. McNeil was still in there, singing.

"We don't care where the oxygen goes
If it doesn't get into the wine. . . ."

Evidently he'd already removed a couple of bottles before Grant had arrived to grab the case. Let them last him two weeks then, Grant thought, if they last the night.

"We don't care *where* the oxygen goes
If it doesn't get into the wine. . . ."

Where the hell had he heard that refrain? Grant, whose education was severely technical, was sure McNeil was deliberately misquoting some bawdy Elizabethan madrigal or the like, just to taunt him. He was suddenly shaken by an emotion which, to do him justice, he did not for a moment recognize, and which passed as swiftly as it had come.

But when he reached the flight deck he was trembling, and he felt a little sick. He realized that his dislike of McNeil was slowly turning to hatred.

XI

Certainly Grant and McNeil got on well enough in ordinary circumstances. It was nobody's fault that circumstances were now very far from ordinary.

Only because the two men had shown wonderfully smooth personality curves on the standard psychological tests; only because their flight records were virtually flawless; only because thousands of millions of pounds and dollars and yen and drachmas and dinars were involved in the flight of *Star Queen* had the Board of Space Control granted the ship a waiver of the crew-of-three rule.

The crew-of-three rule had evolved during a century and a half of space flight and ostensibly provided for a minimally sound social configuration during long periods of isolation—a problem that had not been pressing in the 20th century, before occupied spacecraft had ventured farther than the moon and the time delay for communication with Earth was still measured in seconds. True, in any group of three, two will eventually gang up on the third—

as the ancient Romans learned after several hard political lessons, in human affairs the least stable structure is the tripod. Which is not necessarily bad. Certainly three is better than two, and two is much better than one. And any group larger than three will soon enough degenerate into sub-groups of diads and triads.

A man or woman alone will almost certainly go mad within a relatively short time. It may be a benign madness, even an exemplary madness—taking the form of an obsessive writing of romantic poetry, for example—but no form of madness is encouraging to spacecraft insurors.

Experience shows that a crew of one man and one woman will experience a crisis within days. Their relative ages do not matter. If the text of their conversation is power, the subtext will be sex. And vice versa.

On the other hand, two men alone together or two worn...n alone together, provided their sexual vectors are not convergent, will dispense with the sexual subtext and will get down to the nitty-gritty of power every time: who's in charge here? ... Although in the case of two women the resolution of that question is, for cultural reasons, somewhat less likely to lead to fatal violence.

With three people of whatever sex, everybody will try to get along for a while and eventually two will gang up on the third. Thus the power question resolves itself, and depending on the make-up of the crew, sex will take care of itself also, i.e. two or more may be doing it together and one or more will be doing it alone.

Two men, not close friends, both of them heterosexual and of comparable age and status but fundamentally different in temperament, are the worst possible combination.

* * *

Three days without food, it has been said, is long enough to remove the subtle differences between a so-called civilized man and a so-called savage. Grant and McNeil were in no physical discomfort, nor would they be in extreme pain even at the end. But their imaginations had been active; they had more in common with a couple of hungry cannibals lost in a log canoe than they would have cared to admit.

One aspect of their situation, the most important of all, had never been mentioned; the computer's analysis had been checked and rechecked, but its bottom line was not quite final, for the computer refrained from making suggestions it had not been asked to make. The two men on the crew could easily take that final step of calculation in their heads—

—and each arrived at the same result. It was simple, really, a macabre parody of those problems in first-grade arithmetic which began, "If two men had six days to assemble five helicopters, how long...?

At the moment the meteoroid destroyed the stored liquid oxygen, there were approximately forty-eight hundred cubic feet of air inside the crew module and twelve hundred cubic feet of air in the pressurized compartment of Hold A. At one atmosphere a cubic foot of air weighs one and two-tenths ounces, but less than a fourth of that is oxygen. Adding in the space-suit and emergency supplies, there were less than seventy pounds of oxygen in the ship. A man consumes almost two pounds of oxygen a day.

Thirty-five man-days of oxygen...

The oxygen supply was enough for *two* men for two and a half weeks. Venus was three weeks away. One did not have to be a calculating prodigy to see that one man, one man only, might live to walk the curving garden paths of Port Hesperus.

Four days had passed. The acknowledged deadline was thirteen days away, but the unspoken deadline was ten. For ten more days two men could breathe the air without endangering the chances of the one who might survive alone. Beyond ten days one man only would have any hope of reaching Venus. To a sufficiently detached observer the situation might have seemed highly engaging. Grant and McNeil were not detached, however. It is not easy at the best of times for two people to decide amicably which of them shall commit suicide; it is even more difficult when they are not on speaking terms.

Grant wished to be perfectly fair. Therefore, as he conceived matters, the only thing to do was to wait until McNeil sobered up and emerged from his cabin; then Grant would put it to him directly.

As these thoughts swirled over the surface of his mind Peter Grant was staring through the windows of the flight deck at the starry universe, seeing the thousands upon thousands of individual stars and even the misty nebulas as he had never seen them before. He was moved by a certain conviction of transcendence—

—which mere speech would surely betray.

Well, he would write McNeil a letter. And best do it now, while they were still on diplomatic terms. He clipped a sheet of notepaper to his writing pad and began: "Dear McNeil." He paused, his ballpoint poised above the paper. Then he tore that sheet out and began again: "McNeil."

It took him the best part of three hours to get down what he wanted to say, and even then he wasn't wholly satisfied. Some things were damned difficult to put on paper. At last he finished; he folded the letter and sealed it with a strip of tape. He left the flight deck, taking the letter with him, and closed himself into his cabin. The business of actually handing the letter to McNeil could wait a day or two.

Few of the billions of videoplate addicts on Earth—or the additional thousands on Port Hesperus and Mars and in the Mainbelt and on the colonized moons—could have had any true notion of what was going on within the minds of the two men aboard *Star Queen*. The public media was full of rescue schemes. All sorts of retired spaceship pilots and writers of fantasy fiction had been dredged up to give their opinons over the airwaves as to how Grant and McNeil should comport themselves. The men who were the cause of all this fuss wisely declined to listen to any of it.

Traffic control on Port Hesperus was a bit more disreet. One could not with any decency give words of advice or encouragement to men on death row, even if there was some uncertainty about the date of execution. Therefore traffic control contented itself with few emotionally neutral messages each day—relaying the newsheads about the war in southern Asia, the growing sector dispute in the Mainbelt, new mineral strikes on the surface of Venus, the fuss over the censorship of "While Rome Burns," which had just been banned in Moscow. . . .

Life on *Star Queen* continued much as before, not withstanding the stiffness between the two men that had attended McNeil's emergence—classically hung-over—from his cabin. Grant, for his part, spent much of his time on the flight deck writing letters to his wife. Long letters. The longer the better. . . . He could have spoken to her if he'd wished, but the thought of all those news addicts listening in prevented him from doing so. Unhappily, there were no truly private lines in space.

And that letter to McNeil. Why not deliver it, get it over with? Well, he would do that, within a couple of days ... and then they would decide. Besides, such a delay would give McNeil a chance to raise the subject himself.

That McNeil might have reasons for his hesitation other than simple cowardice did not occur to Grant.

He wondered how McNeil was spending his time, now that he'd run out of booze. The engineer had a large library of books on videochip, for he read widely and his range of interests was unusual. Grant had seen him delving into Western philosophy and Eastern religion and fiction of all kinds; McNeil had once mentioned that his favorite book was the odd early-20th century novel *Jurgen*. Perhaps he was trying to forget his doom by losing himself in its strange magic. Others of McNeil's books were less respectable, and not a few were of the class curiously described as "curious. . . ."

But in fact McNeil, lying in his cabin or moving silently through the ship, was a subtler and more complicated personality than Grant knew, perhaps too complicated for Grant to understand. Yes, McNeil was a hedonist. He did what he could to make life comfortable for himself aboard ship, and when planetside he indulged himself fully in the pleasures of life, all the more for being cut off from them for months at a time. But he was by no means the moral weakling that the unimaginative, puritanical Grant supposed him to be.

True, he had collapsed completely under the shock of the meteoroid strike. When it happened he'd been passing through the life support deck's access corridor, on his way back from the hold, and he understood the seriousness of the violent explosion instantly—it happened hardly a meter away, on the other side of the steel wall—without having to wait for confirmation. His reaction was exactly like that of an airline passenger who sees a wing come off at 30,000 feet: there are still ten or fifteen minutes left to fall, but death is inevitable. So he'd panicked.

Like a willow in the wind, he'd bowed under the strain—and then recovered. Grant was a harder man—an oak—and a brittler one.

As for the business of the wine, McNeil's behavior had been reprehensible by Grant's standards, but that was Grant's problem; besides, that episode too was behind them. By tacit consent they'd gone back to their normal routine, although it did nothing to reduce the sense of strain. They avoided each other as much as possible except when meal times brought them together. When they did meet, they behaved with an exaggerated politeness, as if each were striving to be perfectly normal—yet inexplicably failing.

A day passed, and another. And a third.

Grant had hoped that McNeil would have broached the subject of suicide by now, thus sparing him a very awkward duty. When the engineer stubbornly refused to do anything of the sort it added to Grant's resentment and contempt. To make matters worse he was now suffering from nightmares and sleeping very badly.

The nightmare was always the same. When Peter Grant was a child it had often happened that at bedtime he had been reading a story far too exciting to be left until morning. To avoid detection he had continued reading under the bedclothes by flashlight, curled up in a snug white-walled cocoon. Every ten minutes or so the air had become too stifling to breathe and his emergence into the delicious cool air had been a major part of the fun. Now, thirty years later, these innocent childhood hours returned to haunt him. He was dreaming that he could not escape from the suffocating sheets while the air was steadily and remorselessly thickening around him.

He'd intended to give McNeil the letter after two days, yet somehow he'd put it off again. This procrastination was very unlike Grant, but he managed to persuade himself that it was a perfectly reasonable thing to do. He was giving McNeil a chance to *redeem* himself—

—to prove that he wasn't a coward, by raising the issue first. It never occurred to Grant that McNeil might be waiting for him to do the same. . . .

The all-too-literal deadline was three days off when, for the first time, Grant's mind brushed lightly against the thought of murder. He'd retired to the flight deck after the "evening" meal, trying to relax by gazing at the starry night through the wide windows that surrounded the flight deck, but McNeil was doing a very thorough and noisy job of cleaning up the galley, clattering around with what must surely be an unnecessary, even a deliberate, amount of noise.

What *use* was McNeil to this world? He had no family, no responsibilities. Who would be the worse for his death?

Grant, on the other hand, had a wife and three children, of whom he was moderately fond, even if they were no more than dutiful in their perfunctory displays of affection for him. An impartial judge would have no difficulty in deciding which of them should survive, and if McNeil had had a spark of decency in him he would have come to the same conclusion already. Since he appeared to have done nothing of the sort he had surely forfeited all further claims to consideration. . . .

Such was the elemental logic of Grant's subconscious mind, which of course had arrived at this conclusion days before but had only now succeeded in attracting the attention for which it had been clamoring.

To Grant's credit he at once rejected the thought. With horror.

He was an upright and honorable person, with a very strict code of behavior. Even the vagrant homicidal impulses of what is misleadingly called a "normal" man had seldom ruffled his mind. But in the days—the very few days—left to him, they would come more and more often.

The air was noticeably fouler. Although air pressure had been reduced to a minimum and there was no shortage of the canisters that were used to scrub carbon dioxide from the circulating atmosphere, it was impossible to prevent a slow increase in the ratio of inert gases to the dwindling oxygen reserves. There was still no real difficulty in breathing, but the thick odor was a constant reminder of what lay ahead.

Grant was in his cabin. It was "night," but he could not sleep—a relief in one way, for it broke the hold of his nightmares. But he had not slept well the previous night either, and he was becoming physically run down; his nerve was rapidly deteriorating, a state of affairs accentuated by the fact that McNeil had been behaving with a calmness that was not only unexpected but quite annoying. Grant realized that in his own emotional state it would be dangerous to delay the showdown any longer. He freed himself from his loose sleep restraint and opened his desk, reaching for the letter he had intended to give to McNeil days ago. And then he *smelled* something—

A single neutron begins the chain reaction that in an instant can destroy a million lives, the toil of generations. Equally insignificant are the trigger-events that can alter a person's course of action and so alter the whole pattern of the future. Nothing could have been more trivial than what made Grant pause with the letter in his hand; under ordinary circumstances he would not have noticed it at all. It was the smell of smoke—tobacco smoke.

The revelation that McNeil, that sybaritic engineer, had so little self-control that he was squandering the last precious pounds of oxygen on *cigarettes* filled Grant with a blinding fury. For a moment he went quite rigid with the intensity of his emotion. Then, slowly, he crumpled the letter in his hand. The thought that had first been an unwelcome intruder, then a casual speculation, was now finally accepted. McNeil had had his chance and had proved, by this unbelievable selfishness, unworthy of it.

Very well—he could die.

The speed with which Grant arrived at this self-justifying conclusion would have been obvious to the rankest of amateur psychiatrists. He had needed to convince himself that there was no point in doing the honorable thing, suggesting some game of chance that would give McNeil and him an equal chance at life. Here was the excuse he needed, and he seized upon it. He might now plan and carry out McNeil's murder according to his own particular moral code.

Relief as much as hatred drove Grant back to his bunk, where every whiff of tobacco aroma salved his conscience.

* * *

McNeil could have told Grant that once again he was badly misjudging him. The engineer had been a heavy smoker for years—against his better judgment, it's true, and quite conscious that he was unavoidably an annoyance to the majority of folk who did not care to breathe his exhaust. He'd tried to quit—it was easy, he sometimes quipped, he'd done it often—but in moments of strain he inevitably found himself reaching for those fragrant paper cylinders. He envied Grant, the sort of man who could smoke a cigarette when he wanted one but put them aside without regret. He wondered why Grant smoked at all, if he didn't need to. Some sort of symbolic rebellion . . . ?

At any rate, McNeil had calculated that he could afford two cigarettes a day without producing the least measurable difference in the duration of a breathable atmosphere. The luxury of those six or seven minutes, twice a day— one late at night, one at mid-morning, hidden deep down in the central corridor of the ship—was in all likelihood beyond the capacity of Peter Grant to imagine, and it contributed greatly to Angus McNeil's mental well-being. Though the two cigarettes made no difference to the oxygen supply, they made all the difference in the world to McNeil's nerves, and thus contributed indirectly to Grant's peace of mind.

But no use trying to tell Grant that. So McNeil smoked privately, exercising a self-control that was in itself surprisingly agreeable, even voluptuous.

Had McNeil known of Grant's insomnia, he would not have risked even that late night cigarette in his unsealed cabin. . . .

For a man who had only an hour ago talked himself into murder, Grant's actions were remarkably methodical.

Without hesitation—beyond that necessitated by caution—Grant floated silently past his cabin partition and on across the darkened common area to the wall-mounted medicine chest near the galley. Only a ghostly blue safe-light illuminated the interior of the chest, in which tubes and vials and instruments were snugly secured in their padded nests by straps of Velcro. The ship's outfitters had provided tools and medicines for every emergency they had ever heard of or could imagine.

Including this one. There behind its retaining strap was the tiny bottle whose image had been lying far down in the depths of Grant's unconscious all these days. In the blue light he could not read the fine print on the label—all he could see was the skull and crossbones—but he knew the words by heart: "Approximately one-half gram will cause painless and almost instantaneous death."

Painless and instantaneous—good. Even better was a fact that went unmentioned on the label. The stuff was tasteless.

Most of another day went by.

The contrast between the meals prepared by Grant and those organized with considerable skill and care by McNeil was striking. Anyone who was fond of food and who spent a good deal of his life in space usually learned the art of cooking in self-defense, and McNeil had not only learned it but had mastered it. He could coax a piquant sauce from dried milk, the juices of rehydrated beefsteak, and his private stash of herbs; he could coax flavor from the deep freeze with his flasks of oils and vinegars.

To Grant, eating was one of those necessary but annoying jobs that was to be got through as quickly as possible, and his cooking mirrored this attitude. McNeil had long ago ceased to grumble about it; imagine his bemusement, then, had he seen the trouble Grant was taking over this particular dinner.

They met wordlessly, as usual—only the constraints of habit and civility kept them from grabbing their trays and retreating to their own lairs. Instead they hovered on opposite sides of the little convenience table, each perched in midair at a careful angle, not quite looking at or looking away from the other. If McNeil noticed any increasing nervousness on Grant's part as the meal progressed, he said nothing; indeed they ate in perfect silence, having long since exhausted the possibilities of light conversation. When the last course, succotash, had been served in those bowls with the incurved rims, designed to restrain their contents, Grant cleared the litter and went into the adjacent galley unit to make coffee.

He took quite a long time, considering the coffee was, as always, instant—for at the last moment something maddening happened. He was on the point of squeezing boiling water from one container into another, looking at the two hot-liquid bulbs in front of him, when he remembered an ancient silent film he'd seen on a chip somewhere, featuring a clown who usually wore a bowler hat and a funny mustache—Charlie somebody—who in this movie was trying to poison an unwanted wife. Only he got the glasses accidentally reversed.

No memory could have been more unwelcome. Grant nearly lapsed into psychopathic giggles. Had the erudite McNeil known what was going on in Grant's mind (assuming he could have retained his equanimity and humor), he might have suggested that Grant had been attacked by Poe's "Imp of the Perverse," that demon who delights in defying the careful canons of self-preservation.

A good minute passed before Grant, shivering, managed to regain control. His nerves must be in even worse condition than he had imagined.

But he was sure that outwardly at least he was quite calm as he carried in the two plastic containers and their drinking tubes. There was no danger of confusing them now: the engineer's had the letters M A C painted boldly around it. He pushed that one toward McNeil and watched, fascinated—trying hard to disguise his fascination—as McNeil toyed with the bulb. He seemed in no great hurry; he was staring moodily at nothing. Then, at last, he put the drinking tube to his mouth and sipped—

—and spluttered, staring at the drinking bulb with shock. An icy hand seized Peter Grant's heart. McNeil cleared his throat, then turned to him and said evenly—

"Well na', Grant, you've made it properly for once. And very hot, too."

Slowly Grant's heart resumed its interrupted work. He did not trust himself to speak, but he did manage a noncommittal nod.

McNeil parked the bulb carefully in midair, a few inches from his face. His fleshy face settled into a ponderously thoughtful expression, as if he were weighing his words in preparation for some momentous pronouncement.

Grant cursed himself for making the coffee so hot. Just the sort of detail that hanged murderers. And if McNeil waited any longer to say whatever he was going to say, Grant would probably betray himself through nervousness.

Not that it would do McNeil any good now.

At last McNeil spoke. "I suppose it's occurred to you,"

he said in a quietly conversational way, "that there's still enough air to last one of us to Venus."

Grant forced his jangling nerves under control and tore his eyes away from McNeil's fatal bulb of coffee; his throat seemed very dry as he answered. "It . . . it had crossed my mind."

McNeil touched the floating bulb, found it still too hot, and continued thoughtfully: "Then it would be more sensible—wouldn't it?—if one of us simply decided to walk out the airlock, say—or take some of the poison in there." He jerked his head toward the medicine chest, on the curve of the wall not far from where they were floating.

Grant nodded. Oh yes, that would be quite sensible.

"The only trouble, of course," McNeil mused, "is deciding which of us is to be the unlucky fella'. I suppose we could draw a card . . . or something equally arbitrary."

Grant stared at McNeil with a fascination that almost outweighed his mounting nervousness. He never would have believed the engineer could discuss the subject so calmly. Obviously McNeil's thoughts had been running on a line parallel with his own, and it was scarcely even a coincidence that he had chosen this time, of all times, to raise the question. From his talk it was certain that he suspected nothing.

McNeil was watching Grant closely, as if judging his reaction.

"You're right," Grant heard himself say. "We must talk it over. Soon."

"Yes," McNeil said impassively. "We must." And then he reached for the bulb of coffee and brought the drinking tube to his lips. He sucked at it slowly, for a long time.

Grant could not wait for him to finish. Yet the relief

he had hoped for did not come; indeed, he felt a stab of regret. Regret, not quite remorse. It was a little late now to think of how lonely he would be aboard *Star Queen,* haunted by his thoughts, in the days to come.

He knew he did not wish to see McNeil die. Suddenly he felt rather sick. Without another glance at his victim he launched himself toward the flight deck.

XII

Immovably fixed, the fierce sun and the unwinking stars looked down on *Star Queen,* which on the grand scale of cosmic affairs was as motionless as they were.

There was no way for a naive observer to know that the tiny model molecule of a spaceship had now reached its maximum velocity with respect to Earth and was about to unleash massive thrust to brake itself into a parking orbit near Port Hesperus. Indeed, there was no reason for an observer on the cosmic scale to suspect that *Star Queen* had anything to do with intelligent purpose, or with life—

—until the main airlock atop the command module opened and the lights of the interior glowed yellow in the cold darkness. For a moment the round circle of light hung oddly within the black shadow of the falling ship; then it was abruptly eclipsed, as two human figures floated out of the ship.

One of the two bulky figures was active, the other passive. Something not easy to perceive happened in the shadows; then the passive figure began to move, slowly at first but with rapidly mounting speed. It swept out of the shadow of the ship into the full blast of the sun. And now the cosmic observer, given a powerful telescope, might have noted the nitrogen bottle strapped to its back, the valve evidently left open—a crude but effective rocket.

Rolling slowly, the corpse—for such it was—dwindled against the stars, to vanish utterly in less than a minute. The other figure remained quite motionless in the open airlock, watching it go. Then the outer hatch swung shut, the circle of brilliance vanished, and only the reflected sunlight of bright Venus still glinted on the shadowed wall of the ship.

In the immediate vicinity of *Star Queen,* nothing of consequence happened for the next seven days.

PART FOUR

A QUESTION OF HONOR

XIII

When she caught up with the uniformed man, he was marching along the river walk in the Council of Worlds grounds, heading away from the Earth Central offices of the Board of Space Control. The formal gardens were green with the tender new leaves of budding trees; another spring had come to Manhattan . . .

"Assistant Inspector Troy, Commander. They told me to catch you before you left."

He kept walking. "I'm not going anywhere, Troy. Just getting out of the office." She fell into step beside him. He was a gaunt man, of Slavic ancestry by the look of him, with an iron-gray crewcut and a Canadian-accented voice so hoarse it was hardly more than a whisper. His blue uniform was pressed and spotless; the gold insignia on his collar gleamed; his chest was pinned with only a few ribbons, but they were the ones that count. Despite the blue suit and the headquarters job, the commander's deeply creased face, burned almost black, betrayed his years in deep space. He opened a silver pill case and popped a tiny purple sphere into his mouth—then seemed to remember Sparta, marching beside him. He paused at the steel railing and held out the open case. "Care for one? Rademas." When she hesitated he said, "Lots of us use them, I'm sure you know that—mild boost, wash out of your system in twenty minutes."

"No thank you, sir," she said firmly.

"I was kidding," he rasped. "Actually they're breath mints. Violet flavor. Strongest thing in 'em is sugar." He stretched his face into a shape that was not much like a grin. He still held out the open case. Sparta shook her head again and he flipped it closed. "As you wish." Grimacing in distaste, he spit the mint he'd been holding under his tongue over the rail, into the gelid East River. "Guess I've pulled that dumb stunt too often; you rookies are wise."

He gazed out across the water, its thick green surface crowded with long-legged algae harvesters like water skates on a pond, their stainless steel manifolds reflecting the golden sunlight of early morning. The commander was staring past them, straight at the sun—probably wishing he had a different view of it, one without a lot of muggy atmosphere in the way. After a few moments he turned to Sparta, clearing his throat roughly. "Okay. Seems Inspector Bernstein thinks highly of you. She wrote you a good ER. We're giving you a solo."

Sparta's pulse raced; after two years, the prospect of a mission of her own! "I'm grateful for her recommendation."

"I'll bet you are. Especially since you never thought she'd let you out of her grasp."

Sparta allowed herself to smile. "Well sir, I admit I was getting to know Newark better than I ever wanted to."

"No guarantee you won't go back there when this is over, Troy. Depends."

"What's the assignment, Commander?"

"TDY to Port Hesperus. The *Star Queen* thing. Shouldn't be too hairy. Either the ship was holed by a meteoroid or it wasn't, in which case it broke or somebody broke it. The owner and most of the people concerned are already on their way to Port Hesperus in *Helios*, but we'll get you there first. You'll be working with a guy named Proboda from the local. He's got seniority, but you're in charge. Which reminds me . . ." He reached into the inside pocket of his jacket and took out a leather folder. "Since we don't want the locals to push you around"—he flipped open the folder to reveal a gold shield—"you're promoted." He handed it to her. "Here's the visual aid. Sliver in the case. The electronics are already in the system."

Sparta took the badge case in both hands and studied the intricate shield. A delicate flush bloomed on her cheekbones.

The commander watched her a moment, then said abruptly, "Sorry there's no time for ceremony, Inspector. Congratulations anyway."

"Thank you, sir."

"Here's your ride now." She turned with him as a low-slung white helicopter dropped shrieking toward the helipad in front of the Council of Worlds tower. It touched down gently, its turbines spinning down to idle, its rotors whistling in lazy circles. "Forget your personal gear, you can req what you need," said the commander. "Within reason, of course. You've got a shuttle to catch at Newark and a torch waiting in orbit. Everything you need to know is in the system. We'll update you if we have to."

She was startled at her sudden impending departure, but she tried not to show it. "One question, sir."

"Go ahead."

"Why anyone from Earth Central, sir? Why not leave the investigation to Port Hesperus?"

"Port Hesperus is short a body. Captain Antreen is in charge there; she looked at what we had available and asked for you by name." The commander grinned again. "Be grateful to her. Bernstein never *would* have let you out of Customs."

Sparta saluted and walked briskly toward the waiting helicopter. The commander watched her go on with undisguised envy.

Beside its three-person crew the torch-powered cutter carried Sparta and no one else. The slender white ship, bearing the blue band and gold star of the Board of Space Control, streaked sunward on a hyperbolic orbit and closed on Port Hesperus a week after Sparta's hasty Earthside promotion. Two days out, less than a week from rendezvous with Port Hesperus, a radio message came through. "*This is* Star Queen, *Commander Peter Grant speaking. Engineering Officer McNeil and I have jointly concluded that there is sufficient oxygen remaining for one man . . .*"

Earth Central was on the horn to Sparta in less than an hour; the commander's lined and blackened face appeared on the videoplate in the cutter's comm shack. "All right, Troy, this adds a wrinkle. We need to know whether this crewman went out the airlock this morning on his own, or did he get pushed?"

"Yes, sir. Are the dossiers I requested on the *Helios* passengers available?"

There was a minute's delay while her words made the

trip to Earth and his made their way back. "We're squirting you with what we have on the blackchannels," he said. "I can tell you that you're dealing with an odd bunch there. A guy working for the insurance people who's a known con—they know it too, so apparently it's all right with them. A woman into heavy machinery and old books. Her temperamental girlfriend. A guy who owns a spaceship with a history so odd it had to have its name changed. Another guy with practically no history at all."

"Thanks, Commander."

A minute later he said, "Watch yourself, Inspector." He signed off.

Three days before arriving at Port Hesperus, the cutter crossed *Helios's* path and a day after that, *Star Queen's*. If Sparta had had a telescope, she could have looked at the fast ships with the perspective of a cosmic observer. But it was the people aboard them that interested her.

With its mighty torch blazing, the cutter decelerated toward the great rings and spokes and cylinders of Port Hesperus, that whole spinning conglomerate of a space station hanging in high orbit over the dazzling clouds of Venus, with its axis pointing straight at the center of the planet.

At the radiation perimeter the cutter's torch flamed out. It approached under chemical power, gingerly.

Port Hesperus was one of the triumphs of 21st-century engineering, built almost entirely from the raw materials of captured asteroids. Exploiting the resources of the planet's surface, it had paid back its cost within two decades; it currently housed a hundred thousand people in conditions that ninetenths of Earth's population would have considered luxurious. Parks, for example, and green things . . . The great glass central sphere of the station was filled with lush gardens, some of them in tribute to the old dreams of Venus as a world of swamps and jungles. Come to Venus and you could see jungles, all right, as long as you stuck to the paths of Port Hesperus's brilliantly lit central sphere. Don't try to visit the surface of the planet, don't even ask. Of the five human beings who had made the attempt in armored and heat-shielded landers, only two had returned to tell the tale.

Sparta's cutter matched spin with the star-side docking bay under chemical power; in fifteen minutes, under automated landing controls, it had made it into the huge axial bay, crowded with local traffic.

The high-security side of the docking bay was all business, no nonsense, without amenities—all white steel and black glass, pipes and hoses and blinking lights. A tube like a giant leech closed over the cutter's lock, the air slammed into it under high pressure, and the cutter's hatch popped.

Sparta clapped her hands over her painful ears. Floating in the airlock, she found herself suddenly face-to-face with a delegation from the local Board of Space Control headquarters, advancing toward her in the docking tube. They didn't look all that friendly.

The tallest of the locals facing her was the Port Hesperus unit captain, Kara Antreen. She was dressed in a gray wool suit worth a month of her respectable salary; her gray hair was cut in a severe pageboy, and her pale gray eyes fixed on Sparta from beneath thick black brows.

Even without her hands over her ears, Sparta was at a social disadvantage. It was this matter of her clothes. She had found little to requisition from ship's stores, despite the commander's invitation—the quartermaster's imagi-

nation seemed limited to gym shorts, personal care products, near-beer, and "entertainment" items emphasizing
soft-porn videochips—so besides picking up a few changes
of socks and underwear and acquiring a comb and a
toothbrush, she'd arrived at Port Hesperus still wearing the
mufti of an assistant inspector assigned to shuttleport customs and entry—that is, the plainclothes disguise of a bribable dock rat: plastic patch-pocket cargo pants, olive drab
tank top, polymer canvas windbreaker. The outfit was distinctly on the casual side, but at least it was neat and
clean.

"Ellen Troy, Captain," Sparta said. "I look forward to
working with you and your people."

"Troy." Antreen smiled then, lessening the tension.
"And we look forward to working with you. Any cooperation we can give you—anything at all—we want to be
there helping out."

"That's very . . ."

"Understood?"

"Certainly, Captain. Thanks."

Antreen extended her hand; they shook vigorously.
"Inspector Troy, this is my aide Lieutenant Kitamuki. And
this is Inspector Proboda."

Sparta shook hands with the others—Kitamuki, a slender woman with long black hair knotted back and floating
over one shoulder in a sinuous ponytail, Proboda, a rough-
hewn blond male giant, Polish or maybe Ukrainian, with
a touch of the old hell-for-leather cossacks about his
slanted eyes. Antreen was all smiles, but her two sidekicks
studied Sparta as if considering arresting her on the spot.

"Let's get into some gravity," Antreen said. "We'll
show you to your quarters, Troy. And when you're settled
we'll see if we can clear off a desk for you at unit HQ."

She moved off quickly; Kitamuki and Proboda parted to let Sparta through, then closed in tight formation behind her.

Sparta followed Antreen easily enough through the weightless passage—she'd had three days without acceleration in the middle of her trip and she hadn't lost the body-memory of what it was like to have space legs—passing from the station's motionless hub through the gray metal bulkheads of the security sector. They passed the station's huge sliding collar, and Sparta paused a moment to adjust to the spin. They moved on, through black-and yellow-striped emergency hatches into wider corridors, until they reached one of the main halls in the turning section of the station, far enough outside the hub to create fractional gees which established a "floor," that being the inner cylindrical surface of the hall itself. Once in the hall, Antreen turned planetward, toward the Space Board headquarters in the station's central sphere.

Sparta paused. Kitamuki and Proboda almost tumbled into her. "Something wrong, Inspector?" Antreen asked.

"It's very good of you," Sparta said, smiling. "But time is too short, I'll have to check out my quarters later."

"If you say so. I'm sure we can get you settled at HQ, anyway."

"I'll be going to traffic control first. *Star Queen* is due within the hour."

"We haven't arranged authorization," Antreen said.

"No problem," Sparta replied.

Antreen nodded. "You're right, of course. Your badge is enough. Do you know the way?"

"If any of you want to come with me . . ." Sparta said.

"Inspector Proboda will accompany you. He'll take care of anything you need," Antreen said.

"Okay, thanks. Let's go." Sparta was already moving starward, heading for the transparent traffic control dome that capped the huge space station. Although she had never been beyond Earth's moon, she knew the layout of Port Hesperus in such detail she would have astonished its oldest residents, even its designers and builders.

It took her only moments to thread through the passages and corridors, past busy workers and clerks. By the time she arrived at the center's double glass doors, Proboda had closed in behind her. He was her equal in rank, but older; handling that was going to be the first challenge of her assignment.

The local station patroller glanced at Sparta's badge and then at the hard-breathing Proboda, whom he recognized. The guard waved them both through the glass lock, into the glittering darkness of Hesperus Traffic Control.

Through the arching glass dome Sparta could see the hard points of thousands of fixed stars. Below the dome, row upon circular row of softly glowing terminals were arranged like benches in a Roman amphitheater. In front of each console floated a weightless controller in loose harness. The doors through which Sparta and Proboda had entered were in the center of the ring, and they came in like a pair of gladiators onto the sand, although no one noticed their arrival. High above their heads, higher than the highest row of consoles, the chief controller's platform was suspended on three fine struts at the dishshaped room's parabolic focus.

Sparta launched herself upward.

She turned as she touched down lightly on the platform edge. The chief controller and his deputy seemed only mildly interested in her arrival.

"I'm Inspector Ellen Troy of Central Investigative Services, Mr. Tanaka...."—she'd stored the names of all the key personnel in the station—"And this is Inspector Proboda," she added as the blond hulk arrived behind her, scowling. "I'm instructed to direct the investigation of *Star Queen.*"

"Hi, Vik," the controller said cheerily, grinning at the flustered cop. He nodded to Sparta. "Okay, Inspector. We've had *Star Queen* on auto for the past thirty-six hours. We should have her onboard in about seventy-two minutes."

"Where are you parking the ship, sir?"

"We're not. You're right, normally we wouldn't dock a ship of this mass, we'd stand her in the roads. But Captain Antreen of your office here suggested we bring *Star Queen* on into the security sector to facilitate the removal of the ... survivor. That will be dock Q3, Inspector."

Sparta was mildly surprised at Antreen's order—the crewman on *Star Queen* had survived a week on his own, and the extra half hour it would take to bring him in from a parking orbit on a utility shuttle would hardly make a difference.

"I'd like to stay to observe the docking procedure, if you don't mind," she said. "And I'll want to be first in line when the lock is opened, if you'd be good enough to inform your personnel of that." She turned her head, sensing that Proboda was about to object. "Of course you'll be with me at the airlock, Inspector," she said.

"That's fine with us," Tanaka said. He could care less. "Our job's over when the ship's in and secured. Now if you'll excuse me...." The muscular little man ran a thick hand lightly over his black crewcut. Not until he moved

forward out of the harness in which he'd been floating did
Sparta notice he had no legs.

An hour passed in Traffic Control; the hot sun rose
somewhere below. From her perch on the chief controller's
platform Sparta could see up to the stars and across to the
intense ascending sun; she could see down to the first ring
of multi-ringed Port Hesperus, which turned ceaselessly
about its stationary hub like a heavenly carousel. She
could not see the disk of Venus, which was immediately
under the station, but the glare of the planet's sulfuric-
acid clouds reflected onto the station's painted metalwork
was almost as bright from below as the direct rays of the
sun were from above.

Sparta's attention was not on the station but on the
hundred-meter white ship, standing straight up against the
stars, which lowered itself by inches with spurts of its maneuvering thrusters, toward the gaping bay in the hub below the traffic control dome.

The sight triggered an odd memory, of a backyard barbecue in Maryland—who had been there? Her father? Her
mother? No. A man, a woman with gray hair, other older
couples whom she could not now quite picture or place—
but that was not the memory, the memory was of a bird
feeder suspended from the branch of an elm in the backyard by a long, thin wire, the sort of wire used as baling
wire, and at the end of this wire was the bird feeder full
of seeds, hanging from the wire a good two meters below
the branch and a meter above the ground, to protect the
seeds from squirrels. But one squirrel was not to be
thwarted; this squirrel had learned to grip the wire with
all four paws and slide—slowly, and with obvious trepi-

dation—headfirst down the wire, from the branch above to the feeder below. The people who were giving the barbecue were so impressed by the squirrel's daring they had not even bothered yet with any new scheme to frustrate it. They were so proud they wanted Sparta to see the animal perform its trick.

And here was a huge white space freighter, sliding headfirst down an invisible wire, into the maw of the docking bay. . . .

Something else that memory was trying to tell her . . . but she couldn't dredge it up. She forced her attention back to the moment. *Star Queen* was almost docked.

Outside the security sector the passage to the lock was jammed with media people. Sparta, with Proboda dogging her, arrived at the back of the crowd.

"I wonder what he's feeling like now?" a cameraman was saying, fussing with his videochip photogram.

"I can tell you," replied a sleek brushcut type, a stand-up reporter. "He's so pleased to be alive . . ."

Sparta sensed that Proboda, beside her, was about to pull his rank and clear the mediahounds out of the passage. She gently preempted him. "I want to hear this," she murmured, touching his arm.

". . . that he doesn't give a damn about anything else," the reporter concluded.

"I'm not so sure I'd want to leave a mate in space so I could get home."

"Who would? But you heard the transmission—they talked it over and the loser went out the lock. It was the only sensible way."

"Sensible? If you say so—but it's pretty horrible to let somebody sacrifice himself so you can live . . ."

"Don't act the bloody sentimentalist. If that happened to us you'd shove me out before I'd had a chance to say my prayers."

"Unless you did it to me first . . ."

Sparta had heard enough. She pushed close to the reporter and said quietly, "Space Control. Move aside, please," and kept repeating it, "Space Control, move aside please . . ."—effortlessly opening a path before her. Proboda followed.

They left the pack behind at the security sector lock. Beyond the sealed collar of the core they reached the Q3 lock, which was almost as crowded with technicians and medical personnel. Through the big plate glass port the bulbous head of *Star Queen* was nosing into place a few meters away, patiently tugged and shoved by mechanical tractors. Sparta had a few words with the medics and the others as the tube fastened itself over the ship's main airlock.

When the pressure popped and *Star Queen*'s hatch opened, Sparta was standing in front of it, alone.

The smell from inside the ship was an assault. Nevertheless she inhaled deeply, tasted the air with her tongue. She learned things from the flavor of the air that no subsequent tests could have told her.

Almost a minute passed before, rising from the depths of the ship, a haggard man drifted into the circle of light. He paused while still inside *Star Queen*, just shy of the docking tube. He took a deep, shuddering breath—and another—and then he let his watery eyes focus on Sparta.

"We're happy to have you safe with us, Mr. McNeil," she said.

He watched her for a moment, then nodded.

"My name's Ellen Troy. I'm from the Board of Space

Control. I'll be going with you while the medics assist you. I must ask you not to speak to anyone but me, until I give you permission—no matter who asks, or what they ask. Is that acceptable to you, sir?"

Wearily, McNeil nodded again.

"If you will move toward me, sir . . ."

McNeil did as he was told. When he was clear of the hatch Sparta darted past him and twisted the handle of the exterior lock. The massive outer door slid closed, seating itself with a palpable thud. Sparta pushed her hand into the right thigh pocket of her cargo pants and pulled out a bright red flexible plastic disk, which she slapped over the rim of the hatch—sealing it like a lump of wax over the flap of an envelope. She turned and took McNeil by the arm. "Come with me, please."

Viktor Proboda was blocking the tube exit. "Inspector Troy, it is my understanding that this man is to be placed under arrest, and that the ship is to be inspected without delay."

"You are mistaken, Inspector Proboda." *Good,* she was thinking, *he didn't use the word "orders," as in "my orders are . . ."*—which meant that she could put off the inevitable confrontation a little longer. "Mr. McNeil is to be extended every courtesy. I'm taking him to the clinic now. When he feels up to it, he and I will talk. Until then, no one—not anyone—is to enter *Star Queen.*" Her gaze had not left Proboda's pale blue eyes. "I'm confident you'll be diligent in carrying out Central's orders, Viktor."

It was an old trick, but he was surprised when she used his first name, as she'd intended. This slender girl was perhaps twenty-five, he was well into his thirties, and he'd struggled a decade to achieve his rank—but her easy assumption of authority was genuine, and Proboda, a good soldier, recognized it. "As you say," he gruffly conceded.

Sparta guided engineer McNeil, who seemed on the point of nodding off, to the waiting medics. One of them clamped an oxygen mask over McNeil's face: McNeil's expression was that of a man taking a drink of cold water after a week in the tropical sun. Sparta repeated her injunction to the medics about talking to the media; they would disobey her, of course, but not until she had left McNeil's side.

The little group emerged from the security lock. McNeil, with an oxygen mask over his nose and mouth, guided by medics, with Sparta and Proboda bringing up the rear, ran the gauntlet of frantic questions. . . .

But, after another week of waiting, the media had only the arrival of *Star Queen* and the confirmation of McNeil's survival to add to the electrifying radio message that had initiated their death watch. The broadcast had been as succinct as it was chilling:

"This is *Star Queen,* Commander Peter Grant speaking. Engineering officer Angus McNeil and I have jointly concluded that there is sufficient oxygen now remaining for one man and one man only to live until our ship docks at Port Hesperus. Therefore one of us must die if either of us is to live. We have mutually agreed to decide the matter with a single draw of playing cards. Whoever draws the low card will take his own life."

A second voice had spoken: "McNeil here, confirmin' that I'm in agreement with everything the commander says."

The radiolink had been silent then, for several seconds,

except for the shuffle and snap of playing cards. Then Grant came back on the air. "This is Grant. I've drawn the low card. I want to make it clear that what I'm about to do is the result of my personal decision, freely undertaken. To my wife and children, I should like to affirm my love for them; I've left letters for them in my cabin. A final request: I wish to be buried in space. I'm going to put my suit on now, before I do anything else. I'm asking Officer McNeil to put me out the lock when it's all over and send me away from the ship. Please don't search for my body."

Aside from routine automated telemetry, that was the last anyone had heard from *Star Queen* until today.

The Port Hesperus clinic was in the station's halfgee torus. An hour after his arrival McNeil lay propped up between clean sheets. His color was rosy, although the dark circles under his eyes remained and the once full flesh of his cheeks hung in folds. He was a much thinner man than he had been when he left Earth. There had been more than enough food on *Star Queen,* but for the last few days under deceleration he'd had hardly enough energy to drag himself to the galley.

He'd just begun to remedy that lack with a dinner of medium-rare Chateaubriand, accompanied by puff potatoes and garden vegetables, and preceded by a crisp green salad with a light herb vinaigrette and accompanied by a half-bottle of velvety California Zinfandel—all of which had been laid on by the Board of Space Control according to Sparta's instructions.

She knocked lightly on the door, and when he said "Come in" she entered the room, followed by the brooding Proboda.

"I hope everything was all right?" she asked. The salad

was gone but the Chateaubriand was only half eaten and many of the vegetables were untouched. Not so the wine; bottle and glass were empty. McNeil was wreathed in tobacco smoke, halfway through a pungent unfiltered cigarette.

"It was delicious, Inspector, simply delicious, and I'm sorry to let the rest go. But I'm afraid my stomach's shrunk—that bit just filled me up."

"That's certainly understandable, sir. Well, if you feel rested . . ."

McNeil smiled patiently. "Aye, there'll be lots of questions now, won't there be?"

"If you'd rather we came back later . . ."

"No point in putting off the inevitable."

"We sincerely appreciate your cooperation. Inspector Proboda will record our conversation."

When everyone was settled McNeil launched into his tale. He spoke quite calmly and impersonally, as if he were relating some adventure that had happened to another person, or indeed had never happened at all—which, Sparta suspected, was to some extent the case, although it would be unfair to suggest that McNeil was lying. He wasn't making anything up. She would instantly have detected that from the rhythm of his speech, but he was leaving a good deal out of his well-rehearsed narrative.

When, after several minutes, he'd finished speaking, Sparta sat thoughtfully in silence. Then she said, "That seems to wrap it up, then." She turned to Proboda. "Are there any points you'd like to explore further, Inspector?"

Again Proboda was caught by surprise—any points *he'd* like to explore? He'd already resigned himself to a passive role in the investigation. "One or two," he said, clearing his throat, "as a matter of fact."

McNeil drew on his cigarette. "Have at me," he said with a cynical grin.

"Now, you say you lost your grip—I believe those were your words—when the meteoroid or whatever it was struck the ship? What exactly did you do?"

McNeil's pale features darkened. "I *blubbered*—if you want to know the details. Curled up in my cabin like a little boy with a skinned knee and let the tears come. Grant was a better man than I, calm as could be throughout it all. But I hadn't been a meter away from the oxygen tanks when they exploded, you see—just the other side of the wall in fact—loudest damn noise I've heard in my life."

"How did you happen to be at just that place at just that moment?" Proboda asked.

"Well, I'd been down doing the periodic check on the temperature and humidity in Hold A. The top compartment of that hold's pressurized and temperature-controlled because we're carrying things like specialty foods, cigars and so forth, organics—whereas in the vacuum holds we've got inert stuff, machinery mostly. I'd just come up through the hold airlock and I was in that part of the central corridor that passes through the life support deck, on my way up to the flight deck, when—*blam*."

"The life support deck was also pressurized?"

"We normally keep it that way so we can get into it from inside the crew module. It's really a very small space, crammed with tanks and pipes, but you can reach in there if you have to. When it was hit the inside hatches seized up automatically."

"Now, this business about the wine crate..."

McNeil grinned sheepishly. "Yes, I did behave rather badly. I suppose I'm going to have to pay someone a pretty penny for the bottles I managed to down before Grant caught me."

"That wine was the personal property of the director of the Hesperian Museum, Mr. Darlington," Proboda grunted. "I imagine he'll have something to say about it. ... But you say Grant put the partial crate back where you got it?"

"Yes, and then he changed the combination on the airlock so I couldn't get back in."

A feral gleam appeared in Proboda's pale eye. "You claim the airlock of that hold hasn't been opened since the day after the accident?"

"That's right, sir."

"But the top compartment of that hold is pressurized. It's a vessel almost half the volume of the command module. And it was full of fresh air!"

"Aye, it was, and if we'd had another like it, Peter Grant would be alive today," McNeil said quietly. "Originally we were to carry some seedlings. They wouldn't have saved us, but the extra air that came with 'em might have." He seemed to notice Proboda's confusion for the first time. "Oh, I see your problem, sir. And you're right, about the old ships ... but *Star Queen* and most of the newer freighters are piped to allow any combination of gas exchange through all the airtight compartments, without having to open the airlocks. That allows us to carry cargo that the shipper wouldn't want us to know about or get into, you see. If they're willin' to pay freight on the entire hold. Which is the usual procedure on military contracts."

"So you had access to the air in that compartment even though you couldn't get inside?"

"Right. If we'd wanted, we could have pumped the air out of that hold and jettisoned the whole thing, got rid of the mass. In fact Grant ran some calculations, but we wouldn't have saved enough time."

Proboda was disappointed, but still he persisted. "But after Grant had, uh, left the ship . . . you could have found his new combination for the airlock, couldn't you?"

"Could be, but I doubt it, even if I'd been interested. I'm no computer whiz, and a man's private files aren't easy to crack into. But why would I have wanted to?"

Proboda glanced significantly at the empty bottle and glass beside McNeil's half full plate. "Because there were still three and a half crates of wine in there, for one thing. And no one to stop you from drinking it."

McNeil studied the blond inspector with an expression that struck Sparta as calculating. "I like a glass as well as the next person, Inspector. Maybe better. Maybe a little too much better. I've been called a hedonist and maybe I am that, but I'm not a complete fool." McNeil ground out the remains of his cigarette.

"What did you have to fear," Proboda insisted, "beyond the commission of a felony, of course, if that really *did* concern you?"

"Just this," McNeil said quietly, and the steel edge of his affable personality finally slid out from under the smile, glittering. "Alcohol interferes with the functioning of your lungs and constricts your blood vessels. If you're going to die anyway, you might not mind that. But if you intend to survive in an oxygen-poor environment, you won't be taking a drink."

"And cigarettes? Do they interfere with the functioning of the lungs?"

"After two packs a day for twenty years, Inspector, two cigarettes a day are but a crutch for the nerves."

Proboda was about to plunge on when Sparta interrupted. "I think we ought to leave Mr. McNeil in peace for now, Viktor. We can continue at a later time." She had watched the exchange with interest. As a cop, Proboda had his strong points—she liked his bulldog persistence even when he knew he looked foolish—but his shortcomings were numerous. He was easily sidetracked, having here fixated on the trivial issue of destruction of property—Sparta suspected that was due to an excessive concern for powerful interests in the Port Hesperus community—and he hadn't done his homework, or he would have known about the hold airlocks.

But his most serious error was that he had already passed moral judgment on McNeil. McNeil was not to be judged so easily. Everything he had said about himself was true. He was not a fool. And he intended to survive.

Sparta rose and said, "You are free to go wherever you like on the station when the medics release you, Mr. McNeil, although if you prefer to avoid the media this is probably the best place to do it. *Star Queen* is off limits, of course. I'm sure you understand."

"Perfectly, Inspector. Thanks again for arrangin' this lovely dinner." He gave her a jaunty salute from the comfort of his bed.

Before they reached the corridor, Sparta turned to Proboda and smiled. "You and I make a good team, Viktor. Good guy, bad guy, you know. We're naturals."

"Who's the good guy?" he asked.

She laughed. "Right. You were hard on McNeil, but I

read you as the good guy when it comes to your neigh-
bors. Whereas I intend to show them no mercy."

"I don't follow. How could anybody on Port Hesperus
be involved in this?"

"Viktor, let's go climb into spacesuits and take a look
at that hole in the hull, shall we?"

"All right."

"But first we've got to get through the mob."

They stepped lightly through the clinic doors, into a
crowd of waiting mediahounds. *"Inspector Troy!" "Hey,
Vik, old buddy . . ." "Please, Inspector, what have you got
for us? You've got something for us, right . . . ?"*

XIV

They left the howling newspack outside the security sector. "I've never seen them like this," Proboda muttered. "You'd think they'd never had a chance to report a real story before."

Sparta had no experience with the media. She'd thought she could use the standard techniques of command and control, the voice and personality tricks, and they did work up to a point, but she had underestimated the mob's ability to tear at her concentration, to sour her internal functions. "Viktor, excuse me—I've got to have a moment." She paused in a corner of the empty passage, closing her eyes, floating in midair, willing the tension in her neck and shoulders to dissolve. Her mind emptied itself of conscious thought.

Proboda eyed her curiously, hoping no one would come along and he would have to explain. The formidable young Inspector Troy was suddenly vulnerable, her eyes closed and her head pitched forward, floating with her hands up like a small animal's paws; he could see the down on the back of her slender white neck, bared where her straight blond hair had fallen clear.

Seconds later, Sparta allowed her eyes to open fully. "Viktor, I need a spacesuit. I'm a size five and a half," she said, and just like that her expression was firm again.

"I'll see what I can find in the lockers."

"And we'll need some tools. Limpet clamps and suction cups. Grip struts. Inertial wrench with a full set of heads and bits. Bags and tape and stuff."

"That's all in a grade ten mechanic's kit. Anything special?"

"No. I'll meet you at the lock."

She moved forward, toward the *Star Queen* docking tube, and Proboda went off to the tool shed.

Two patrollers were on duty beside the entrance to the tube, wearing blue spacesuits with helmets on, although unlatched. They were armed with stunguns—air rifles using rubber bullets that were capable of severely injuring a human, even one in a spacesuit, although not likely to puncture crucial space station systems. Metal cartridges and the weapons that fired them were barred on Port Hesperus.

Through the double glass windows behind the guards the enormous bulk of *Star Queen* almost filled the docking bay. *Star Queen* was of average size as freighters go, but she was much larger than the tenders, launches, and shuttles that normally docked inside Port Hesperus.

"Has anyone been here since McNeil was taken off the ship?" Sparta asked the guards.

They glanced at each other and shook their heads. "No, Inspector." "No one, Inspector." They betrayed it in their voices and they smelled of it: they were lying.

"Good," she said. "I want you to report to me or Inspector Proboda if anyone attempts to get past you. Anyone at all, even someone from our office. Understood?"

"Right, Inspector."

"Certainly, Inspector. You bet."

Sparta went into the boarding tube. The red plastic seal was still in place over the rim of the hatch. She laid her hand over it and leaned close to it.

The plastic seal was little more than it seemed, an adhesive patch. It concealed no microcircuitry, although its conducting polymers were sensitive to electric fields and preserved the patterns of any that had recently been applied. By placing her hand over the patch, by leaning close to it and inhaling its odor, Sparta learned what she needed.

The field detectors under her palm picked up the strongly impressed pattern of a diagnostic device—someone had passed a field detector of their own over the plastic, hoping to discover its secrets. Doubtless they had learned that it had no secrets. Then they'd grown bold enough to handle the seal, presumably with gloves. The inquisitive one had left no fingerprints, but from the odor that clung to the surface of the plastic, Sparta had no difficulty identifying who had been there.

Each person's skin exudes oils and perspiration that contain a blend of chemicals, especially amino acids, in a combination as unique as the pattern of the iris. When Sparta inhaled these chemicals she instantly analyzed them. She could call the specific chemical formulas into consciousness or, more usefully, match them to patterns she had already stored. She routinely stored the amino acid signatures of most people she met, eventually discarding those of no interest.

Two hours ago she had stored the amino acid signature

of Kara Antreen. She was not surprised to recognize it here. Nor could she blame the guards for lying to her. They'd been told to keep quiet; and they'd have to live with Antreen long after Sparta had gone back to Earth.

Sparta couldn't blame Antreen for her curiosity, either. She'd examined the seal, but there was no evidence she had opened the hatch. The only other entrance to the ship was through the midships airlock aft of the cargo holds, and Sparta doubted she'd used that. Antreen would have been in full view of a hundred controllers and dockside workers had she donned a spacesuit and gone into the ship that way.

Viktor arrived, pulling the tool bag and a suit for her—a blue one, the uniform suit of the local law. He'd already climbed into his own suit; his gold badge was blazoned on his shoulder.

Minutes later they were drifting close to the spotlit hull of *Star Queen*, their attention concentrated on a small round hole in a metal plate.

Behind them in the cavernous docking bay great metal clamps clashed, shackling craft to the station, and self-guiding hoses and cables snaked out from the refueling manifolds, seeking the orifices of fuel tanks and capacitors. Tugs and tenders were arriving and launching from the bay, sliding in and out of the huge bay doors open to the stars. All this activity took place in the dead silence of vacuum. The Space Board cutter was moored next to *Star Queen* in the security sector. A launch stood by at the commercial lock across the way, fueled and ready to bring passengers into the station when the liner *Helios* arrived. Over the whole scene the clear dome of Traffic Control presided.

They'd gone through one of the worker's locks, dragging the translucent nylon bag of tools, tethered to Proboda's wrist, behind them. Sparta had carefully worked her way around the superconducting coils of the radiation shield that looped in a lacy hemisphere over the top of *Star Queen*'s crew module, keeping a respectful distance. If Proboda wondered why, he said nothing, and she didn't care to explain what she'd learned through unsettling personal experience, that strong electric and magnetic fields were dangerous to her in intimate ways that other people could not sense: induced currents in the implanted metal elements next to her skeleton were disorienting and, *in extremis*, threatening to her vital organs.

But she maneuvered to hull plate L-43 without difficulty. It was not easily accessible for even one person in a spacesuit, since it was tucked away on the underside of the crew module just above the convex end of the long cylinder of Hold C.

"I'll take a look," she said, squeezing close. "Here, put this someplace else." She popped the crablike robot eye off the hull where it perched over the hole and handed it to Proboda; the magnetic rollers on the ends of its legs were whirring as it searched for a grip. Proboda put it up higher on the module and it scurried away toward its home hatch.

Sparta got her head up next to the damaged plate and focused her right eye upon the hole. She zoomed in and examined it in microscopic detail.

"Doesn't look like much from here," Proboda's voice said from the commlink in her right ear.

"Wait 'til you see inside. But let me get a picture of this first," she murmured. She snapped it with the ordinary photogram camera looped around her left wrist.

What Sparta could see on the outside of the hull, even at a magnification that would have astonished Proboda, corresponded to just what she would have expected from the collision with the hull plate of a one-gram meteoroid traveling at forty kilometers per second—a hole the size of a BB, in the center of a small circle of gleaming smooth metal that had melted and recrystallized.

The damage done to a ship's hull by a meteoroid travelling at typical interplanetary velocities approximates what happens when, say, a hypervelocity missile strikes armor. The indentation on the outside of the plate may be modest in itself, but the deposited energy creates a cone-shaped shock wave travelling inward that spalls a wide circle of material off the inside of the plate. This molten material keeps on moving and does its own damage; meanwhile, if the interior of the hull is filled with air, the shock wave quickly expands, producing overpressures which are intensely destructive near the hole, although they fall off rapidly with distance.

"Is that one of the ones that comes off easily?" Proboda asked.

"We're not quite that lucky," she said. "Want to hand me that wrench and a standard Philips?"

Almost a third of the surface area of the life support deck consisted of removable panels, and L-43 was one of these—not, unfortunately, a door that conveniently swung open like others nearby, but a plate that could be removed by patiently unscrewing some fifty flathead bolts around its edges. Proboda took a power drill from the nylon tool bag and fixed a bit to it. "Here," he said, handing it to her, "anything I can do to help?"

"Catch these damn little screws." It took her almost ten

minutes to remove the bolts. He plucked them from the vacuum and corralled them in a plastic bag.

"Let's try the limpet now."

He handed her a small, massive electromagnet and she set it against the painted yellow triangle in the center of the plate, which marked the presence of a ferrous laminate hardpoint. She flipped the magnet's switch and tugged hard. The magnet stuck fast to the hardpoint, but—

"That's what I was afraid of. Can you get your feet on something? Then tug on my legs." He braced himself and grabbed her feet. He tugged on her and she tugged on the plate, but the plate was stuck fast in the hull.

"We'll have to set up the grip rig."

Proboda reached into the tool bag and withdrew a set of steel rods with sliding couplings. He fed her the pieces one by one, and in a few minutes she had rigged a bridge of parallel rods over the recalcitrant hull plate, set against the hull to either side on gimbaled feet. She mounted a worm gear in a heavy bracket in the center of the bridge. She fitted a crossbar handle to its top; its lower end rotated in a joint on the back of the magnet. When Sparta twisted the crossbars the worm gear turned and began to exert an inexorable pull. After three complete turns the bulging plate, like a stiff cork sliding out of a bottle, popped free.

"This is what was holding it." She showed him the inside of the plate. "Sealant all over the place."

Blobs of hardened yellow plastic had held the plate tight, plastic foam that had spewed from emergency canisters inside the deck. Some of it had been carried by the outrush of air into the meteoroid hole, where it congealed and sealed the leak as it was designed to; the rest had simply made a mess.

Sparta inspected the inner side of the plate and the hard dark mound of plastic that covered the hole. She photogrammed it, then peered back over her shoulder. "Let me see that knife kit." He held it out and she took a curved, thin-bladed knife from the set. "And give me some of those little bags." She carefully worked the edge of the blade under the brittle plastic. She began peeling back the plastic, which came away in thin layers like sediment, like wood grain.

"What are you doing that for?"

"Don't worry, I'm not destroying any evidence." She saved the shavings in a clear bag. "I want to see what the hole looks like under the goop." Beneath the plastic was the wide side of the conical hole, as big as a nickel, surrounded by an aureole of bright recrystallized metal. "Well, that's certainly by the book." She photogrammed it again, then passed him the hull plate. "Let's put all this in the sack."

Sparta shone her hand-lamp into the blackened interior of the life support deck. In her private way she spent a moment studying what she saw. Then she took more photograms. "Can you get your head in here, Viktor? I want you to see this."

He squeezed his helmet in close beside hers, so that they were touching. "What a mess." His voice was as loud by conduction through their helmets as it was by commlink.

Everything within two meters of the point of the hole in the hull was severely damaged. Pipes writhed crazily and ended in jagged mouths, like frozen benthic worms.

"Both oxygen tanks in one whack. Hardly a more vulnerable spot in the whole ship." One oxygen sphere was torn open, while another lay in shards like a broken egg shell. Fragments of the shattered fuel cell still floated near the ceiling, where they had collected under the gentle deceleration of docking. " 'Scuse me a minute, I've got to get my arm in there." Sparta reached up and gathered glittering bits of debris from the ceiling. She carefully placed these and other samples in plastic bags. She took a final look around inside the ravaged deck, then withdrew.

They replaced the tools and the evidence they had gathered in the net bag. "That should do it here."

"Did you find what you expected?"

"Maybe. We'll have to wait for the analysis. Before we go back let's have a peek inside the ship."

They pulled themselves along the bulging cylinder of Hold C, tugging themselves from one handhold to the next, until they reached *Star Queen*'s midships airlock.

The midships airlock was set into the long central shaft that separated *Star Queen*'s fuel tanks and nuclear engines from the holds and the crew module, just aft of the holds themselves. Sparta manipulated the external controls that opened the hatch—controls that by law were standardized on all spacecraft—then entered the cramped space. Proboda squeezed in behind her, towing the tool bag.

She closed the outer hatch. From inside she could pressurize the lock, if there were no overriding commands from inside the spacecraft. But a big red sign lit up beside the inner hatch wheel: WARNING. VACUUM.

"I'm going to pressurize," she said. "This won't smell too good."

"Why don't we just stay suited?"

"We've got to face it sooner or later, Viktor. Keep your helmet on, if you want."

He didn't discuss it with her, but he did keep his helmet

on. She didn't let him see her grin. He had delicate feelings for a man of his size and profession.

She used the controls to pressurize the interior of the ship's central shaft. After a few moments the warning indicator shifted from red to green—"Atmospheric pressure equalized"—but she did not yet open the inner hatch. First she pulled off her helmet.

Crashing into Sparta's brain came the smell of sweat, stale food, cigarette smoke, spilled wine, ozone, new paint, machine oil, grease, human waste . . . and above it all, carbon dioxide. The air was not nearly as bad as it had been for McNeil in those final days, for it had already mingled with fresh air from the station, but it was bad enough; Sparta needed a moment of conscious effort to clear her head.

What she didn't tell Proboda was that she wasn't doing this for the sake of torturing herself.

Eventually she could not only directly sense the chemical constituents of her surroundings, but evaluate and bring to consciousness what she sensed. She had an urgent question to ask here, before going inside: had anyone used this lock during the voyage? The main airlock was not a problem. If either Grant or McNeil had left the ship through it during the flight, the other man would have known about it—until they went through it the last time together, of course, and only McNeil returned. But this airlock was another matter. Conceivably one of them might have snuck outside the ship through this secondary airlock while the other slept or was busy elsewhere. The question had recently assumed new importance.

The smell of the place answered her question.

"Okay, I think I can take it now." She grinned at Proboda, who looked at her dubiously from within the safety of his helmet.

She twisted the wheel, opened the inner hatch, and entered the central corridor. For a moment the experience was profoundly disorienting: she was in a narrow shaft a hundred meters long, a constricted polished tube so straight that it seemed to vanish aft to a black point. For a moment she had the unsettling sensation of staring into a rifle barrel.

"Anything wrong?" Proboda's voice was loud in her commlink.

"No . . . I'm fine." She looked "up," toward the bow of the ship, to the hatch of the hold airlock a few meters overhead. Above that hatch was access to the cargo hold, and then to the crew module itself.

The light beside it was green: "Atmospheric pressure equalized." She turned the wheel, lifted the hatch, and entered the large airlock that segregated the huge detach-able holds—each of which had its own airlock—from the crew module. The outer hatches of the four hold airlocks surrounded her: bright red signs gleamed on three of them. DANGER. VACUUM.

The notice beside the hatch to Hold A, however, glowed a less frantic yellow: "Unauthorized entry strictly forbid-den."

All of them were of the standard design, heavy-duty wide spoked wheels in the midst of circular, hinged steel doors. Anyone who could strike the correct combination of numbers into the pad beside the wheel would gain quick entry.

She took a moment to bend her head close to each in turn, before Proboda clambered up from below with his bag of tools. Holds B and D hadn't been touched in weeks, but Hold A's keyboard and wheel showed expected signs of handling. So, less expectedly, did Hold C's.

"A's the only one that's locked, Viktor," as he climbed up beside her. "We'll have to retrieve the combination later, or force it. Want to look in B? I'll check out C."

"Sure," he said. He punched buttons to pressurize B's airlock. She latched her helmet and entered Hold C. The ritual of closing the outer hatch behind her, evacuating the lock, and opening the inner hatch to the airless hold—restraining any temptation to impatience—had to be performed carefully. Then she was inside.

It was a steel cylinder as big as a grain silo, dark but for a worklight beside the airlock. In the dim green worklight the metal monsters, each almost six metric tons in mass, stood against the wall like a *zaftig* chorus line. They were all strongly shackled to the hold's steel-alloy ribs and stringers. In the shadows they seemed to expand as she approached them, and their compound eyes of diamond seemed to follow her like the eyes in *trompe l'oeil* portraits.

They were nothing but inert machines, of course. Without their fissile fuel rods, stacked nearby within shielding assemblies of graphite, the huge robots could not move a millimeter. Yet Sparta could not deny the impression they made upon her, their segmented titanium bodies made to withstand furnace temperatures, their insectlike legs made for negotiating the most abrupt terrain, their diamond-edged mouth parts and claws made for shredding the most recalcitrant natural matrices . . .

And those glittering diamond eyes.

As Sparta floated closer to the nearest robot she felt a tingling in her inner ear. She paused a moment before recognizing the effects of latent radioactivity, recognizable by the same sort of induction currents—minute, in this case—that she had feared from the ship's radiation shield. A glance at the machine's serial number confirmed that it was the one Sondra Sylvester had had tried at the Salisbury proving grounds three weeks before it was loaded aboard *Star Queen.*

She cautiously moved past the first robot and inspected the others, one by one, peering at their erect and fearsome heads. All but the first were cold as stones.

Back in the hold access, with the airlock sealed behind her, Sparta waited for Proboda to climb out of Hold D. Apparently he had satisfied himself with whatever he saw in B and had gone on into the remaining vacuum hold while she was still admiring the robots. The top of his head stuck out of the hatch, his helmet looking like an ant's head. She tapped his blue plastic noggin. "Why don't you take that thing off?" she said. "The stink won't kill you."

He looked at her and twisted the helmet off his head. He got one whiff and his bold Slavic nose wrinkled all the way up into his forehead. "He lived in this for a week," he said.

She thought maybe the smell gave him a little better appreciation of McNeil, if not more respect for him. "Viktor, I want you to do something for me. It means us splitting up for a few minutes."

"Before we're finished in here? We still have to check on McNeil's story."

"I'm pretty sure we've already got the important stuff. I want you to get this evidence to the lab."

"Inspector Troy"—going all formal on her—"my orders are to be with you. Not to leave your side."

"Okay, Viktor, tell Captain Antreen everything you think you have to."

"First you have to tell *me*," he said, exasperated.

"I will. Then as soon as you get that stuff into the lab I want you to go out and intercept *Helios*. Before anybody disembarks. Keep them busy. . . ."

As soon as she had explained her suspicions and he understood them, he left. This business of being persuasive was draining, she found. Social intelligence—the people-manipulative intelligence—came hardest to her. Almost immediately, almost involuntarily, she collapsed into trance again.

The brief meditation restored her. As she allowed the external world to trickle back into her awareness, she began to *listen.* . . .

At first she did not filter or focus what she heard but took in the whole symphony of the great space station, spinning in space above Venus, its sounds vibrating through the wall of *Star Queen*. Gases and fluids coursed through its pumps and conduits, the bearings of its great hubs and rings rolled smoothly on their eternal rounds, the hum of thousands of circuits and high-voltage buses made the aether tremble. She could hear the muted voices of the station's hundred thousand inhabitants, a third of them at work, a third breathing deeply, asleep, a third concerned with the rich trivia of existence, buying, selling, teaching, learning, cooking, eating, fighting, playing. . . .

Simply by listening, she could not pick out individual conversations. No one seemed to be talking in the immediate neighborhood. She could have tuned in on the radio transmissions and the communications links, of course, had she chosen to go into receptor state, but that was not her purpose. She wanted a feel for the place. What was it like to live in a metal world constantly orbiting a hell planet? A world with parks and gardens and shops and schools and restaurants, to be sure—a world with unparalleled views of the starry night and the brilliant sun—but a contained world, one from which only the rich could easily get relief. It was a world where people from disparate cultures—Japanese, Arab, Russian, North American—were thrown into close proximity under conditions that inevitably produced strain. Some came for the money, some because they had imagined that space would somehow be free of the restrictions of crowded Earth. Some came, of course, because their parents brought them. But only a few had the pioneering spirit that made hardship an end itself. Port Hesperus was a company town, like an oil platform in the North Atlantic or a mill town in the Canadian forest.

The message Sparta had through the metal walls was one of tension in reserve, of time bided, of a feeling close to indentured servitude. And there was something more, partly among the recent, reluctant immigrants but especially among the younger residents, those who had been born on the station—a sense of humdrum, a certain resentment, the half-conscious undercurrent of brewing discontent—but for now the older generation was firmly in charge, and they had little in mind beyond vigorously exploiting the resources of Venus's surface, making themselves as comfortable as possible while they did so, and earning the wherewithal to get off Port Hesperus forever. . . .

Almost a kilometer away from where Sparta drifted dreaming in the freighter, the off-duty life of Port Hesperus was at its busiest. The enormous central sphere of the station was belted with tall trees—their tops all pointing inward—and ribbed with louvered glass windows that continually adjusted to compensate for the whirl of Venuslight and sunlight. Among the trees, paths wove among lush gardens of passion flowers and orchids and bromeliads, under cycads and tree ferns, beside trickling brooks and still reflecting ponds of recirculated water, over arched bridges of wood or stone.

A stroller who made the entire three-and-a-half-kilometer circuit would come upon seven strikingly different views, separately climate-controlled, laid out by the master landscape architect Seno Sato to suggest the diversity of cultures that had contributed to build Port Hesperus, and the mythic past of its mother planet. Step through this *torii*: here is Kyoto, an eaved castle, raked pebbles, twisted pines. Brush aside these tamarisk branches: Samarkand, its arabesque pavilions of inlaid blue stone reflected in perfumed pools. Through these bare birches to Kiev, blue onion domes above a frozen canal, where today two skaters circle. The snow underfoot becomes powdered marble, then plain sand: here is the Sphinx, in a garden of bare red rocks. Up this rocky path and past this flowering plum to vanished Changan, a seven-story stone pagoda with gilded finials. Through these yellow ginkgos the boat pond of New York's Central Park appears, complete with toy schooners, watched over with perplexed amusement by the well-polished bronze of Alice. An aisle of silent hemlocks leads to Vancouver, dripping cedars and totem poles and verdigrised gargoyles. And under these dripping tree ferns to the fern swamps of legendary, fictitious Venus, with a notable collection of carnivorous plants glistening in the eternal rain. Around this tall monkey-puzzle: Kyoto's gate...

On either side of the magnificent gardens, in parallel belts around the central sphere, were the Casbah, plaka, Champs Élysées, Red Square, Fifth Avenue, and Main Street of Port Hesperus—shops, galleries, dime stores, Russian tea shops, rug merchants, restaurants of fifteen distinct ethnic persuasions, fish markets (aquacultured bream a specialty), fruit and vegetable markets, flower stands, temples, mosques, synagogues, churches, discreetly naughty cabarets, the Port Hesperus Performing Arts Center, and the streets outside jammed with shoppers and hawkers, jugglers and strolling musicians, people wearing bright metals and plastics and their own colorized skin. Sato's gardens brought wealthy tourists from throughout the solar system. Port Hesperus's merchants and boosters were ready for them.

The central sphere was frequented by the station's workers and families too, of course. It's just that a Disney kind of world—even a Disney world equipped with a cosmopolitan selection of foods and beverages and real, sometimes kinky people—grows familiar after the fifth or sixth visit, and deadly dull after the hundredth. Every excuse for news, for a diversion, becomes precious....

Which is why Vincent Darlington was in a snit.

Darlington waddled about the spectacularly gaudy main hall of the Hesperian Museum aimlessly straightening the baroque and rococo paintings in their ornate frames, trying to keep his fingers out of the piles of cultured shrimp and caviar and tiny lobster tails and synthetic ham rolls the caterers had hauled in by the kilo and which now gleamed oilily beneath the odd light of the room's stained glass dome. Every few seconds Darlington returned to the empty display case at the head of the room—positioned where, had this place been a church, as its spectacularly intricate overarching stained glass apotheosis suggested, the altar would have stood. He drummed his chubby fingers on the gilt frame. It had been specially built to hold his newest acquisition, and he'd placed it where no one entering the museum could *possibly* miss it—especially that Sylvester woman, if she had the brass to come.

One reason he'd staged the reception. And invited someone, that oh-so-special someone, who was quite likely to *drag* her along. He hoped she did come; he couldn't *wait* to see the hunger on her face....

But now the whole thing was off. Or at least postponed. First the news that his acquisition had been *impounded*. Then the news just now that the police were *delaying* the disembarkation of *Helios!* What in heaven's name could be so *complicated* about a simple accident in space...?

Horribly embarrassing, but he certainly had no *intention* of reopening the Hesperian Museum until his treasure was safely enthroned.

Darlington pushed himself away from the empty altar. He'd recoiled from the notion of mingling with the crowd of media persons and other rabble that had rushed to the security sector when *Star Queen*, at last, had arrived. He had subsequently placed one discreet call to the powers-that-be, urging—one might in fact say *pleading*, but only really in the *gentlest* possible fashion—that something be done about the red tape that prevented him from taking *immediate* delivery of the most valuable book in the entire history of the English language—and honestly now, if it *weren't* the most valuable book, then why had he been forced to pay such an outrageous *sum* for it, surely the largest sum ever paid for a book in the English language in the history of the English language itself, and that surely said *something* ... and out of his own pockets, which weren't, shall we say, *bottomless*, after all ... ?

Not, of course, that he cared about the book, actually, the actual contents of the book, that is to say, the *words* in the book. War stories, you know. Given that this fellow Lawrence was said to have written rather well, and there were those endorsements, G. B. Shaw, Robert Graves, whoever *they* were, but they were said to have written well themselves, for the period, that is, anyway someone said so, and really, any reputation that lasts a century has *some* value, wouldn't-you-say? But not really what he thought he was getting, in fact—permitting himself to make a small confession to himself—some confusion actually, quite understandable, another chap named Lawrence from the same period, after all it *was* more than a hundred years ago.

Which was quite beside the point. He'd paid money for this bloody book. There were only five copies in the universe, and three of those were *lost*, and now there was only the one in the Library of Congress of the United States of America and *his*—the Hesperian Museum's, which itself was his. And he'd bought it for one reason, to humiliate that woman, who had humiliated him in the aftermath of her disgraceful public pursuit of his ... well, that oh-so-special someone. His legal companion, once.

He supposed he should simply say good riddance to the little slut. But he couldn't. She had her quite remarkable charms, and Darlington was not likely to find her equivalent on *this* sardine-can-in-space.

Which set him to brooding, as he did endlessly, over whether he would ever get off Port Hesperus, whether he could ever go home again. He knew, deep down, that he wouldn't. They'd bury poor Vince Darlington in space, unless by some miracle they buried his sisters first. Not a matter of fighting extradition to Earth, nothing so public, or so legal. No, it was the price the family—the poisonous *sisters*, actually—had exacted for keeping their persimmon-lips puckered tightly—for keeping him out of a Swiss *jail*, to be precise. Of course it would have had to be *their* money . . .

This was the retreat he'd made for himself, and here he would stay, in these few small rooms with their velvet walls and this . . . really *amazing* glass dome (perhaps it really had been built as a church?), surrounded by his dead treasures.

He eyed the shrimps. They weren't getting any fresher.

He set off on another round of picture straightening. When *would* he be allowed to take possession? Perhaps he should cancel now. Captain Antreen had been *most* unhelpful. Oh, smiles and all that, said she'd do the best she could, but *results*? No promises there, darling. It all had a sour taste to it, rather curdling his intended triumph over Sylvester.

Darlington passed nervously into one of the smaller, darker side rooms, He stopped beside a glass case, caught by his reflection in its lid. He patted his thinning black hair and adjusting his old-fashioned horn-rimmed eyeglasses—hadn't lost his looks *quite* yet, thank God—twitching his lips in a little moue, then moving on, ignoring the contents of the case.

What Darlington left behind in this small room were his real treasures, although he refused to acknowledge them. Here were those odd scraps of fossil imprints, found on the surface of Venus by robot explorers, which had made the Hesperian Museum a place of intense interest to scientists and scholars, and, after Sato's gardens, one of the chief tourist attractions of Port Hesperus. But Darlington, absurdly wealthy even on a negotiated allowance, was a collector of second-rate European art of the melodrama-and-curlicue periods, and to him rocks and bones belonged in some desert gas station or Olde Curiosity Shoppe on Earth. His Venusian fossils brought him system-wide attention, so he grudgingly allowed them their space.

He continued to pace, staring at his garish paintings and sculptures and expensive bric-a-brac and brooding on what that busybody police person from Earth was up to, poking about on the derelict ship that held *his* precious book.

Shortly before *Helios* was due to rendezvous with Port Hesperus and shortly after Sparta had asked him to assure its quarantine while she went off on business of her own, Viktor Proboda presented himself at the Board of Space Control's local headquarters. Captain Antreen called him into her office; Lieutenant Kitamuki, her aide, was already in the room.

"Your instructions were simple, Viktor." Antreen's smiling mask had slipped; she was rigid with anger. "You were not to leave Troy's side."

"She trusts me, Captain. She has promised to inform me promptly of everything she finds."

"And you trust her?" Kitamuki demanded.

"She seems to know what she's doing, Lieutenant." Proboda felt it was getting awfully warm in this office. "And Central did put her in charge."

"We requested a replacement. We didn't ask that the investigation be taken away from us." Antreen said.

"I didn't like that any better than you did, Captain," Proboda said stoutly. "In fact I took it personally at first, considering you'd already given me the assignment. But after all, most of the principals in the case are Earth-based. . . ."

"Most of the principals are Euro-Americans," Kitamuki said. "Does that give you a clue?"

"Sorry," Proboda said stoutly. He could see the conspiracy theory coming—Kitamuki was big on them—but conspiracy theories were not his thing. He put his faith in simpler motivations, like vengeance, greed, and stupidity. "I really think you ought to take a look at these lab results. We did—Troy did, in fact—a very close inspection of the impact site, and what she found . . ."

"Someone back there has passed the word that this department is to be discredited," Kitamuki interrupted. "Here on Port Hesperus, Azure Dragon is producing spectacular results, and some among the Euro-Americans, on the station and back on Earth, don't like it." She paused to let her dark suspicions sink in.

"We've got to watch our step, Viktor," Antreen said evenly. "To preserve our integrity. Port Hesperus is a model of cooperation, and unfortunately some would like to destroy us."

Proboda suspected somebody was blowing smoke in his face—he wasn't sure who. But while Captain Antreen didn't always choose to make her reasoning clear, she did make her point. "How do you want me to handle it, then?"

"You do as Troy asks you. Just know that we'll be working with you too, sometimes behind the scenes. Troy is not to be made aware of this. We want the situation resolved, but there's no need to go beyond the pertinent facts."

"All right, then," Proboda concurred. "Shall I see to *Helios?*"

"You do that," Lieutenant Kitamuki said. "Leave Troy to us."

"Now what did you want to tell us about these lab results?" Antreen asked him.

XV

Alone in *Star Queen*, Sparta started her investigation from the top down.

Immediately below the inner hatch of the main airlock was a claustrophobic space jammed with stores and equipment lockers. Three spacesuits normally hung against the wall in one quadrant of the round deck. One was missing. Grant's. Another appeared unused. Wycherly's, the unfortunate pilot's. Curious, Sparta checked its oxygen supply and found it partially charged—enough there for half an hour. Had McNeil been saving it, in case things went wrong, and he too decided to lose himself in space? Sparta poked here and there among the supply lockers—tools, batteries, spare lithium hydroxide canisters and such—but she found nothing of significance here. She quickly moved down to the flight deck.

The flight deck was spacious by comparison, taking up a slice through the wide tropics of the crew module's sphere. The consoles that circled the deck beneath the wide windows were alive with flickering lights, their blue and green and yellow indicator lamps glowing softly on auxiliary power. Facing them were seats for commander, second pilot, and engineer—although *Star Queen*, like other modern freighters, could be flown by a single crewmember or none, if placed under remote control.

The room was a pragmatic mix of the exotic and the mundane. The computers were state of the art and so were the window shades, although the state of the window-shade art had not changed a whole lot in the past century, and the fire extinguishers were still just red-painted metal bottles, clipped to the bulkheads. There were racks and cabinets of machines, but there was also plenty of good working space and a good view out the surrounding windows; the deck had been designed in the awareness that crews would spend many months of their lives within its confines. Sparta was struck, however, that there were no personalizing touches, no cut-out cartoons or posters or pin-ups, no cute notes. Perhaps neo-commander Peter Grant had not been the sort to tolerate individual litter.

Besides the ship's working programs, the logs—Grant's verbal log and the ship's black-box recorders—were accessed from these consoles. In fact almost all of the codable information about the ship and its cargo, except Grant's and McNeil's personal computer files, was accessed from this deck.

Sparta expelled a breath and got down to work. From the chemical traces left on the consoles, armrests, handrails, and other surfaces she confirmed that no one besides Grant and McNeil had been on this deck for several weeks. There were still a jumble of traces, but most were months old, left by the workmen who had refurbished the ship.

Sparta had internalized the computer's standard access

codes. In little more time than it took to slip her gloves off and slide her PIN probes into the ports, she'd off-loaded its memory into her own much denser, much more capacious cellular storage mechanisms.

She raced lightly through the first few files of interest. The cargo manifest was as she had memorized it on the trip from Earth—no additions, no subtractions, no surprises. Four detachable cargo holds, capable of pressurization. On this voyage, only the first compartment of Hold A pressurized—the usual foodstuffs, medicines, so on—and that diminutive bit of mass worth two million pounds Sterling, a book in its carrying case. . . .

A few other items in Hold A were insured for relatively large amounts of money per unit of mass: two crates of cigars consigned to none other than Kara Antreen, valued at a thousand pounds each—Sparta smiled at the thought of the stiff Space Board captain savoring her stogies—and four crates of wine, one of which McNeil had already confessed to looting, worth a total of fifteen thousand American dollars and consigned to the same Vincent Darlington who was the new owner of the very famous book.

But there were also items that had cost more to ship than they were worth to insure: the newest BBC epic on videochip, "While Rome Burns," massing less than a kilo (and almost all of that was protective plastic packaging), wholly *un*insured. Although the original had cost millions to produce, the chips were much cheaper to *re*produce than an old-fashioned celluloid-based movie or a tape cassette, and indeed (admittedly with some loss of fidelity) the whole show could have been beamed to Venus for the cost of transmission time. Plus an item that had earlier struck Sparta as worthy of close attention: a case of "miscellaneous books, 25 kilos, no intrinsic value" consigned to Sondra Sylvester.

The contents of Holds B, C, and D, which had remained in vacuum throughout the flight, were of much less interest—tools, machinery, inert matter (a tonne of carbon in the form of graphite bricks, for example, marginally cheaper to ship from Earth than to extract from the atmospheric carbon dioxide of Venus)—except for the "6 Rolls-Royce HDVM," Heavy Duty Venus Miners, "at 5.5 tonnes each, total mass 33.5 tonnes gross including separate fuel assemblies," etc., consigned to the Ishtar Mining Corporation. Sparta satisfied herself that the onboard manifest was identical with the one that had been published. And she and Proboda had already confirmed its accuracy.

Sparta turned quickly to the mission recorder, which contained the entire public record of the voyage. Bringing the full record to consciousness, with the time-slip that involved, would be a lengthy process. For the time being she contented herself with a rapid internal scan, searching for anomalies.

One anomaly stood out, in data space, in smell space, in harmony space—an explosion, secondary explosions, alarms, calls for help . . . human voices, shocked, coping, accusing—the black-box mission recorder contained the entire sequence of events attendant upon the meteoroid strike.

Sparta heard it through at lightning speed and played it back to herself mentally. It confirmed in fine detail what she had learned in her firsthand look at the site of the accident.

One other anomaly stood out in the mission recorder's

datastream, a conversation, taking place immediately before Grant's fateful radio message had been beamed to
Earth and Venus. "This is *Star Queen*, Commander Peter
Grant speaking. Engineering Officer McNeil and I have
jointly concluded that there is sufficient oxygen remaining
for one man...."

But in the moments preceding the announcement,
Grant and McNeil had not been on the flight deck.... The
two men's voices were muffled by the intervening bulkhead. One voice was momentarily raised to the threshold
of audibility—McNeil's—and his words were stern: "*You're
in no position to accuse me of anything....*"

Accuse him...?

The whole conversation might be recovered, but Sparta
would have to put herself into light trance to do it. And
there were other chunks of data that might yield to analysis, but she must set aside the time to deal with them. It
was too soon to sacrifice alertness again. For now she had
to move quickly....

The fast liner *Helios*, driven by a powerful gaseous-
core atomic reactor, had been a week out of Earth, a week
and a day from Port Hesperus, when that somber message
had been received throughout the solar system: "This is
Star Queen, Commander Peter Grant speaking..."

Within minutes—even before Peter Grant had left the
Star Queen's airlock for the last time—the skipper of *Helios*
had received orders from the Board of Space Control, acting under interplanetary law, to notify his passengers and
crew that all transmissions from *Helios* were being recorded and that any pertinent information thus obtained
would be used in subsequent administrative and legal pro-

ceedings, including criminal proceedings, if any, bearing on the *Star Queen* incident.

In other words, everyone aboard *Helios* was a suspect in the investigation of some as yet unspecified misdeed on *Star Queen.*

Not without reason. *Helios* had left Earth on a hyperbolic orbit for Venus two days after the meteoroid struck *Star Queen.* The departure date for the fast liner had been on the boards for months, but at the last minute, after the meteoroid strike, *Helios* acquired several new passengers. Among them was Nikos Pavlakis, representing the owners of the stricken freighter. Another was a man named Percy Farnsworth, representing the Lloyd's group who had insured the ship, its cargo, and the lives of its crew.

Other passengers had booked the flight long in advance. There was an emeritus professor of archaeology from Osaka, three Dutch teenage girls setting forth on a grand planetary tour, and half a dozen Arabian mining technicians accompanied by their veiled wives and rebellious children. The Dutch girls rather relished the notion of being suspected of interplanetary crime, while Sondra Sylvester, another passenger who had booked in advance, did not. Sylvester's young travelling companion, Nancybeth Mokoroa, was simply bored rigid by the whole affair.

These were not the sort of passengers who mixed easily: the Japanese professor smiled and kept to himself, the Arabs kept to themselves without bothering to smile. The teenagers staggered about in their high-heeled shoes during periods of constant acceleration and twitched uncomfortably in their unaccustomed tight dresses, whether under acceleration or not, and at all times made a point of ogling the one unaccompanied male passenger over fifteen and under thirty. He did not return their compliment. He was Blake Redfield, a last minute addition to the manifest who kept very much to himself throughout the voyage.

Such social encounters as did occur took place in the ship's lounge. There Nikos Pavlakis did his nervous best to be gracious to his client Sondra Sylvester whenever their paths crossed. That wasn't often, as she generally avoided him. The poor man was distracted with worry anyway; he spent most of his time nursing a solitary ouzo and a plastic bag of Kalamata olives. Farnsworth, the insurance man, was often to be found lurking in the nearby shadows, sipping on a bulb of straight gin and ostentatiously glowering at Pavlakis. Pavlakis and Sylvester both made it a point to avoid Farnsworth altogether.

But it was in the lounge, not long after Grant's public sacrifice, that Sylvester found Farnsworth plying Nancybeth with a warm bulb of Calvados. The middle-aged man and the twenty-year-old woman were floating, weightless and slightly giddy, before a spectacular backdrop of real stars, and the sight infuriated Sylvester—as Nancybeth had no doubt intended. Before approaching them Sylvester thought about the situation—what, after all, should she care? The girl was possessed of heart-stopping beauty, but she had the loyalty of a mink. Nevertheless, Sylvester felt she could not afford to ignore the sly Farnsworth any longer.

Nancybeth watched Sylvester's approach, her malice diffused only slightly by weightlessness and alcohol. " 'Lo, Sondra. Meet m' friend Prissy Barnsworth."

"Percy Farnsworth, Mrs. Sylvester." One did not get to

one's feet in microgravity, but Farnsworth straightened admirably nonetheless, and tucked his chin in a credible bow.

Sylvester looked him over with distaste: although he was approaching fifty, Farnsworth affected the look of a young army officer, off duty for the weekend to do a bit of pheasant slaughtering, say—Sylvester's recent acquaintance at the Salisbury proving grounds, Lieutenant Colonel Witherspoon, was a model of the type. Farnsworth had the mustache and the elbow-patched shooting jacket and the rigid set of the neck right down. The public school accent and the clipped Desert Rat diction were strictly second-hand, however.

Sylvester looked past his outstretched hand. "You'll want to be careful, Nancybeth. A brandy hangover's not pleasant."

"Dear mother Sylvester," she simpered. "What'd I tell you, Farny? Expert on everthn'. *I* never heard of this stuff 'fore she innerduced me." Nancybeth batted her bulb of apple brandy from hand to hand. On the third toss she missed, and Farnsworth snatched it out of the air for her, returning it without comment.

"Understand you had a very pleasant visit to the south of France, Mrs. Sylvester," Farnsworth said, braving her determined unpleasantries.

Sylvester gave him a look intended to silence him, but Nancybeth piped up brightly. "*She* had verry pleasan' two days. Three days? *I* had verr' *boring* three *weeks*."

"Mr. Farnsworth," Sylvester hastily interrupted, "your attempt to pump my companion for information that you imagine may somehow be of use to you is . . . is transparent."

Nancybeth's eyes widened—"Pump me? Why, *Mis*ter

Farmerworthy"—and she snatched dramatically at the billowing skirt of her flowery print dress.

"And despicable," Sylvester added.

But Farnsworth pretended to take no notice. "No offense meant, Mrs. Sylvester. Light chat, that's all. Comes to business, much prefer to talk to you straight from the shoulder. Eh?"

Nancybeth growled, "Man to man, so to speak," then pretended to flinch when Sylvester glared at her. Evidently she was farther into her cups than Sylvester had feared.

"Got me wrong, Mrs. Sylvester," Farnsworth said smoothly. "Represent your interests too, y'know. In a sense."

"In the sense that you'll be forced to pay your clients whatever sum you can't weasel out of?"

He drew himself up a bit. "*You've* nothing to fear, Mrs. Sylvester. *Star Queen* would dock safely with your cargo even if she were a ghost ship. Take more than a measly meteoroid to do in a Rolls-Royce robot, what?"

Throughout their exchange Nancybeth was contorting her face into a series of exaggerated masks, miming first Sylvester's aloof contempt, then Farnsworth's wounded innocence. It was the sort of childish display that under some circumstances lent her a gamin attractiveness. At the moment she was about as attractive as a two-year-old on a tantrum.

"Thanks for your interest, Mr. Farnsworth," Sylvester said coldly. "And perhaps you would leave us alone now."

"Let me be blunt, Mrs. Sylvester, begging your pardon—"

"No, why don't you be pointed?" Nancybeth suggested brightly.

Farnsworth pushed on. "After all, we're both aware of the difficulties of the Pavlakis Lines. Eh?"

"I'm aware of no such thing."

"Doesn't take much imagination to see what Pavlakis had to gain by doing in his own ship. Eh?"

"Nancybeth, I'd like you to leave with me, this moment," Sylvester said, turning away.

"But he did it rather badly, didn't he?" Farnsworth said, floating closer to Sylvester, his voice deeper and harsher. "No significant damage to the ship, no damage whatever to the cargo? Not even that famous book you were so interested in?"

"Don' forget crew," cried Nancybeth, still the giddy imp. "Tried to kill 'em all!"

"Good God, Nancybeth . . ." Sylvester glanced across the lounge to where Nikos Pavlakis hovered over his ouzo. "How can you say such a thing? About a man you've never met?"

"Only got half of 'em, though," the girl finished. "Good ol' Angus won through."

"That's a shrewd guess, Mrs. Sylvester, and I'd lay odds she's right." Farnsworth's insinuating gaze narrowed melodramatically. "Pavlakis Lines holds rather large accidental-death policies on its crewmembers—did you know that?"

Her eyes fastened on his, almost against her will. "No, Mr. Farnsworth, actually I didn't."

"But *suicide*, though. Now there's another matter. . . ."

Sylvester jerked her gaze away from him. Something about his teeth, his gingery hair, set her stomach to seething. She glared at Nancybeth, who peered back in fuddled and exaggerated innocence. Taking hold of a nearby convenience rail, Sylvester turned her back on both of them and launched herself hastily outward, into the gloom.

"Bye-bye, Sondra . . . sooorry we made you mad," Nancybeth crooned as Sylvester disappeared through the nearest doorway. She squinted at Farnsworth. "Suicide? 'Sat mean you don' have to pay Grant? I mean, *for* Grant? 'Cause he killed himself?"

"Might mean." Farnsworth peered back owlishly. "Unless he didn't, of course."

"Didn't? Oh, yeah . . . an' if he *was* murdered?"

"Ah, murder. Gray area, that." Farnsworth tugged at the knot of his blood-colored polymer tie. "I say, been awfully good. But 'fraid I must run."

"Yes, Wusspercy," cooed the abandoned Nancybeth. So that's what he'd wanted from her, nothing more than a conversation with Syl. "Run along, why don't you? And while you're at it, take a hint from Commander Grant . . . ? Lose *your* body too."

Across the room, not far away, Nikos Pavlakis floated near the bar with his bulb of ouzo and his bag of olives. He was well aware that they had been talking about him. His temper urged him to confront Farnsworth, to call him to immediate account, but his business sense urged him to stay calm at all costs. He was frantic over the condition of his beautiful new ship. He was almost equally sorrowful for the man Grant, who had been a dependable employee of his and his father's for many years, and for Grant's widow and children. He was even more apprehensive about the prospects of McNeil, another good man. . . .

Pavlakis thought he knew what had happened to *Star Queen*. To him it was retrospectively obvious, transparently so—but not, he hoped, to anyone else. Nor could he afford to breathe a word of his suspicions to anyone. Farnsworth least of all.

As *Helios* slid into its parking orbit near Port Hesperus, Sparta was poking about in Angus McNeil's private cabin on *Star Queen.*

She'd quickly looked through the galley, the personal hygiene facility, the common areas. She'd found nothing inconsistent with McNeil's account. A slot in the medicine chest which would have held a tiny vial of tasteless, odorless poison was vacant. There were two packs of playing cards in the drawer of the table in the common room, one of which had never been opened, one of which had been handled by both McNeil and Grant—McNeil's traces were strongest, although Grant had gripped one card tightly. She noted its face.

After the common areas Sparta had visited the pilot's cabin next. It had not been entered since Wycherly was last on the ship, before it left Falaron Shipyard.

Grant's cabin, then—notable mostly for what it failed to reveal. His bed was still made, the corners squared off and the blanket so tight one could have bounced a nickel off it at one gee. His clothes were neatly folded in the restraining hampers. His bookshelf and personal-computer files were mostly electronics manuals and self-improvement books; there were no signs that Grant did any reading for pleasure or had any hobbies except fiddling with microelectronics. The promised letters to his wife and children were clipped to the little fold-down writing desk, and Sparta left them there after ascertaining that no one except Grant had touched them. McNeil, if he'd been curious about their contents—as well he might have been—had had the integrity to leave them strictly alone.

In fact there was no trace of McNeil's presence anywhere in the room.

There was another letter, addressed to McNeil himself, in Grant's desk drawer. But as McNeil had not searched the drawer, presumably he did not know of its existence.

McNeil's cabin painted a portrait of quite a different man. His bed had not been made for days, perhaps weeks—Sparta noted purplish splotches of spilled wine on the sheets that, if he'd been telling the truth about not getting into Hold A after Grant changed the combination, had been there since four days after the explosion. His clothes were in a jumble, jammed into the hampers of his locker. His chip library was a fascinating mix of titles. There were works of mysticism: the *Tao Te Ching* of Lao Tsu, a treatise on alchemy, another on the Cabala. And of philosophy: Kant's *Prolegomena to Any Future Metaphysic*, Nietzsche's *The Birth of Tragedy*.

Some of McNeil's books were real, photogrammed onto plastic sheets that imitated the paper of a hundred years ago. Games: a slim little book on parlor magic, another on chess, another on go. Novels: Cabell's odd *Jurgen*, a recent work of the Martian futurists, *Dionysus Redivivus*.

McNeil's personal computer files revealed a different but similarly wide range of interests—it took Sparta only moments to discover that he had been playing master level chess with his machine, that he had carefully followed the London, New York, Tokyo, and Hong Kong stock exchanges, that he subscribed to a variety of clubs, from rose-of-the-month to wine-of-the-month. Wine and roses—he must collect several months' worth of each, between trips.

There were other files on the computer, protected by passwords that would have stopped a casual browser but which were so trivial Sparta barely noted them—files that made full use of the machine's high-resolution graphics. The invention of the home video player a century ago had brought erotic films into the living room, but that was a mild innovation compared to what followed when the invention of the cheap supercomputer-on-a-chip brought new meaning to the phrase "interactive fantasy." McNeil's id was much on display in these private files, which Sparta closed hastily; despite her opinion of herself as sophisticated beyond her years, her face had turned bright pink.

She made her way into the corridor that passed through the center of the life support deck. Just on the other side of these close, curving, featureless steel walls the fatal explosion had occurred; at the same moment the access panels had been automatically dogged shut to prevent decompression of the crew module.

She went through the lock into the hold access then, to the three locks that warned VACUUM and the one that sternly wagged its bright yellow finger: "Unauthorized entry strictly forbidden."

McNeil had told the truth. The traces of his and many other hands resided on the keypad, but the most recent trace was Peter Grant's—his touch on six of the keys overlaid all others. Sparta could not recover the order of touch—six keys gave rise to six-factorial possible combinations—but if she'd wanted to play a game with herself she probably could have deduced the likelier possibilities within a few seconds, from her knowledge of probabilities and, mostly, from what she'd learned of the man himself.

There was no point in taking the time. She'd already uncovered the combination where Grant had noted it in his personal computer files.

She tapped the keys. The indicator diode beside the lock blinked from red to green. She turned the wheel and tugged on the hatch. Inside the airlock the indicators confirmed that the interior pressures of the hold were equal to those outside the lock. She turned the wheel on the inner hatch and a moment later floated into the hold.

It was a cramped circular space, hardly big enough to stand erect in, ringed by steel racks filled with metal and plastic bags and cases. The roof of the compartment was the reinforced cap of the hold itself; the floor was a removable steel partition, sealed to the walls. The wooden ships that once plied Earth's oceans commonly carried sand and rocks for ballast when travelling without a paying cargo, but ballast was worse than useless in space. Aft of the few stacked shelves ringing the pressurized top of the hold, the vessel was just a big bottle of vacuum.

The pallets near the airlock were strapped down securely, carrying sacks of wild rice, asparagus tips in gel, cases of live game birds frozen in suspended animation— delicacies that, having made the trip from Earth, were worth far more than their weight in gold.

And of course that miscellany which had snagged Sparta's attention in the manifest. Kara Antreen's Cuban cigars. Sondra Sylvester's "books of no intrinsic value." Sylvester's books were in a gray Styrene case which showed little sign of handling—Sparta noted Sylvester's own traces, McNeil's, Grant's, others unknown, but none recent. Sparta quickly deduced the simple combination. Inside she found a number of plastic-wrapped paper and plastic books, some bound in cloth or leather, others with quaint and lurid illustrated covers, but nothing she did not expect to find. She resealed the case.

She moved next to Darlington's consignment, a similar

but not identical gray Styrene case equipped with an elaborate magnetic lock, something even more complex than the numeric pad on the airlock. The case showed no signs of tampering. Oddly, it showed no signs of having been handled at all. The only chemical signals on the entire case were the strong contending odors of detergent, methyl alcohol, acetone, and carbon tetrachloride. It seemed to have been throughly scrubbed.

A defensive measure, that, like the human hair laid across the crack in the closet door, intended to divulge any attempts at searching or tampering? Well, there had been no tampering.

Sparta proceeded to tamper with it. The lock's code was based on a short stack of rather small primes. No one without Sparta's sensitivities could have cracked the combination in less than a few days, without the aid of a sizable computer—it would take that long just to run through half the possible combinations. But Sparta eliminated possibilities by the millions and billions, instantly, simply by reading electronic pathways deep in the lock's circuitry and discarding those that were dormant.

She was in trance while she did it. Five minutes later she had the lock open. Inside the case was the book.

The man who had had this book made for himself had reveled in fine things. He had valued the presentation of his hard-wrought words so much that he would not let those he hoped to impress with it, or even his friends, see anything but the best. *The Seven Pillars of Wisdom* had not only been given the trappings of a marbled slipcase, leather binding, and beautiful endpapers, it had been printed like the King James Bible itself, on Bible paper, set in double columns of linotype.

Sparta had heard about metal type, although she had

never actually seen the effect of it. She slid the book from its case, let it gently push itself open. Sure enough, each single letter and character was pressed onto the paper, not simply appearing there as a filmy overlay but as a precise quantity of ink pushed crisply into the pulp. That sort of craftsmanship in an object of "mass production" was beyond Sparta's experience. The paper itself was thin and supple, not like the crumbling discolored sheets she had seen in the New York library, displayed as relics of the past. . . .

The richness and glory of the book in her hand was hypnotic, calling her to handle its pages. For the moment she forgot investigation. She only wanted to experience the thing. She studied the page to which it had spontaneously opened.

"An accident was meaner than deliberate fault," the author had written. "If I did not hesitate to risk my life, why fuss to dirty it? Yet life and honour seemed in different categories. . . . or was honour like the Sybil's leaves, the more that was lost the more precious the little left . . . ?"

An odd thought. "Honour" considered as a commodity, the more that was lost the more precious what was left.

Sparta closed the fabulous book and slid it back into its slipcase, then settled the whole thick package into its padded case. She had seen what she needed to of *Star Queen.*

XVI

"Ladies and gentlemen, I regret to announce that there will be a delay in the disembarkation process. A representative from Port Hesperus will be joining us shortly to explain. To facilitate matters, all passengers should report to the lounge as soon as possible. Stewards will assist you."

Unlike *Star Queen*, *Helios* had arrived at Port Hesperus in the normal way, grappled into parking orbit by short-range tugs. Plainly visible through the windows of the ship's lounge, the space station hung in the sky a kilometer away, its wheels revolving grandly against the bright crescent of Venus, the green of its famous gardens glinting through the banded skylights of its central sphere. Murmuring resentment, the passengers gathered in the lounge; the most reluctant found themselves "helped" by stewards who seemed to have forgotten deference. All aboard the ship, passengers and crew, were frustrated to have travelled millions of kilometers across a trackless sea and at the last moment to be prevented from setting foot on the shore.

A bright spark moved against the insect cloud of other spacecraft drifting about the station, and soon resolved itself into a tiny white launch bearing the familiar blue band and gold star insignia. The launch docked at the main airlock and a few minutes later a tall, square-jawed blond man pulled himself briskly into the lounge.

"I'm Inspector Viktor Proboda, Port Hesperus office of the Board of Space Control," he said to the assembled passengers, most of whom were unhappily glowering. "You will be detained here temporarily while we continue our investigation into the recent events aboard *Star Queen*; we sincerely regret any inconvenience this may cause. First I'll need to establish that your registration slivers are in order. Then I will soon be approaching some of you individually and asking you to assist us in our inquiries. . . ."

Ten minutes after she left *Star Queen*, Sparta knocked on the door of Angus McNeil's private ward. "Ellen Troy, Mr. McNeil."

"C'm in," he said cheerily, and when she opened the door he was standing there smiling at her from his freshly shaved face, wearing a freshly pressed, luxurious cotton shirt with its sleeves folded above the elbows and crisp plastic trousers, and puffing lightly on a cigarette he had evidently lit only moments before.

"I'm sorry to interrupt you," she said, seeing the open kit on the bed. He had been packing bathroom articles; she noted that they seem to have been issued from the same government stores as her own hastily acquired toothbrush.

"Good time for a fresh start. Sorry you had to see that

mess of mine—might just chuck the lot, whenever you decide to let me back aboard."

"That will be a while yet, I'm afraid."

"More questions, Inspector?" When she nodded yes, he gestured to a chair and took another for himself. "Better make ourselves comfortable, then."

Sparta sat down. For a moment she watched him without speaking. McNeil's color was much better, and although he would be gaunt for some time to come, he appeared not to have lost his muscle tone. Even after days of near-starvation, his forearms were powerfully muscled. "Well, Mr. McNeil, it's fascinating what the latest diagnostic techniques can recover from even the most obscure pools of data. Take *Star Queen's* mission recorder, for example."

McNeil drew on his cigarette and watched her. His pleasant expression did not change.

"All the data from the automatic systems is complete, of course. And the microphones get every word spoken on the flight deck. What I listened to confirmed your account of the incident in every detail."

McNeil raised an eyebrow. "You've hardly had time to screen a couple of weeks' worth of real-time recordings, Inspector."

"You're right, of course. A thorough review will take months. I employed an algorithm that identifies areas of maximum interest. What I want to talk to you about now is the discussion that took place in the common area shortly before you and Grant made your last broadcast."

"I'm not sure I recall . . ."

"That's where these new diagnostic techniques are so helpful, you see." She leaned forward, as if to share her enthusiasm. "Even though there are no microphones in the living areas, enough sound carries to be picked up by the main flight recorder. In the past we wouldn't have been able to recover the exact words."

She let that sink in. His expression still didn't change, but his features almost imperceptibly stiffened. She knew he was wondering whether she was bluffing.

She would remove that hope. "You'd just eaten dinner together. Grant had served you coffee—it was hotter than usual. He left you there and started for the corridor. 'What's the hurry?' you asked him. 'I though we had something to discuss. . . .' "

Now the last hint of relaxation left McNeil's eyes. As he crushed his cigarette his fleshy cheeks jiggled.

"Well, Mr. McNeil," Sparta said softly, "do you and I have something to discuss?"

For a moment McNeil seemed to look past her, into the blank white wall behind her head. Then his eyes refocused on her face. He nodded. "Aye, I'll tell you everythin'," he whispered. "I would make one request—not a condition, I know better than that—but simply a request, that once you've heard me out, if you agree with my reasonin', you'll keep what I'm about to say off the record."

"I'll bear that request in mind," she said.

McNeil sighed deeply. "Then here's the whole truth, Inspector. . . ."

Grant had already reached the central corridor when McNeil called softly after him, "What's the hurry? I thought we had something to discuss."

Grant grabbed a rail to halt his headlong flight. He turned slowly and stared unbelievingly at the engineer. McNeil should be already dead—but he was sitting quite comfortably, looking at him with a most peculiar expression.

"Come over here," McNeil said sharply—and in that moment it suddenly seemed that all authority had passed to him. Grant returned to the table without volition, hovering near his useless chair. Something had gone wrong, though what it was he could not imagine.

The silence in the common area seemed to last for ages. Then McNeil said rather sadly, "I'd hoped better of you, Grant."

At last Grant found his voice, though he could barely recognize it. "What do you mean?" he whispered.

"What do you think I mean?" replied McNeil, with what seemed no more than mild irritation. "This little attempt of yours to poison me, of course."

Grant's tottering world collapsed at last. Oddly, in his relief he no longer cared greatly that he'd been found out.

McNeil began to examine his beautifully kept fingernails with some attention. "As a matter of interest," he asked, in the way that one might ask the time, "when did you decide to kill me?"

The sense of unreality was so overwhelming that Grant felt he was acting a part, that this had nothing to do with real life at all. "Only this morning," he said, and believed it.

"Hmm," remarked McNeil, obviously without much conviction. He rose to his feet and moved over to the medicine chest. Grant's eyes followed him as he fumbled in the compartment and came back with the little poison bottle. It still appeared to be full. Grant had been careful about that.

"I suppose I should get pretty mad about this whole business," McNeil continued conversationally, holding the bottle between thumb and forefinger. "But somehow I'm not. Maybe it's because I've never had many illusions about human nature. And, of course, I saw it coming a long time ago."

Only the last phrase really reached Grant's consciousness. "You . . . saw it coming?"

"Heavens, yes! You're too transparent to make a good criminal, I'm afraid. And now that your little plot's failed it leaves us both in an embarrassing position, doesn't it?"

To this masterly understatement there seemed no possible reply.

"By rights," continued the engineer thoughtfully, "I should now work myself into a good temper, call Port Hesperus, denounce you to the authorities. But it would be a rather pointless thing to do, and I've never been much good at losing my temper anyway. Of course, you'll say that's because I'm too lazy—but I don't think so." He gave Grant a twisted smile. "Oh, I know what you think about me—you've got me neatly classified in that orderly mind of yours, haven't you? I'm soft and self-indulgent, I haven't any moral courage—any morals at all, for that matter—and I don't give a damn for anyone but myself. Well, I'm not denying it. Maybe it's ninety percent true. But the odd ten percent is mighty important, Grant. At least to me."

Grant felt in no condition to indulge in psychological analysis, and this seemed hardly the time for anything of the sort. He was still obsessed with the problem of his failure and the mystery of McNeil's continued existence. And McNeil, who knew this perfectly well, seemed in no hurry to satisfy his curiosity.

"Well, what do you intend to do now?" Grant asked, anxious to get it over.

"I would like," McNeil said calmly, "to carry on our discussion where it was interrupted by the coffee."

"You don't mean . . ."

"But I do. Just as if nothing had happened."

"That doesn't make sense! You've got something up your sleeve!" cried Grant.

McNeil sighed. "You know, Grant, you're in no position to accuse me of plotting anything"—he released the little bottle to float above the surface of the table between them; he looked up sternly at Grant. "To repeat my earlier remarks, I am suggesting that we decide which one of us shall take poison. Only we don't want any more unilateral decisions. Also"—and he drew another vial from his jacket pocket, similar in size to the first but bright blue in color; he allowed it to float beside the other—"it will be the real thing this time. The stuff in here," he said, pointing to the clear bottle, "merely leaves a bad taste in the mouth."

The light finally dawned in Grant's mind. "You changed them."

"Naturally. You may think you're a good actor, Grant, but frankly, from the balcony, I thought the performance stank. I could tell you were plotting something, probably before you knew it yourself. In the last few days I've deloused the ship pretty thoroughly. Thinking of all the ways you might have done me in was quite amusing; it even helped pass the time. The poison was so obvious that it was almost the first thing I fixed." He smiled wryly. "In fact I overdid the danger signal. I nearly gave myself away when I took that first sip—salt doesn't go at all well with coffee."

McNeil fixed unblinking eyes on the embittered Grant before going on. "Actually, I'd hoped for something more subtle. So far I've found fifteen infallible ways of murdering anyone aboard a spaceship." He smiled again, grimly. "I don't propose to describe them now."

This was simply fantastic, Grant thought. He was being treated, not like a criminal, but like a rather stupid schoolboy who hadn't done his homework properly. "Yet you are willing to start all over again?" he asked, unbelieving. "And you'd take the poison yourself if you lost?"

McNeil was silent for a long time. Then he said, slowly, "I can see that you still don't believe me. It doesn't fit at all nicely into your tidy little picture, does it? But perhaps I can make you understand. It's really simple." He paused, then continued more briskly. "I've enjoyed life, Grant, without many scruples or regrets—but the better part of it's over now and I don't cling to what's left as desperately as you might imagine. Yet while I *am* alive I'm rather particular about some things." He allowed himself to drift farther from the table. "It may surprise you to know that I've got any ideals at all. But I've always tried to act like a civilized, rational being, even if I've not always succeeded. And when I've failed I've tried to redeem myself. You might say that's what this is about." He gestured at the tiny weightless bottles.

He paused, and when he resumed it was as though he, and not Grant, were on the defensive. "I've never exactly liked you, Grant, but I've often admired you and that's why I'm sorry it's come to this. I admired you most of all the day the ship was hit." He seemed to have difficulty finding his words: he avoided Grant's eyes. "I didn't behave well then. I've always been quite sure, complacent really, that I'd never lose my nerve in an emergency—but then it happened right beside me, something I understood instantly and had always thought to be impossible—happened so suddenly, so *loud*, that it bowled me over."

He attempted to hide his embarrassment with humor. "Of course I should have remembered—practically the same thing happened on my first trip. Spacesickness, that time ... and I'd been supremely confident it couldn't happen to me. Probably made it worse. But I got over it." He met Grant's eyes again. "And I got over this ... and then I got the *third* big surprise of my life. I saw *you*, of all people, beginning to crack."

Grant flushed angrily, but McNeil met him sharply. "Oh yes, let's not forget the business of the wines. No doubt that's still on your mind. Your first good grudge against me. But that's one thing I *don't* regret. A civilized man should always know when to get drunk. And when to sober up. Perhaps you wouldn't understand."

Oddly, that's just what Grant was beginning to do, at last. He had caught his first real glimpse of McNeil's intricate and tortured personality and realized how utterly he had misjudged him. No—misjudged was not the right word. In some ways his judgment had been correct. But it had only touched the surface; he had never suspected the depths that lay beneath.

And in his moment of insight Grant understood why McNeil was giving him a second chance. This was nothing so simple as a coward trying to reinstate himself in the eyes of the world: no one need ever know what happened aboard *Star Queen*. And in any case, McNeil probably cared nothing for the world's opinion, thanks to the sleek self-sufficiency that had so often annoyed Grant. But that very self-sufficiency meant that at all costs he must preserve his own good opinion of himself. Without it life would not be worth living; McNeil had never accepted life save on his own terms.

McNeil was watching Grant intently and must have

guessed that Grant was coming near the truth. He suddenly changed his tone, as if sorry he had revealed so much of his own character. "Don't think I get some quixotic pleasure from turning the other cheek," he said sharply, "it's just that you've over-looked some rather basic logical difficulties. Really, Grant—didn't it once occur to you that if only one of us survives without a covering message from the other, he'll have a very uncomfortable time explaining what happened?"

Grant was dumbstruck. In the depths of his seething emotions, in the blindness of his fury, he had simply failed to consider how he was going to exculpate himself. His righteousness had seemed so . . . so *self evident.*

"Yes, I suppose you're right," he murmured. Still, he privately wondered if a covering message was really all that important in McNeil's thoughts. Perhaps McNeil was simply trying to convince him that his sincerity was based on cold reason.

Nevertheless, Grant felt better now. All the hate had drained out of him and he felt—almost—at peace. The truth was known and he accepted it. That it was rather different from what he had imagined hardly seemed to matter. "Well, let's get it over," he said, unemotionally. "Don't we still have that new pack of cards?"

"Yes, a couple of them in the drawer there." McNeil had taken off his jacket and was rolling up his shirtsleeves. "Find the one you want—but before you open it, Grant," he said with peculiar emphasis, "I think we'd better speak to Port Hesperus. Both of us. And get our complete agreement on the record."

Grant nodded absently; he did not mind very much now, one way or the other. He grabbed a sealed pack of the metallized cards from the game drawer and followed McNeil up the corridor to the flight deck. They left the glinting poison bottles floating where they were.

Grant even managed a ghost of a smile when, ten minutes later, he drew his card from the pack and laid it face upward beside McNeil's. It fastened itself to the metal console with a faintly perceptible snap.

McNeil fell silent. For a minute he busied himself lighting a fresh cigarette. He inhaled the fragrant, poisonous smoke deeply. Then he said, "And the rest you already know, Inspector."

"Except for a few minor details," Sparta said coolly. "What became of the two bottles, the real poison and the other?"

"Out the airlock with Grant," he replied shortly. "I thought it would be better to keep things simple, not run the risk of a chemical analysis—revealing traces of salt, that kind of thing."

Sparta brought a package of metallized playing cards from her jacket pocket. "Do you recognize these?" She handed them to him.

He took them in his large, curiously neat hands, hardly bothering to look at them. "They could be the ones we used. Or others like them."

"Would you mind shuffling the pack, Mr. McNeil?"

The engineer glanced at her sharply, then did as he was told, expertly shuffling the thin, flexible cards in midair between his curved palms and nimble fingers. Finished, he looked at her inquisitively.

"Cut, if you don't mind," she said.

"That would be your privilege, wouldn't it?"

"You do it."

He laid the deck on the nearby lamp table and swiftly moved the top section of the deck to one side, then placed the bottom section on top of it. He leaned away. "What now?"

"Now I'd like you to shuffle them again."

The look on his face, as blank as he could make it, nevertheless barely concealed his contempt. He had shared one of the more significant episodes of his life with her, and her response was to ask him to play games—no doubt in some feeble attempt to trick him into something. But he shuffled the cards quickly, making no comment, letting the hiss and snarl of their separation and swift recombination make the comment for him. "And now?"

"Now I'll choose a card."

He fanned the deck and held it toward her. She reached for it but let her fingers hover over the cards, moving back and forth as if she were trying to make up her mind. Still concentrating, she said, "You're quite expert at handling these, Mr. McNeil."

"Nor have I made a secret of it, Inspector."

"It was no secret to begin with, Mr. McNeil." She tugged a card from the edge of the deck and held it up, toward him, without bothering to look at it herself.

He stared at it, shocked.

"That would be the jack of spades, wouldn't it, Mr. McNeil? The card you drew against Commander Grant?"

He barely whispered yes before she plucked another card from the deck he still rigidly held out to her. Again she showed it to him without looking at it. "And that would be the three of clubs. The card Grant drew, which sent him to his death." She flipped the two cards onto the bed. "You can put the deck down now, Mr. McNeil."

His cigarette burned unnoticed in the ashtray. He had already anticipated the point of her little demonstration, and he waited for her to make it.

"Metallized cards aren't allowed in professional play for a simple reason," she said, "with which I'm sure you're quite familiar. They aren't as easy to mark with knicks and pinholes as the cardboard kind, but it's a simple matter to impose a weak electric or magnetic pattern on them that can be picked up by an appropriate detector. Such a detector can be quite small—small enough, say, to fit into a ring like the one you're wearing on your right hand. That's a handsome piece—Venusian gold, isn't it?"

It was handsome and intricate, portraying a man and woman embracing; if examined closely, in fact, it was more than a little curious. Without hesitating, McNeil twisted the heavy sculpted ring over his knuckle. It came off easily, for his finger was thinner than it had been a week ago. He held it out to her, but to his surprise, she shook her head—

—and smiled. "I don't need to look at it, Mr. McNeil. The only coherent patterns on these cards were imposed by me, a few minutes ago." She leaned away from him, relaxing in her chair, inviting him to relax as well. "I used other methods to determine which cards had been drawn by you and Grant. They were the only two cards in the deck which seemed to have been handled beyond a light shuffle. Frankly, I was partly guessing."

"You made a lucky guess, then," he said hoarsely, having found his voice. "But if you aren't accusing me of cheating on Grant, why this demonstration? Some people might call it unusual, maybe even cruel."

"Oh, but *you*," she said fiercely. "*You* wouldn't have needed electromagnetic patterns to cheat, would you, Mr.

McNeil?" She glanced at his forearms, which rested on his thighs, his hands clasped between his knees. "Even with your sleeves rolled up."

He shook his head no. "I could have cheated him easily enough, Inspector Troy. But I swear I didn't."

"Thank you for saying so. Although I was confident that you would admit the truth." Sparta got to her feet. " 'Life and honour seemed in different categories. . . . the more that was lost the more precious the little left.' "

"What's that mean?" McNeil growled.

"From an old book I glanced at recently—a passage that made me want to read the whole thing someday. It gave me considerable insight into your situation. You're quite good at concealing truths, Mr. McNeil, but your particular sense of honor makes it very difficult for you to lie outright." She smiled. "No wonder you almost choked on that coffee."

McNeil's expression was puzzled now, almost humble. How could this pale, slim child have peered so deeply into his soul? "I still don't understand what you mean to do."

Sparta reached into her jacket again and brought out a small plastic book. "*Star Queen* will be inspected by other people after me, and they will be at least as thorough as I've been. Since you and I know you didn't cheat Grant out of his life, it's probably a good thing you thought to bring this book out with you, and that I never found it, and that I never had any suspicion of what a gifted amateur magician you are."

She tossed the book on the bed, beside the cards. It landed face up: *Harry Blackstone on Magic.*

"Keep the cards, too. Little gift to help you get well soon. I bought them ten minutes ago at a kiosk in the station."

McNeil said, "I'm having the feelin' that nothing I said came as much of a surprise to you, Inspector."

Sparta had her hand on the door panel, poised to leave. "Don't think I admire you, Mr. McNeil. Your life and the way you choose to live it is your business. But it so happens I agree that there's no justification for destroying the late, unfortunate Peter Grant's reputation." She wasn't smiling now. "That's me speaking privately, not the law. If you've kept anything else from me, I'll find it out—and if it's criminal, I'll have you for it."

PART FIVE

BLOWOUT

XVII

Sparta reached Viktor Proboda on the commlink: he could stop playing games now. The passengers from *Helios* could come aboard.

Spaceports in space—unlike planetside shuttleports, which resemble ordinary airports—have a flavor all their own, part harbor, part trainyard, part truckstop. Small craft abound, tugs and tenders and taxis and cutters and self-propelled satellites, perpetually sliding and gliding around the big stations. There are very few pleasure craft in space (the eccentric billionaire's hobby of solar yachting provides a rare exception) and unlike a busy harbor, there is no swashing about, no bounding over wakes or insolent cutting across bows. The daily routine is orbit-matching— exquisitely precise, with attendant constant recalculation of velocity differentials and mass/fuel ratios—so that in space even the small craft are as rigidly constrained to preset paths as freight cars in a switching yard. Except that in space, gangs of computers are continually rearranging the tracks.

And aside from local traffic, spaceports are not very busy. Shuttles from the planet's surface may call a few times a mouth, interplanetary liners and freighters a few times a year. Favorable planetary alignments tend to concentrate the busy times; then local chambers of commerce turn out costumed volunteers in force, greeting arriving liners the way Honolulu once greeted the *Lurline* and the *Matsonia*. Lacking indigenous grass skirts or flower leis, space station boosters have invented novel "traditions" to reflect a station's ethnic and political mix, its economic base, its borrowed mythologies: thus, arriving at Mars Station, a passenger might encounter men and women wearing Roman breastplates, showing their bare knees, and carrying red flags emblazoned with hammers and sickles.

At Port Hesperus the passengers from *Helios*, disembarking after a long delay, traversed a winding stainless steel corridor rippling with colored lights, garish signs boasting of the station's mineral products in English and Arabic and Russian; *kanji*-splashed paper banners, fluttering in the breeze from the exhaust fans, added an additional touch of festivity.

When the passengers reached a glass-roofed section of the corridor they were distracted by a silent commotion overhead; looking up, they were startled to see a chitoned Aphrodite riding a plastic seashell, smiling and waving at them, and near her a Shinto sun goddess wafting prettily in her silk kimono. Both women floated freely in zero-gee, at odd angles to each other and everyone else. These apparitions of the station's goddess (the Japanese were stretching the identity some) were haloed by a dozen grinning men, women, and children gesturing with fruit-and-flower baskets, products of the station's hydroponic farms and gardens.

The passengers, before being allowed to ascend to the level of these heavenly creatures, faced one last obstacle. At the terminus of the corridor Inspector Viktor Proboda, flanked by respectful guards with stunguns at their sides, ushered them into a small cubical room upholstered on all six sides with dark blue carpet. Some were admitted individually, some in groups. On one wall of the carpeted cube a videoplate displayed the stern visage of Inspector Ellen Troy, bigger than life-size. She was ostentatiously studying a filescreen in front of her, its surface invisible to the videoplate watcher.

Sparta was actually in a hidden room not far from the disembarkation tube, and in fact she was paying no attention to the filescreen, which was a prop. She had arranged with Proboda to bring the passengers into the room in a specific order, and she had already disposed of most of them, including the Japanese professor and the Arabs with their families, and various engineers and travelling salesmen.

At the moment she was trying to hustle the Dutch schoolgirls on their way. "We won't have to detain you any longer," she said with a friendly smile.

"Hope the rest of your trip is more fun."

"*This* has been the *best* part," one of them said, and another added, with much batting of lashes at Proboda, "We really are *liking* your comrade." The third girl, however, looked as prim as Proboda himself.

"Through here, please," he said, "all of you. To your right. Let's move it along."

"Bye, Vikee..."

"Vikee" felt Sparta's amused gaze from the videoplate,

but he managed to hurry the girls out and get Percy Farnsworth into the room without having to look her image in the eye. "Mr. Percy Farnsworth, London, representing Lloyd's." Farnsworth came into the interrogation cube with mustache twitching. "Mr. Farnsworth, Inspector Troy," Proboda said, indicating the videoplate.

Farnsworth managed to be brisk and breathless at the same time. "Eager to be of assistance in your investigation, Inspector. Say the word. This sort of thing my specialty, you know."

Sparta watched him, expressionless, for two seconds: a veteran confidence man who'd done his time, now working for the other side. That was the story, at any rate. "You've already been helpful, sir. Given us a great many leads." She pretended to peruse his file on her dummy filescreen. "Mm. Your Lloyd's syndicate seems to have been quite enthusiastic about *Star Queen*. Insured the ship, most of the cargo, the lives of the crew."

"Quite. And naturally I'd like to contact Lloyd's as soon as possible, file a preliminary . . ."

She interrupted. "Well, off the record, I'd say the underwriters have gotten off lightly."

Farnsworth mulled this bit of information—what exactly did she mean?—and apparently decided the inspector was willing to play cozy with him. "Encouraging, that," he said, and dropped his voice to a confidential murmur. "But would you mind terribly . . . this business with Grant . . ."

"I suppose you'd like to know if it was legally an accident or a suicide. That's the big question here. Unfortunately the solicitors will just have to fight it out, Mr. Farnsworth. I have nothing to add to the public record." Her tone conveyed no coziness. "I'll accept your kind offer of further assistance. Please move through that door on the left and wait for me inside."

"There?" A door into a grim steel tube had suddenly opened in the carpetry. He peered through it hesitantly, as if expecting to meet a wild animal.

Sparta prodded him. "I won't keep you more than ten minutes, sir. Carry on. Eh?"

With a mumbled "Quite," Farnsworth moved through the door. The moment he was clear it popped shut behind him. Proboda quickly opened the door to the disembarkation tube. "Mr. Nikos Pavlakis, Athens, representing Pavlakis Lines," Proboda said. "This is Inspector Troy."

Pavlakis bobbed his big head and said, "Good day, Inspector." Sparta did not acknowledge him until she had finished reading something from her filescreen. Meanwhile he tugged nervously at the cuffs of his tight jacket.

"I see this is your first visit to Venus, Mr. Pavlakis," she said, looking up. "Regrettable circumstances."

"How is Mr. McNeil, Inspector?" Pavlakis asked. "Is he well? May I talk to him?"

"The clinic has already released him. You'll be able to talk to him soon." His concern struck her as sincere, but it did not deflect her from her line. "Mr. Pavlakis, I note that *Star Queen* is a new registry, yet the ship is actually thirty years old. What was her former registry?"

The heavyset man flinched. "She has been completely refurbished, Inspector. Everything but the basic frame is new, or reconditioned, with a few minor . . ."

Viktor Proboda cut into Pavlakis's nervous improvisation. "She asked for the former registry."

"I . . . I believe the registry was NSS 69376, Inspector."

"*Kronos,*" Sparta said. The word was an accusation. "Ceres in '67, two members of the crew dead, a third woman injured, all cargo lost. Mars Station '73, docking collision killed four workers on the station, cargo in one hold destroyed. Numerous accidents since involving loss of cargo. Several people have been injured and at least one other death has been attributed to below-standard maintenance. You had good reason to rechristen the ship, Mr. Pavlakis."

"*Kronos* was not a good name for a spaceship," Pavlakis said.

She nodded solemnly. "A titan who ate his own children. It must have been difficult to line up qualified crews."

Pavlakis's amber beads were working their way over and through his strong fingers. "When will I be allowed to examine my ship and its cargo, Inspector?"

"I'll answer your questions as best I can, Mr. Pavlakis. As soon as I finish this procedure. Please wait for me—through that door to your left."

Again the invisible door yawned unexpectedly on the cold steel tube. Grimly, staring down over his mustache, Pavlakis moved through it without another word.

When the door closed Proboda admitted the next passenger from the disembarkation tube. "Ms. Nancybeth Mokoroa, Port Hesperus, unemployed." She came in mad, glared at Proboda wordlessly, sneered at the videoplate. As the corridor door closed, sealing her inside, Proboda said, "This is Inspector Troy."

"Ms. Mokoroa, a year ago you sued to break a three-year companionship contract with Mr. Vincent Darlington, shortly after you both had arrived here. The grounds were sexual incompatibility. Was Mr. Darlington aware at the time that you had already become the de facto companion of Mrs. Sondra Sylvester?"

Nancybeth stared silently at the image on the video-plate, her face set in a mask of contempt that was the product of long practice—

—and which Sparta easily recognized as cover for her desperate confusion. Sparta waited.

"We're friends," Nancybeth said huskily.

Sparta said, "That's nice. Was Mr. Darlington aware at the time that you were also lovers?"

"Just friends, that's all!" The young woman stared wildly around at the claustrophobic carpeted room, at the hulking policeman beside her. "What the hell do you think you're trying to prove? What is this . . . ?"

"All right, we'll drop the subject. Now if you would . . ."

"I want a lawyer," Nancybeth shrieked, deciding that offense was better than defense. "In here, right now. I know my rights."

". . . answer just one more question," Sparta finished quietly.

"Not another damned word! Not one more word, blue-suit. This is unlawful detainment. Unreasonable search. . . ."

Sparta and Proboda traded glances. Search?

"Impugnment of dignity," Nancybeth continued. "Slanderous implication. Malicious aforethought . . ."

Sparta almost grinned. "Don't sue us until you hear the question, okay?"

"So we don't have to arrest you first," Proboda added.

Nancybeth choked on her anger, realizing she'd jumped the gun. They hadn't arrested her yet. Possibly they wouldn't. "What d'you wanna know?" She sounded suddenly exhausted.

"Nancybeth, do you think either of them—Sylvester or

Darlington—would be capable of committing murder...
for your sake?"

Nancybeth was startled into laughter. "The way they
talk about each other? They *both* would."

Proboda leaned toward her. "The Inspector didn't ask
you what *they*..."

But Sparta silenced him with a glance from the videoplate. "Okay, thanks, you can go. Through that door to
your right."

"Right?" Proboda asked, and Sparta nodded sharply.
He opened the doorway.

Nancybeth was suspicious. "Where's that go?"

"Out," Proboda said. "Fruits and costumes. You're
free."

The young woman stared wide-eyed around the room
again, her flaring nostrils seeming almost to quiver. Then
she darted through the door like a wildcat freed from a
trap. Proboda looked at the videoplate, exasperated. "Why
not her? It looked to me like she had a lot to hide."

"What she's hiding has nothing to do with *Star Queen*,
Viktor. It's from her own past, I'd guess. Who's next?"

"Mrs. Sylvester. Look, I have to say I hope you'll handle this with more tact than..."

"Let's play the game the way we agreed."

Proboda grunted and opened the door to the tube.
"Mrs. Sondra Sylvester, Port Hesperus, chief executive of
the Ishtar Mining Corporation." His voice was as formal,
as heavy with respect as a majordomo's.

Sondra Sylvester floated smoothly into the small carpeted room, her heavy silks clinging about her. "Viktor?
Must we go through this yet again?"

"Mrs. Sylvester, I'd like to present Inspector Troy," he
said apologetically.

"I'm sure you're eager to get to your office, Mrs. Sylvester," Sparta said, "so I'll be brief."

"My office can wait," Sylvester said firmly. "I'd like to unload my robots from that freighter."

Sparta dipped her gaze to the phony filescreen, then up to Sylvester's eyes. The women stared at each other through the electronics. "You've never dealt with Pavlakis Lines before," Sparta said, "yet you helped persuade both the Board of Space Control and the ship's insurers to waive the crew-of-three rule."

"I believe I've just told Inspector Proboda why. I have six mining robots in the cargo, Inspector. I need to put them to work soon."

"You were very lucky, then." Sparta's relaxed voice conceded no sign that she was being pressured. "You could have lost them all."

"Unlikely. Less likely, even, than that a meteoroid would strike a ship in the first place. Which at any rate has nothing to do with the size of *Star Queen*'s crew."

"Then would you have preferred to trust your robots—insured for approximately nine hundred million dollars, I believe—to an unmanned spacecraft?"

Sylvester smiled at that. It was an astute question, with political and economical overtones one hardly expected from a criminal inspector. "There *are* no unmanned interplanetary freighters, Inspector—thanks to the Space Board, and a long list of other lobbyists, the predictable sort of special interest groups. I don't waste time on hypothetical questions."

"Where did you spend the last three weeks of your Earth holidays, Mrs. Sylvester?"

A decidedly non-hypothetical question—and it cost

Sylvester effort to cover her surprise. "I was vacationing in the south of France."

"You rented a villa on the Isle du Levant, in which, except for the first day and last day and two occasions when you visited, Ms. Nancybeth Mokoroa stayed alone. Where were you the rest of the time?"

Sylvester glanced at Proboda, who avoided her look. His earlier superficial questioning had not prepared her to face this level of detail. "I was . . . I was on private business."

"In the United States? In England?"

Sondra Sylvester said nothing. With visible effort she settled her features.

"Thank you, Mrs. Sylvester," Sparta said coldly. "Through that door to the left"—and Sparta noted that Proboda took just a little too long opening the hidden door, softening the impact of its surprise. "It will be necessary to detain you a short while longer. Not more than five or six minutes."

Sylvester kept the mask in place as she went through the door, but she could not disguise her apprehension.

Proboda hurried the next passenger into the room.

"Mr. Blake Redfield. London. Representing Mr. Vincent Darlington of the Hesperian Museum."

In the instant Proboda was opening the corridor door, Sparta's fingers flicked out to the monitoring lens, degrading the videoplate image visible to Redfield. He came into the small room, looking alert, relaxed, proper in his expensive English suit, but showing just the edge of a young man's temptation to strut his stuff in that certain cut of the lapels, that certain length of his shiny auburn hair.

"Inspector Troy, Space Board," Proboda said, nodding at the videoplate, failing to notice the image had lost its crips focus. Blake turned toward the screen with the reserved, expectant half-smile that marks the socially adept. If he recognized her he did not betray himself, but she knew he was as good at this game as she was. If he had a reason to hide, he could hide better than any of the others.

She inspected him intensely, although her macrozoom eye was largely disabled by the limited resolution of the videoplate, and she had no sense whatever of his chemical presence. She had not seen him in two years; he did not look older so much as more sure of himself. He was holding something in reserve, something she had not known in him before. The only sound from him, floating weightless in the acoustically deadened room, was his quiet breathing. He waited for her to speak.

If someone had made a voiceprint graph when she did finally speak, its very flatness would have been suspicious. "You acted as Mr. Darlington's agent in the purchase of *The Seven Pillars of Wisdom*, Mr. Redfield?"

"That's correct." His voice, by contrast, was warm and alert; its graph would have said, if you're not giving anything away, neither am I.

"The purpose of your trip?"

"I'm here to see that the famous book you just named is safely delivered to Mr. Darlington."

Sparta paused. It seemed an illogical reply, deliberately provocative, which she could not let pass without challenge. "If you were planning to personally insure its delivery, why ship it aboard *Star Queen*? Why not keep it with you?"

Redfield grinned. "Perhaps I did."

He knew she knew he didn't. "I've confirmed that the book is aboard *Star Queen*, Mr. Redfield."

"That's reassuring. May I see it too?"

Sparta's heart thudded, hard and quick. Well below the level of anything she could bring quickly to consciousness, she knew something was happening that she had not anticipated. On the spot she decided that Mr. Blake Redfield was not to be given more information than he had already. "Soon, Mr. Redfield. Through that door to your right, please. Sorry to keep you waiting."

As he went out she could see that he was smiling broadly. He meant for her to see it. Impatiently she said, "All right, Viktor, he was the last of the sheep."

"The last of the what?"

"The goats are in the pen. Let's get 'em."

The tiny room into which Farnsworth, Pavlakis, and Sylvester deposited themselves after negotiating a dogleg twist in the steel tube was another cube—this one of raw steel, as featureless as a submarine's brig. The cell had no visible exit; the way back had been closed off by sliding panels. The blank videoplate overhead filled the entire ceiling.

The sullen conversation among the three inmates was on the verge of slicing into vicious bickering when the dark videoplate suddenly brightened. A close-up image of Inspector Ellen Troy, now three times life size, formed on the screen.

"I promised that this wouldn't take long, and it won't," the iconic face announced. Sparta's image was replaced by a crisp view of a convexly curving metal plate. "This hull plate from *Star Queen*'s life support deck, designated

L-43, has a hole in it." The image zoomed in rapidly to
the upper right corner, to the neat black hole in the paint.

The screen switched to another view of the plate, its
inner surface blackened, concave. "The plate displays internal spalling characteristic of a high-velocity projectile,
such as a meteoroid"—and again the image changed, moving in closer to show a crater in the steel as vast as
Aetna's—"which was covered by hardened plastic foam,
making the hole airtight." A new image showed a shiny,
viscid lump of yellow plastic mounded over the spot in
the plate where the crater had been displayed—a view of
the hole before the protective plastic had been removed.

Sparta's pedantic, almost hectoring voice continued
over the succession of images. "The significant damage to
Star Queen was done by an explosion that destroyed both
major oxygen tanks and a fuel cell," she said, as a view
of the blackened mess inside the flight deck came up on
the screen.

She paused a moment to let them study the wreckage
before saying, "Neither the hole in the hull plate nor the
internal explosion was caused by a meteoroid, however."

Their solemn faces were washed in the screen's cold
light. If her audience of three were surprised by this news,
none betrayed it except by the deepening silence.

Another close-up, this one a micrograph, snapped into
view. "The melt pattern around the hole shows large, irregular metal crystals, characteristic of slow melting and
cooling—not the fine regular crystals that would have resulted from an instantaneous deposition of energy. This
hole was probably cut with a plasma torch." Another micrograph. "Here you see that there are in fact two separate
strata of the hardened plastic plug—the first is very thin
and its laminations do not show the turbulence patterns

expected from a supersonic airflow through the hole—you can see the smooth exfoliation here." A computerized chart, this time. "As this spectrograph proves, this layer of plastic was actually catalyzed over two months ago. In other words, the hole was in the plate and sealed with plastic before *Star Queen* left Earth. Note that this same thin layer has been shattered in the center, blasted outward. The explosion occurred inside the ship—blew the hole open, allowing the air to escape—then was quickly sealed again by the ship's emergency systems."

More charts and graphs. "The interior explosion was caused by a charge of fulminate of gold, detonated by acetylene, placed inside the casing of the fuel cell—these spectrographs reveal the nature of the explosives. Ignition was electrical and was probably triggered through the fuel cell monitor, by a preset signal in the ship's computer."

Sparta's stern image reappeared, fiercely bright in the stark steel cell. "Who sabotaged *Star Queen*? Why was it sabotaged? Anyone who can shed light on this may speak now. Or if you prefer, please privately contact the local office of the Board of Space Control. *Star Queen* will remain off limits pending the completion of our investigation."

A shaft of light pierced the room and partially washed out the screen. A double door had opened at the back of the cell; right outside was one of the core's busiest hallways.

Meanwhile Sparta had flipped a switch that cycled her austere videoplate image. Her tiny control room, hardly more than a closet full of glittering panels, was tucked into a crevice between corridors. She was physically closer to them than any of the people in the cell realized. Under cover of the cycled frame she turned to Proboda, who hovered near her in the control room. "Viktor, you thought I was impertinent with Mrs. Sylvester. You follow her, then. If she goes to her office or approaches *Star Queen*, signal me right away. Wherever she goes, call me in five minutes. She's already leaving—get going!"

Sparta flipped her videoplate image back to live feed. Farnsworth and Pavlakis were still in the room, although Pavlakis had one tentative foot out the door and Farnsworth was walking boldly up to the videoplate.

"Odd, that," Farnsworth said to the giant screen over his head. "Revealing your evidence without making an accusation."

"We're aboard a space station, Mr. Farnsworth. More isolated than a town in Kansas."

"And if the villain isn't here with us?"

"Then no harm done," she said.

The man was transparent, but bold—standing there as much as telling her he knew what she knew about his past, that she would be mistaken to suspect him. "D'you expect your revelations to remain secret more than a few minutes? Even from Earth?"

"Did you have a specific comment to make, Mr. Farnsworth?"

Farnsworth jerked his thumb toward Pavlakis, who was still hulking in the background, silhouetted against the brightly lit corridor outside. "That one. Family history of defrauding insurors. Never been able to prove it. But if he's not your man he can tell you who is."

He was an insolent man, even if in this case he was, as she had already decided, quite innocent. "What would you say if I told you Sylvester did it?" Sparta asked. Good. That set him back a bit—

He took it seriously. "Jealousy, you mean?"—as if he'd

never thought of it. "This fellow Darlington buys the book she wanted, so she makes sure he never . . . and so forth?"

"And so forth."

"Novel theory, that. . . ." Farnsworth muttered.

"It's not a *theory*, Farnsworth." Her face, three times life size, leaned toward him.

"Not a theory?"

"Not a theory at all."

"Quite enough said then. Do forgive . . ." He was suddenly in a hurry to radio his employers. He swam off awkwardly toward the door.

Pavlakis had disappeared.

The commlink chimed in her right ear. "Go ahead."

"This is Proboda. Mrs. Sylvester went straight to the headquarters of the Ishtar Mining Corporation. I'm outside the Ishtar Gate right now." The Ishtar Mining Corporation was located almost two kilometers away, at the far end of the space station; there its windows and antennas could look straight down on the bright clouds of Venus.

"That seems to eliminate her, too. Meet me back here as soon as you can."

"What happens next?" Proboda sounded irritated. She'd sent him on another wild goose chase.

"We'll wait. Our list is very short, Viktor. I think we're going to see a confession or an act of desperation. Not long. Maybe ten or fifteen min—"

She felt as much as heard the massive thud. The lights went out, all of them, all at once, and in the blackness the low moan of the warning sirens rose quickly to a thin, desperate wail. Wall speakers urgently addressed everyone within hearing, repeating themselves in English, Arabic, Russian, Japanese: *Evacuate core section one immediately.*

There is a catastrophic loss of pressure in core section one.
Evacuate core section one immediately....

Proboda shouted into the commlink, loud enough to deafen her. "Are you all right? What happened up there? Troy?" But no one answered him.

XVIII

A space station's vital systems are both independent and redundant. Someone who knew Port Hesperus well had managed to isolate the entire starward quarter of the hub, interrupting main bus power from the nuclear reactor and cutting the lines from the solar arrays. All this in the instant that a pressure hatch blew out in the security sector—

Until emergency batteries cut in, it was going to be very dark.

But not to Sparta, who tuned her visual cortex to infrared and made her way swiftly through a strange world of glowing shapes, an environment eerily resembling some giant plastic model of a complex organism lit only in red neon. Otherwise-dark light fixtures still glowed from the warmth in their diodes. Wires in the wall panels still glowed from resistance to the electricity that had recently flowed through them, and the panels themselves glowed faintly with borrowed heat.

Although most of the microminiaturized devices in the station consumed only trickles of electricity, their extreme density made for glowing hotspots in every phonelink and datalink. Every flatscreen and video-plate glowed with the alphanumerics or graphics or images of human faces they had displayed when the power was cut. Every place that human hands and feet had touched within the last hour glowed with the warmth of their passage. If there were rats in the walls, Sparta would see them.

Out in the halls and corridors the emergency lights flashed on quickly, drawing from their own self-contained batteries, throwing hard beams and stark strobing shadows down crowded passages. People swam swiftly through this flashing world like schools of squid, moving with single purpose toward the central part of the core—moving, for the most part, soundlessly, except for a few frightened cries, quickly answered by quiet commands, as emergency personnel took frightened newcomers in tow and firmly steered them to safety.

Pressure loss was the primal fear in space, but the regular inhabitants of Port Hesperus had run drills for just this sort of thing so often that when the reality occurred, it was almost routine. Old-timers were comfortable in the knowledge that so huge was the volume of air in even one quarter of Port Hesperus's core that it would be eight hours before the pressure dropped from its current luxurious sea-level value to the thinness of a mountaintop in the Andes. Long before then the repair crews would have done their job.

Sparta stayed in the dark, avoiding the corridors and the crowds, swimming through the dull infrared glow of access passages, along freight shafts, past pipes and cable racks in the ventilation tunnels, toward the site of the blown hatch. She was moving against the crowds but with the air; she'd needed only a moment of listening to pinpoint the wind's destination, for it wailed through the blown pressure plate, playing the core like a vast organ pipe.

As she flew she felt the breeze, stirring gently at first, steadily freshening. Twenty or thirty meters from the hole the airflow reached hurricane velocity, and if she were to slip over that imaginary boundary she would be sucked into a supersonic funnel and shot into space like a rifle bullet. She would have to get close, but not that close.

The open hatch was in the Q3 security lock, and the purpose of this second act of sabotage was clear to her— someone had needed to create a diversion that would draw people away from *Star Queen,* that would make the neighborhood unsafe. Someone much cleverer than Sparta had suspected. So Sparta took the shortcut through the alleys and backyards of the space station, dashing to get to *Star Queen,* while the culprit was still aboard.

It occurred to her, as she approached the lock through a final stretch of ventilator duct, that the diversion had been not just clever but shrewd, provoking maximum terror with minimum risk of injury—the only people in the immediate vicinity of the blown hatch were the spacesuited guards, and even if they had been sucked into the vacuum of the docking bay they would have been protected. A softhearted villain, then?

Not the one who blew up *Star Queen's* oxygen supply. Perhaps safety in this case was more apparent than real, the accidental byproduct of a fundamentally pragmatic scheme.

Sparta knocked the panel from the end of the ventilator

and saw it skitter away, dragged by the wind; she peered
from her hole into dark, howling desolation. The approach
to the security lock was deserted. The guards, if not in the
wrong place at the wrong time and thus instantly sucked
out, would by now have been ordered to clear out. That
would have been what the perpetrator planned, *needed.*

And if Sparta was right, the individual was still aboard
the ship, having left the hatch wide open—with no time to
waste putting on a spacesuit—and would be coming out
again any second.

Sparta would forestall the escape. She pulled herself
out of the ventilator. Clinging to the walls against the
sucking vacuum, she pulled herself hand over hand into
Star Queen's docking tube. She pulled herself along by
inches while the excruciating wind tore at her ears. Finally
she reached *Star Queen's* main hatch.

Inside the ship she punched the switches and watched
as the hatch slowly sealed itself shut behind her; inside
the airlock there was silence. She saw the red glow of
handprints on the switches and on the ladder rungs, one
person's handprints.

The two of them were in here together. Sparta leaned
close to a glowing print and inhaled its chemical essence.
Not anyone she had met on Port Hesperus, not anyone she
had touched in weeks. The spicy amino acid pattern, called
to full visualization, teased at her memory but was nowhere within its access. . . .

In one scenario, Sondra Sylvester was to have been in
the hold, attempting to steal *The Seven Pillars of Wisdom;*
two minutes ago, Sylvester was two kilometers away. In
another scenario—Sparta's favorite—Nikos Pavlakis was to
have been in the ship, on the flight deck, setting its automatic systems to undock and blast its way out of the

station, into the sun, forever burying the evidence of his and his partners' treachery. But without accomplices, Pavlakis had had no time to rig the diversion.

Sparta pulled herself cautiously into the ship, past the stores deck—paused—then floated down through the flight deck. The glow of the console lights, running on batteries, made a soft circular kaleidoscope in the darkness. She paused again, *listening*—

A distant careful movement, the brush of a glove, perhaps, or the scrape of a shoe against metal. She pinpointed it: her quarry was in Hold A. It was no one she had expected to find.

If whoever was in the hold was not Sylvester, it was one of her agents. Not Nancybeth, who was as somatically focused as an infant, incapable of concentrating on anything but her own needs and pleasures for more than a minute at a time. All communications to and from *Helios* had been tightly monitored; someone who had been aboard *Helios*, then. Sparta knew she'd been a fool. . . .

She crept weightless through the life-support-deck corridor with every augmented sense atingle, through the hatch of the hold airlock—which was ajar—until her face was inches from the outer hatch of Hold A. It too stood open. She moved as silently as she could, pulling herself along by the friction of the merest pressure of her fingertips, into the lock.

"Don't be afraid of me," he said. His voice was as warm as before, but this time it rose from a deeper, firmer base. He was quite near. "I needed to learn something."

His control was extraordinary, she thought. If she'd made a voiceprint of his words, they would have betrayed no insincerity.

She stopped where she was, breathless, pausing for

thought. She could hear him and smell him, she knew approximately where he was, but she had no weapon and he was not in the line of sight.

"You don't have to show yourself," he said. "I'm not sure where you are, in fact, although I think you can hear me easily. Let me explain."

Seconds passed while she inched closer to the inner hatch. The empty interior darkness of the hold was cold and black, what she could see of it, except for the dull red glow of the places he had touched.

Their pattern made plain what he was after—the space where the book's Styrene case had rested was a cold, empty pit.

"I'm going to make the assumption that you're willing to listen," he said.

She had him located now, but still not as precisely as she wanted. He was lurking just inside the airlock. That sound—that was probably his hand, maybe his hip, rubbing lightly against the shell of the hold, no more than a foot or two from her head. Keep him talking, talking and moving in the way that talking entrains unconsciously, keep him talking a half a minute more and she would know where to grab. . . .

"I needed to look at this book before you let it off the ship," he said. "You said it was here, but I needed to know if the book you saw was the *real* book. You're not an expert. I am."

She inched closer, breathing in and breathing out in long, slow, controlled inhalations and exhalations that no ear but her own could hear. His breath, because she was so close to him, was a visible cloud of warmth, pulsing slowly in the dark air beyond the lock.

A foot away in the darkness he was explaining himself

to her. "Someone with time and a lot of money to spend could, just conceivably, have counterfeited a book from the early 20th century. They would have had to find craftsmen who could set metal type, to begin with—printers who were willing to print a book in the old way, line by line, from a text a third of a million words long. They would have had to cast the type—it would take months, if the person had the skills—unless the original type was still in existence and they could get hold of it. They would have had to find old paper of the right sort—or reproduce it, watermarks and all, and make it look old. Then the bindings, the marbled slipcase, the leather covers . . . think of the craftsmanship, the incredible skill!"

In his passion for the thing he was describing, that peculiar old book, he seemed momentarily to have forgotten about Sparta.

She hesitated, then spoke in a whisper that would carry only to him. "I'm listening." No answer. Perhaps he was startled by her closeness. "Why so important to look at it now? Why not wait?" she whispered.

"Because the real book may still be aboard."

Had he hoped to find the *real* book first? Or was all this an elaborate alibi because she'd already caught him with the *real* book in his hands?

"Sondra Sylvester flew to Washington, then back to London three weeks before she boarded *Helios*," she said. "She made other trips from France to England. What was she doing there?"

"She was in Oxford. She had a book made." His voice was bolder now, darker, like old hardwood. "I have it in my hand."

A shutter clicked in her mind, a wall descended, a decision was made. She slipped her hands over the rim of the hatch and pulled hard, darting into the hold. She brought herself up against the steel racks opposite the hatch and turned to face him. He was a glowing blob of red in the darkness, beside the open hatch. The thing in his hand was . . . a book—

—only a book.

"Can we have some light now?" he asked.

"Go ahead."

He reached up and hit the switch beside the hatch. Green worklights illuminated the hold and her vision shifted into the visible spectrum. For a moment Blake's eyes held hers. He looked a bit sheepish, as if regretting all the fuss.

She had an odd thought, then—she thought he looked rather charming with his reddish hair awry and his thoroughly rumpled suit.

He held up the book. "A beautiful counterfeit. The typeface is perfect. The paper is perfect—the kind they still print Bibles on. The binding is extraordinarily good. Chemical analysis will prove the book is new, but if you'd never seen the original, you would have to read a lot of it even to become suspicious."

She was watching him, listening to him. He was different indeed. "What gives it away?" she asked.

"There must have been a gang of them at different print shops, whacking the linotype keyboards. Three hundred thousand words. Some of the typesetters weren't as careful as others."

"Errors?"

"A few typos. Only a few, remarkably." He smiled. "There really wasn't time for a thorough proofreading."

She saw what he was driving at. "But Darlington probably wouldn't have read it anyway."

"From what I know of the man he would never have opened it." He smiled. "Well, maybe to the title page."

"What makes you think the original is still on board?"

"Because I personally brought the book up by shuttle and saw it secured in that rack only a few hours before *Star Queen* left Earth. Unless it went back off the ship immediately, it's got to be here."

"Is that the case it came in?" The gray Styrene case floated beside him.

"I'm pretty sure. I wasn't that worried about the lock. A determined thief with plenty of time and access to the ship's computer . . . I thought I knew what Sylvester was up to, you see, but it hadn't occurred to me that she would move so quickly. News of the meteoroid strike started me thinking about how anxious she'd been for *Star Queen* to leave on schedule. Then I learned Inspector Ellen Troy had been assigned. . . ."

How had he learned that? She'd worry about it later—she was going to have plenty of time to interview Blake Redfield. "All right, Mr. Redfield. Let me have this exquisite counterfeit. Exhibit A." Ruefully she added, "Thanks for your help—I'll put in a good word at your trial. If you're lucky you can get a change of venue."

"Sorry I had to blow a hole in the station. But the fuss I made wasn't just for the book's sake—not that it isn't worth it." He made no move to hand it to her. "A wise salesman once told me that anything for sale is worth exactly what the buyer and seller agree it's worth. By that standard the real *Seven Pillars* is worth a million and a half pounds. This fake could have cost Sondra Sylvester a half a million pounds. Labor and materials. Bribes and payoffs."

She liked his voice, but he was talking too much. "The book, please."

His eyes never left hers. "You see, I knew if anyone came before I left *Star Queen*, it would be you. In fact, I counted on it."

Again something had escaped her. Again her heart was suddenly racing. Once she'd known Blade Redfield well, as well as one child could know another. Why was he a mystery to her now?

"SPARTA," he said, quietly. "I never believed what they told us about what happened to you, what happened to your folks, why they closed the program. I recognized you the second I saw you on that street in Manhattan. But you didn't want me to know you even existed. So I . . ."

A great rending and tearing of metal cut him off in midsentence, its obscene screech crushing the warmth of his voice.

Creeping up on him, before she knew who he was, she'd seen that other hold open, but she'd ignored it. "Follow me," she shouted, diving past him into the airlock.

In the corridor a blast of heat seared her face. The open Hold C airlock was the mouth of a furnace. She slammed the hatch shut and spun its wheel. "Blake, move!"

He scrambled out of the hold, still clutching the counterfeit book. "Get up there," she urged him. "We've got to get off the ship, fast!"

Blake pulled himself out of the access lock—just as the hatchcover bulged from a massive impact, slamming him sideways off the ladder. Sparta boosted him and leaped after him, an instant before the diamond-edged proboscis ripped through the hatch's steel plate like a chainsaw through plywood, spraying weightless shrapnel. The Rolls-

Royce robot was rapidly carving a hole for itself through the sealed lock.

The mining robot, which had been loaded through an outer pressure hatch, was not only too big for the airlock but too big for the corridor; that it had to tear the ship to pieces to make progress did not deter it.

Blake sailed up past the cabins, through the flight deck, through the stores deck, toward the main airlock, pulling and steering himself with one hand in the darkness, holding his book in the other. Sparta followed closely, pausing only to slam the lower corridor hatch after herself.

Blake reached the top of the crew module. He careened to a halt against the outer hatch of the main airlock, reached to punch the switches—

—and yanked his hand back as if he'd been scalded.

Sparta pulled herself to a stop below him. "Go, Blake, go!" she barked, before she saw what he saw, the red sign blazing: WARNING. VACUUM. "They must've sealed off the security area," she said, "let it go to vacuum."

"Spacesuits—on the wall beside you."

The robot's progress was a demolition derby; an endless mashing and tearing of metal and plastic. Any moment it would rip through the hull, and then they would perish in vacuum.

"No time," she said. "Our only chance is to disable it."

"Do what?"

"Not here. We're trapped."

She dived back down to the flight deck. He fumbled after her. To him the place was pitch dark but for the glow of the console lights, but she saw everything. She could see through the steel deck to what looked like the glow of an oncoming white dwarf star.

"Forget that damned book!" she yelled at Blake—but

he held onto the exquisite counterfeit as if it were worth as much as his life. The robot arrived on the flight deck at the same time he did, a creature of nightmare preceded by the flare of its radiators. Having widened the corridor opening with its saw-toothed proboscis, its bristling sensors appeared first above the edge of the hole, followed in milliseconds by its great samurai-helmet head thrusting into the room. Its head swiveled in rapid jerks, diamond-paned compound eyes reflecting the multi-colored glow from the instrument panel.

The wave of heat from its radiators was enough to send Blake and Sparta thrashing away in retreat.

The robot's glittering eyes fixed on Sparta. Its leg motors accelerated with a whine, and it jumped—five and a half weightless tonnes, its ore-scoops out-stretched—toward the corner of ceiling where she cringed. She possessed a small fraction of the machine's mass and could accelerate much faster; by the time it had smashed into the flight deck ceiling she was bouncing off the floor.

"Fire extinguisher," Blake cried, and for a half second she thought he'd panicked, lost his wits—what good's a fire extinguisher against a nuclear reactor?—but in the next half second she realized that the heat had inspired him.

That the mining robot was not built to work in free-fall gave them a slim advantage in the battle. One other advantage, hardly more robust, had occurred to her when she'd leaped to evade its grasp. The brute machine acted as if it had a personal grudge—against *her*. It didn't want to just punch a hole in the ship and let her die, drunk on hypoxia. It wanted to tear her to pieces. It wanted to watch.

Someone was looking through its eyes, controlling its every move—

•

—until Blake flew deftly toward its head, aiming a fire extinguisher as he came, pressing its trigger, covering its eyes with thick foam. . . .

"*Aaahh!*" Blake's cry was sharp, quickly stifled. The robot had swiveled as he'd passed; a radiator had come within inches of his arm; *The Seven Pillars of Wisdom* had exploded in flames. Frantically he turned the fire extinguisher on the book, then on himself, on his burning jacket.

The huge robot was thrown into a frenzy, writhing and slashing. It had lost its purchase, lost its view, like a beetle flipped on its back. But in seconds it would get a grip on something, tear into some fixed structure. Then surely its remote operator, forced to settle for efficient death, would ignore personal revenge and simply use the machine to smash through *Star Queen*'s windows.

Meanwhile the berserk and fiery robot dominated the flight deck, blocking their escape; even if it never got a good foothold it would kill them by setting them afire, melting the cabin around them.

Sparta knew what she had to do. It would leave her utterly vulnerable. The thought flashed through her brain that she couldn't trust Blake Redfield, and instantly the rest of her brain said *store it, first things first.*

She fell into trance. The ultra-high frequency datastream—the frantic-smelling datastream, the hate-filled datastream of the robot's controlling transmission—flowed into her mind. She raised her arms and hands and curved them in an antenna's arc. Her belly burned. She beamed the message.

The robot jerked spasmodically and then froze.

She had it like a cat, by the scruff of its neck, clamped

in her mind instead of her fist—but it took all her concentration to do it. She could override the strong signal from the nearby transmitter only because she was a few feet from the robot; the power stored in the batteries beneath her lungs would trickle away in less than a minute.

"Blake!" The word was plosive, hollow. "Pull the fuel capsule," she gasped. Her beam wavered and the creature twitched violently.

Blake gaped at her. She hung like a levitating Minoan priestess in the lurid light, her arms curved into hooks, conferring a savage benediction. She forced out the words, thin as husks: "In its belly. Pull it."

He moved at last, under it, between its wavering legs and claws. Above the paralyzed machine the ceiling was charring from the heat of the radiators; the smoldering plastic padding began pouring acrid smoke into the room. Blake fumbled at the fuel port—she wanted to tell him what to do but she didn't dare—and after a moment he figured it out and got the port open.

Then he was stymied again. He paused to study the fuel cell assembly for endless seconds.

He saw that it was made for safety, for simplicity. It was, after all, a Rolls-Royce. He wrapped his fingers around the chrome staples of the fuel assembly, braced his feet against the robot's shell, and pulled.

The fuel assembly slid out. Its cladding telescoped to shield it as he withdrew it. In that instant the massive robot was gutted, dead. Its radiators cooled—

—not soon enough to prevent the ceiling exploding into flames.

"Damn it, there'd better be another fire extinguisher in here," he shouted.

There was. Sparta yanked it from its bracket, shot past him, and covered the blazing padding with creamy foam. She emptied the bottle on it, then flung it away.

They looked at each other—keyed up, the pair of them—exasperated, singed and sooty, choking on smoke, and then he managed a grin. She forced herself to return it. "Let's get those suits on before we suffocate."

He put on McNeil's, she Wycherly's. As she was bleeding some of Wycherly's oxygen into McNeil's empty tank, she paused. She'd had another inspiration.

"Blake . . . it was Sylvester who stole the book—who had it stolen. And I think I know where it is now."

"She had a case of other books aboard, but I looked in there. . . ."

"So did I. This is a guess. Don't hold it against me if I'm wrong." She twisted the oversize spacesuit's gloves and yanked them off.

"Where are you going?"

"I need my fingers for this."

She pulled herself back to the flight deck. She moved between the claws and legs of the inert robot until she found its main processor access. She opened the port and reached inside.

Blake watched her from the ceiling, barely visible in the dark. "What are you doing in there?" She'd been at it for what seemed a long time.

"I'm going to have to reinsert the fuel assembly. Don't worry, it's lobotomized now."

He said nothing. He couldn't think of anything to say except, you must be crazy.

When the fuel assembly slid into the robot its head wobbled, its claws clashed feebly, but its movements were those of a drugged rhinoceros. Sparta, tiny inside Wycherly's borrowed suit, moved into the robot's sluggish embrace again and reached into the processor. Motors whined. The robot's abdomen split down the center and unfolded in layer upon layer of compound chambers, until the complex metal intestines of the ore-processing cavity lay exposed. In the grisly light the machine seemed to have disemboweled itself.

Sparta pulled herself over the carapace of the gutted robot and peered inside. There, propped between two massive worm gears in a mesh of tube snouts and grillwork, nestled a fragile, beautiful book, snug in its slipcase.

XIX

The lights came on first, and spacesuited teams of workers moved efficiently into the empty security sector, evacuated both of people and of air, to replace the blown pressure hatch. Within half an hour of the emergency, the core had been repressurized and business had resumed as usual.

Before that, while air was still flowing back into the Q3 lock, a patrol squad, pressure-suited and with stunguns drawn, burst into Star Queen. They were hardened cops, used to dealing with drunkenness and homicidal rage and other forms of insanity that commonly afflict the human residents of space stations, but the destruction astonished them.

For one thing, they'd had few occasions to see, up close, the mining robots that prowled the surface of the planet beneath them, the machines that paid all their salaries, and to find one looming amid the wreckage of *Star Queen*'s bridge, even exposed and enfeebled, was plain terrifying. They approached the machine as divers might approach a comatose great white shark.

Except for the robot, which proved disabled, the ship was deserted. For a long time none of the patrollers noticed that the two spacesuits which had hung on the stores deck were missing.

Sparta and Blake had ditched the suits five minutes after they'd put them on. Again they'd taken to the darkened ventilator shafts, the conduits. She knew the back ways as he could not, having stored a thousand engineering diagrams in her memory, but he'd been careful to memorize what he needed to know about the internal layout of Port Hesperus before he'd left Earth, even then planning his assault on *Star Queen*.

"Three half-ounce wads of plastique on a timer for the pressure hatch," he told her. "Cutter charge on the auxiliary cables, also on a timer. Threw the main bus breakers myself—wanted to make sure I didn't do any real damage. A couple of the power plant workers will have ether hangovers. . . ."

"C-4? Not fulminate of gold? Acetylene detonators?" They spoke on the move, chasing each other through the shadowy maze.

"Who'd use that junk? That's dangerous as hell."

"Somebody who didn't care about danger and wanted the debris to look like an explosion in a fuel cell."

"*Star Queen* was sabotaged?"

"You may be the last person in the solar system to hear the news. Assuming you didn't do it yourself."

He laughed.

"I need the rest of your story, Blake, before I make up my mind what to do with you."

"Let's stop here a minute," he said. Following a man-ifold of pipes and cables, they had reached the mid-region of the core. They were in a substation, surrounded by huge pumps and fat gray transformers; the twilight gloom was striped with bright bars of light projected from a grating below, creeping slowly with the station's rotation. Through the bars they could see straight into the central sphere, ringed with trees and gardens and the twin concourses of the station's social center.

"I didn't take explosives courses in SPARTA, Linda—"

"Don't call me that, ever." Her angry warning echoed in the metal chamber.

"It's too late. They know who you are."

"Yeah? Well I know who they are." Her voice betrayed her, for she was tired, and the fear surfaced. "What I don't know is where they are."

"One of them is here, on this station. Looking for you. That's why I went for all the fireworks—so I could get to you alone. Before they did."

"Who is it?"

"I don't think I'd recognize him. Or her. Maybe you would."

"Dammit." She sighed. "Start from the beginning, will you?"

He took a breath, closed his eyes, and let his breath out slowly. When he opened his dark eyes they glowed in the warm light from below. "SPARTA broke up a year after you left it. There were probably a dozen of us at my level then, the sixteen-and seventeen-year-olds—Ron, Khalid, Sara, Louis, Rosaria . . ."

She interrupted him. "That far back my memory is ex-cellent."

"The spring after you left some weird characters came

around to see us from a government agency. These people were recruiters, looking for volunteers for a 'supplementary training program,' making lots of heavy hints about the black side. We were given the distinct impression that *you* had gone before us . . . and you were everybody's idol, of course."

"Everybody's scapegoat, you mean."

"That too, sometimes." He smiled at the memory. "Anyway, we were suckers for the pitch. I was, anyway. I signed up—got into a shouting match with my mom and dad, but they finally gave in—and I went off to summer camp with a few of the others. This was in eastern Arizona, high up on the Mogollon Rim. We were there maybe three weeks. They knew we were in good shape, so they got right into the intellectual stuff. Survival. Ciphers. Demolition. Silent killing. Later I realized it was all lightweight, child's play. An audition—a sieve, really, to catch those of us who were talented. Psychologically susceptible."

"Who'd they catch? You and who else?"

"Nobody. Your father showed up one afternoon. He had plainclothes heavies with him, FBI maybe. I never saw him so angry; he just terrorized these selfstyled tough guys who were running the place. To us kids he didn't say much, but we could see his heart was breaking. We were on carriers back to Phoenix an hour later. That was the end of summer camp." Blake paused. "That was the last time I saw your father. I never saw your mother again, either."

"They're dead. Officially. Chopper crash in Maryland."

"Yes. Did you go to the funeral?"

"Maybe. Maybe not. That's the year that's missing from my memory."

"Nobody I've talked to went to the funeral. We heard

that—about the crash—a month, after we got home. SPARTA just fell apart, then. Next fall we were dispersed, most of us in private colleges—surrounded by people we thought of as retarded. We still had a whole lot to learn. What happened to you, nobody ever heard."

"What did happen to me?"

Blake looked at her, his warm eyes softening. "This isn't from experience, this is from research," he said. "In some of the journals you'll find that about that time, there was a program to inject self-replicating biochips into human subjects. This program was supposed to be under Navy control, because they were the biochip experts, instead of under Health or Science as you'd expect. The first subject was somebody who was supposedly clinically dead, brain-dead."

"A neat cover story." She laughed, but there was bitterness in her voice. "All they did was reverse cause and effect."

He waited, but she said no more. "This subject supposedly showed remarkable improvement at first, but then became severely disturbed and had to be placed in permanent care. A private place in Colorado."

"Biochips wasn't all they did, Blake," she whispered. "They had a lot to hide."

"I've begun to gather that," he said. "They did their best. Four years ago the place in Colorado burned down. Killed a dozen people. End of trail."

"Everything you've told me I've already reconstructed for myself," she said impatiently.

"If I hadn't already seen you alive, I would have given up. How did you escape?"

"The doctor who was supposed to be my watchdog—his conscience must have started bothering him. He used biochips to repair the lesions they'd made. I started re-membering. . . ." She turned to him and without thinking gripped his arm, hard. "What happened during that miss-ing year? What were they really trying to do? What did I do that scared them, made them turn me into a vegeta-ble?"

"Maybe you learned something," he said.

She started to speak but hesitated; his tone alerted her that she might not like what she heard. She withdrew her hand and quietly asked, "What do you suppose it was?"

"I think you learned that SPARTA was more than your father and mother claimed. The tip of a huge iceberg, an ancient iceberg." He studied her while the station rolled in space and the bright bars of light through the grill sliced his shadowy features to ribbons. "There's a theory. An ideal. Men and women have been burned in the service of that ideal. Others who believed in it have been praised as great philosophers. And some believers gained power and became monsters. The more I study this subject, the more connections I find, and the farther back they reach—in the 13th century they were known as adepts of the Free Spirit, the *prophetae*—but whatever name they used, they've never been eradicated. Their goal has always been god-hood. Perfection in this life. Superman."

Sparta's mind was tingling; images danced in the half-light but flickered strobing away before she could raise them to consciousness. The peculiar vibration overcame her ordinary sight; she pressed her fingers to her closed eyelids. "My parents were psychologists, scientists," she whispered.

"There has always been a dark side and a light side, a black side and a white side." Patiently he waited until she opened her eyes again. "The man who ran M.I. was named

Laird," he said. "He tried to keep his involvement a secret."

"I recognize the name."

"Laird knew your parents for years, decades. Since before they immigrated. Maybe he knew something that
would embarrass them."

"No," she whispered. "No, Blake, I think he seduced
them with visions of an easier route to perfection."

"You've remembered something new?"

She looked around, distracted and nervous. "You've
been helpful, Blake. It's time we got to the rest of our
business."

"Laird's changed his name, maybe his appearance, but
I think he's still influential in the government."

"I'll worry about it later."

"If he could have controlled you, he could have made
himself anything he wanted." He paused. "Maybe even a
president."

"He failed to control me. He also failed to make me
perfect."

"I think he'd like to bury the evidence of his failure."

"I know that well enough. But that's my problem."

"I've made it mine," he said.

"Sorry. You can't play this game." Her voice had re-
gained its confidence. "Let's get on with the game we're
already playing. Catching a thief."

"Inspector Ellen Troy, Board of Space Control."

The expression on Vincent Darlington's round face
wavered between disgust and disbelief—"What*ever* could
have . . . ?"—and finally settled on deference to authority.
He reluctantly opened the doors of the Hesperian Museum.

Sparta pocketed her badge. She was still wearing her

dock rat disguise, and at the moment she felt more like the dock rat than the cop. "I believe you know Mr. Blake Redfield of London."

"Goodness, Mr. Redfield," Darlington fluttered. "Oh, come in, inside, both of you. Do please excuse the frightful disarray. There was to have been a celebration. . . ."

The place looked like a mortuary. White cloths covered lumpy mounds on long tables standing against the walls. Lush and reverent scenes in thick oils hung in ornate frames. Colored light from the glass dome lay over everything.

"Well!" Darlington hesitantly extended a plump hand to Blake. "It is . . . good to meet you personally at last."

Blake shook hands firmly, while Darlington's scandalized gaze fell to the charred sleeve of his jacket. Blake followed his glance. "Sorry, I've just been involved in the pressure-loss incident," he said, "and I haven't had time to clean up."

"My goodness, that was *terrifying*. Whatever *happened*? It's the sort of thing that makes one long to be back on solid ground."

"It's under investigation," Sparta said. "Meanwhile it has been decided to release your property from *Star Queen*. I think it will be just as safe here with you."

In the crook of his left arm Blake held a blocky package wrapped in white plastic. "Here's the book, sir," Blake said, holding out the package. He let the plastic fall away to reveal the pristine marbled paper of the slipcase.

Darlington's eyes widened behind his thick round glasses and his mouth pursed with delight. He quietly took the book from Blake, gazed at it a moment, then carried it with ceremony to the display case at the head of the hall.

Darlington laid the book on top of the glass and slid the leather-covered volume from its slipcase. The gilt edges of the pages glittered in the strange, dramatic light. Darlington stroked the tan cover as gently as if it had been living skin, turning the precious object in his hands to inspect its flawless binding. Then he reverently set it down again and opened it—to the title page.

He left it there. Blake looked at Sparta. She smiled.

"Did you ship it like *this?*" Darlington said abruptly. "This beautiful book might have been . . . badly soiled."

"We're keeping the carrying case in evidence," Sparta replied. "I asked Mr. Redfield to inspect the book and vouch for its authenticity."

"I wanted to see it safely into your hands, Mr. Darlington."

"Yes, indeed. Well!" Darlington smiled cheerily, then glanced around the room with sudden inspiration. "The reception! What do you know, it's not too late after all! I'm going to call everyone *at once.*"

Darlington started off toward his office, got two steps, and remembered that he'd left *The Seven Pillars of Wisdom* sitting in the open. Sheepishly, he returned.

He fiddled with the complex locks of the display case and carefully arranged the book on velvet pillows inside. He slid the case closed.

When Darlington had reset the magnetic locks he looked up, simpering at Sparta, and she nodded approvingly. "We'll be going, then. Please keep the book available in the event it may be required in evidence."

"Right here, Inspector! It will be right here!" Darlington patted the display case, then dashed to one of the tables and pulled off the shroud with a flourish, unveiling a mound of cracked prawns. He was so excited he almost clapped.

Blake and Sparta walked to the doors.

"Oh, by the way, you must come to the party," Darlington called after them as the entrance slid open. "Both of you! . . . After you've had a chance to freshen up."

The concourse outside the museum was crowded with pedestrians. They were opposite the Vancouver garden; they walked swiftly across metal paving and down a path among fern-covered granite rocks, seeking the shelter of arching pine branches and totem poles. When they were alone Blake said, "If you won't let me come with you, I'm going to take Darlington up on his offer. I'm starved."

She nodded. "I notice, Blake, that you're as accomplished a dissimulator as I am. 'Involved in the incident . . .' "

"It's a distinction without a difference, isn't it? Knowingly conveying a false impression is lying, period."

"It's the nature of my job," she said shortly. "What's your rationale?"

As she turned he seized her gently by the elbow. "Guard your back. I don't know what they fixed you up with, but they left out the killer instinct."

She recovered the package she'd hidden in the transformer room, then pressed the commlink in her ear, whose insistent chiming she'd switched off half an hour ago.

"Where have you *been?*" Proboda's half-concern, half-panic, was almost touching.

"I underestimated our quarry, Viktor. I went to *Star Queen* hoping to . . ."

"You were *aboard?*" he shouted, so loudly she yanked the commlink from her ear.

"Dammit, Viktor . . . I was hoping to catch the culprit in the act," she resumed, gingerly bringing the link to her ear. "Unfortunately, I ran into a large robot."

"My God, Ellen, did you hear what went on inside that ship?"

"I just told you I was *there*," she said, exasperated. "I want you to meet me at the offices of the Ishtar Mining Corporation. By yourself. Right now."

"Commander Antreen is terribly angry, Ellen. She wants you to report back here immediately."

"I have no time. Tell her I'll make a full report as soon as I can."

"I can't—I mean, on my own initia—"

"Viktor, if you don't meet me at Ishtar I'll have to handle Sondra Sylvester on my own. And I'm much too tired to be polite." She disconnected. This time she wasn't lying; to her dismay, she found herself trembling with fatigue. She hoped she wasn't too tired for the task remaining.

The two major mining companies on Port Hesperus provided the economic base for the entire colony; Ishtar and Azure Dragon were cordial but serious rivals, their headquarters located opposite each other in projecting arms on the planetward end of the station. Outside, these facilities bristled with antennas that transmitted and received coded telemetry. Only spies saw the interiors of their competition's armored ore shuttles, and the smelting and finishing facilities were located on satellite stations several kilometers away.

After displaying her badge to a videoplate monitor, Sparta was allowed to enter Ishtar through its bronze-studded front doors, the so-called Ishtar Gate, which opened on a long spiraling corridor, paneled in dark leather, leading outward from the weightless core toward Earth-normal gravity. No guards were in evidence, but she was aware that her progress was monitored throughout the approach.

At the end of the corridor she found herself in a room lavishly paneled in carved mahogany, carpeted in Chinese and Persian rugs. There was no other apparent exit from the room, although Sparta knew better. In the center of the shadowy room a small spotlight illuminated a gold statuette of the ancient Babylonian goddess Ishtar, a modern interpretation by the popular Mainbelt artist Fricca.

Sparta paused, taken by it, her macrozoom eye drawn to a microscopic inspection. It was a stunning work, tiny yet swelling with power, supple yet knotted, like one of Rodin's studies in wax. Around the base were carved, in letters meant to suggest cuneiform, verses from a primeval hymn: *Ishtar, the goddess of evening, am I. Ishtar, the goddess of morning, am I. The heavens I destroy, the earth I devastate, in my supremacy. The mountain I sweep away altogether, in my supremacy.*

"How may I assist you?" The question, phrased not helpfully but with disdain, came from a young woman who had stepped silently from the shadows.

"Inspector Troy. Board of Space Control," Sparta said, turning to her. The tall receptionist was wearing a long purple gown of something with the texture of crushed velvet; Sparta was acutely conscious of her own singed hair and smudged cheeks, her torn, stained trousers. "Please inform Mrs. Sylvester"—she cleared her throat—"that I'm here to talk to her."

"Is she expecting you, Inspector?"—smooth and cold, definitely uncooperative . . .

The receptionist's name was engraved on a solid gold

pin beneath her throat, a pin that would have been invisible to ordinary eyes. Not to Sparta's.

One talent of a better-than-average cop is to be able to say more than one thing at once; some simple statements carry a wealth of implication (obey me or go to jail), and the first-name trick never hurts, even if it only makes 'em mad. "I require your full cooperation, Barbara."

Barbara responded with a jerk, freezing the image on the handheld videoplate she'd been consulting.

"I'm here to see Sondra Sylvester on urgent official business," Sparta told her, "regarding *The Seven Pillars of Wisdom.*"

The receptionist stiffly poked out a three-digit code and spoke softly to the gadget. A moment later Sylvester's lush, husky voice filled the room. "Bring Inspector Troy to my office at once." The young receptionist lost her hauteur. "Follow me, please," she whispered.

Sparta followed her through double locking panels that slid silently aside. One curving hall led to another, and that soon opened upon scenes of Escherlike ambiguity: below Sparta and beside her, curving smoky windows overlooked control rooms peopled by dozens of operators in front of green and orange flatscreens and videoplates. Other curving glass corridors crossed above and below, and other control rooms were visible through distant windows. Many of the screens Sparta could see displayed graphics or columns of numbers, but on others live video pictures of a bizarre fishbowl world unreeled like the view from a carnival ride.

Somewhere on the surface of the planet below—on the bright visible side or away in the darkness beyond the terminator—radio signals relayed by synchronous satellites moved robots by remote control, to prospect, to delve, to mill, and to stockpile. The views through the moving screens were robot-eye views of hell.

Abruptly they were past the control rooms. Sparta followed the receptionist through a door, down another corridor, and finally into an office of such opulence that Sparta hesitated before entering.

A desk of polished chalcedony stood before a wall of rough-textured, curving bronze. Ruddy light fell fitfully over the surface of the wall, illuminating statues in their niches, exquisite works by the solar system's major artists: a duplicate cast of Fricca's Ishtar, flanked by Innanna, Astarte, Cybele, Mariana, Aphrodite, Lakshmi. Another wall contained shelf upon shelf of books bound in colored leather and stamped with gold and silver. Through heavily filtered windows the sulfurous clouds of the planet rolled in twilight.

It was a room that spoke, paradoxically, of despair—a prison, its static luxuries meant to substitute for the random simplicities of freedom.

"You may leave us, Barbara."

Sparta turned to find Sylvester behind her, wearing the same dark silk gown she'd worn disembarking from *Helios*. And when Sparta glanced around, the receptionist had gone; these women had an uncanny trick of moving silently. Sparta found herself wishing that Proboda had made his appearance.

"You're much smaller than I expected, Inspector Troy."

"Videoplate images have that effect."

"And I have no doubt you intended the effect," Sylvester said. She crossed the carpeted room to her stone desk and sat down. "Normally I'd ask you to make yourself comfortable, but in fact I am extremely busy just now. Or perhaps you are ready to release my cargo?"

"No."

"What can I tell you about *The Seven Pillars of Wisdom?*"

Sparta realized that she was too tired to work at subtlety; the directness of her question surprised even her. "How much did you spend counterfeiting it? As much as you would have paid for the real thing?"

Sylvester laughed, a startled bark. "An ingenious question—for which there is no answer." But unlike Sparta, Sylvester was a bad liar; she held herself on a tight leash, and what passed for coolness was the result of long practice at restraining a tempestuous nature.

"You left your rented villa on the Isle du Levant the day after you arrived there, took a magneplane from Toulon to Paris, a ramjet to Washington, D.C., where you spent a day in the Library of Congress recording on chip the entire contents of the only remaining Oxford edition of *The Seven Pillars of Wisdom* still accessible to the public. You then flew to London, where with the help of the bookseller Hermione Scrutton—whose record of involvement in literary fraud might almost be considered distinguished in some circles—you arranged to meet certain parties in Oxford, a city where the craft of printing is cherished and its ancient tools preserved, where even the working typefonts of the past are displayed as treasures in museums, where the revered techniques are still occasionally practiced. With the help of several printers and a bookbinder, people whose love of the making of books is so great they allowed themselves to engage in counterfeiting for the sheer joy of practicing their skills—although the very substantial amounts you paid them didn't dampen their enthusiasm—you made an almost perfect copy of *The Seven Pillars of Wisdom*. It was even easier to bribe a notoriously luxury-loving member of *Star Queen*'s crew to practice his calculating skills on a locked case and steal a book from the cargo of his own ship, replacing it with your counterfeit."

As Sylvester listened to this recitation the color in her pale cheeks deepened. "That is an extraordinary scenario, Inspector. I can't imagine what comment you wish me to make."

"Only confirm it."

"I am not a pond for you to fish in." Sylvester willed herself to relax. "Please leave now. I have no more time."

"I was very careless on my first inspection of *Star Queen*—I knew that one of your robots had been field tested; I thought that explained its residual radioactivity. I didn't bother to examine the fuel assemblies."

"Get out," Sylvester said flatly.

". . . but sometimes a little knowledge is dangerous. If I'd checked the hot robot I would have seen that McNeil had reinserted the fuel rods so that he could open the machine. The oversight almost cost Blake Redfield and me our lives. At your hands."

"You're talking utter nonsense. . . ."

In two quick steps Sparta was at the desk. She raised the package wrapped in plastic she'd been holding at her side and slammed it down on the polished stone. "Here's what's left of your book, Mrs. Sylvester."

Sylvester froze. She stared at the package. Her indecision was so transparent, so agonizing, that Sparta could feel the woman's apprehension and pain.

"A bluff will gain you nothing but a little time," Sparta said. "I may not have all the details right, but I'll get at your financial records, I'll talk to the people who know. McNeil, for starters. The details and the witnesses will be along shortly. And there's your book."

It lay there, a rectangular bundle wrapped in plastic.

"Difficult to recognize in its present condition," Sparta said harshly, her own fear and resentment for the attack on her life finally spilling into anger, wiping out the empathy that had threatened her judgment, "so perhaps you will be good enough to tell me which of the two copies it is."

Sylvester sighed. Trembling, she reached to the flimsy plastic, threw it back. . . . The charred block of pages lay in flakes of ash, in the crumbling fragments of its slipcase. "This is too cruel," she whispered. Sylvester steadied herself in her chair, grasping the edge of her desk so tightly that her knuckles whitened. "How can I know?"

Sparta pulled the book around and pried open its baked pages. " 'The dreamers of the day are dangerous men,' " she read, " 'for they may act their dreams with open eyes, to make it possible.' 'Dreams' should be 'dream,' singular." Sparta turned the wrecked book and, leaning over the desk, pushed it toward Sylvester. "Blake Redfield informs me that the text contains many similar errors. This is the counterfeit. The original has been returned to its owner."

"To Darlington?"

"That is corr . . ."

In her near exhaustion, in the heady rush of revenge on the woman who'd tried to take her life, Sparta had not been *listening* . . . Her reaction to the black pistol that appeared in Sylvester's hand, arcing toward her, was woefully sluggish.

XX

Blake Redfield spent a few quick minutes in his Venus-view room at the Hesperus Hilton; then, in a white shirt, maroon tie, and dark silk suit of stylish cut, he sallied forth to make a second, more respectable appearance at the Hesperian Museum.

His adventures of the past hour had left him curiously undecided, unsettled. His chance sighting of Linda on that Manhattan street corner had awakened something in him, a feeling not urgent at first, but insistent and increasingly intense.

He'd found it a simple matter to combine his researches into his childhood friend's mysterious disappearance with his own collector's passion, for he was nowhere more at home than in old bookstores and library stacks and data files, whether electronic or "fiber-based." Thus he had stumbled upon the long, deliberately obscured trail of the shadowy international cult he had only recently been able to tie to the *prophetae* of the Free Spirit. With his nose for inference and testable hypothesis, he'd learned more than he'd expected.

Long before that, other, more savage passions had been awakened, ones he'd indulged as a teenage boy playing half-serious secret-agent games with his peers in the Arizona mountains. Smearing themselves with shoe polish. Sneaking up on each other. Plinking at each other with capsules of red paint. Blowing things up. Etc.

He'd resumed his lessons, privately. No more games with paint.

But tracking down Linda, Ellen as she called herself, had lacked something of the fantastic quality he'd anticipated. When he finally found her—a nice surprise he'd arranged, too—he'd expected to be greeted as a kindred soul; instead she'd seemed preoccupied by matters she was unwilling to share, layers of concern, woven branches of potential—so many crimes, so many villains, doing an invisible gavotte. So many loyalties to balance. So many corners to watch. She'd grown skilled at hiding her thoughts and feelings from people, too skilled. And he had hoped to touch her feelings.

Now he wondered how much of a surprise his dramatic revelations had been. She was mysteriously adept at things he was hardly aware of.

Vincent Darlington, giddy with social success, greeted Blake lavishly and ushered him into the ersatz chapel. Space station society was a hothouse affair, fluid and incestuous, and gaudy display was part of the game. Plumes and trapezes of glitter bobbed on heads whose hair, when not shaved off altogether, had been tortured into extraordinary shapes, wagon wheels and ratchets and Morning Star maces, ziggurats, corkscrews. The faces below came in every natural color and several artificial ones, enlivened by splashes of paint and, on the men, odd swatches of whiskers. The room was filled to capacity and it seemed like everybody was trying to stand in the same place, next to the food tables. These were obviously people who appreciated Darlington's taste, if not in art, then in champagne and hors d' oeuvres.

Blake recognized a few of his recent companions aboard *Helios*, including, to his mild surprise, Sondra Sylvester's companion Nancybeth, who welled up in front of him as he tried to push closer to the display case containing *The Seven Pillars of Wisdom*. Nancybeth was resplendent in green plastic kneeboots, and above them a miniskirt of real leather, dyed white and hanging in fringes all the way from her raw hemp belt. Her top was thinly veiled in low-slung, purple-anodized aluminum mesh, which went well with her violet eyes.

"Open your mowffy," she coaxed, her chin raised and her lips pooched, and when he started to ask her "what for" he got no further than the "what," which gave her the opening she needed to shove a tube of something pink and orange and squishy between his teeth. "You looked hungry," she explained as he masticated.

"I was," he said, when he'd swallowed, wincing.

"Not just your tummy, Blakey. You have hungry eyes." Her voice fell a few decibels, so that he had to lean closer to hear her. Her six-inch mirrored earrings swung like pendulums, threatening to hypnotize him. "All the way here on the liner I could feel your hungry eyes eating at me."

"How ghastly for you," he said. He said it louder than he'd intended; adjacent heads turned.

Nancybeth recoiled. "Blake, silly! Don't you understand what I'm saying?"

"I wish I didn't." He took advantage of her temporary retrenchment to gain a few inches toward his goal. "Have you seen the book yet? Do you think Darlington's given it a decent burial in this mausoleum?"

"What do you mean?" she asked suspiciously. Her chin was abeam his shoulder now, and there was danger she would be swept aft. "Vince has very good taste. I think the gold on the edge of the pages goes really well with the ceiling."

"That's what I meant." He'd finally reached the altar that enshrined the relic, only to discover that it was almost impossible to see; the party guests in the vicinity were using the glass top of the display case as a handy tabletop for their plates and wine glasses. Blake turned queasily away, Nancybeth still with him.

"I'm surprised to see you here without Mrs. Sylvester," he said bluntly.

She wasn't sophisticated, but she had a sixth sense for the needs of others, and Blake's matter-of-factness got through to her; she answered in kind. "Vince won't talk to Sondra. He invited me ages ago—because he thought I'd drag her along. His idea was that she was going to rub me in his face, and he was going to rub that book in hers."

Blake smiled. "You're okay, Nancybeth. You call it the way you see it."

"I'm seeing it now. And I'm calling it. But it's not answering."

"Sorry. Fact is, I'm looking for someone else."

Her eyes went cold. She shrugged and turned her back on him.

He moved through the crowd searching the faces of strangers. After filling a plate he tried to get away from the crowd and found himself alone for the moment in a small chapellike room off the grotesque glass-domed nave of Darlington's cathedral. In this small room were cases displaying objects quite different from the run of execrable gimcracks Darlington had pushed to center stage. Inside the cases Blake recognized the fossils of Venusian life that had gotten Darlington's silly art gallery a place on the map of the solar system.

They were dusty red and gray things, fragmented, morphologically ambiguous. He knew nothing of paleontology, but he understood that these had been authenticated as the remains of creatures that had burrowed and crawled, maybe flapped and glided, during a brief paradise of liquid water and free oxygen that had prevailed millions of years ago, before the catastrophic positive feedback of the greenhouse effect had turned Venus into the acid-drenched, high-pressure inferno it was now.

The remains were more suggestive than descriptive. Scholarly volumes had been devoted to these dozen scraps of stone, but no one could say for sure what things had made them, or left them behind, except that whatever they were, they'd been alive.

Blake brooded unhappily on the puzzle, hardly new to him, that so many people like Vincent Darlington possessed so many treasures of which they had not the slightest conception of value—aside from money, aside from possession itself.

His ponderings were abruptly interrupted.

In the adjoining room a woman's scream rose above the babble, a man yelled, and in quick succession there were seven very loud *whacks*—overtaken by a long splintering of glass.

For a moment the air hung still, echoing, before everyone in the crowd began screaming and shouting and fighting each other to get out. Blake dodged panicked refugees and seconds later found himself in an empty room, confronting a bloody tableau.

Sondra Sylvester was writhing in the grip of Percy Farnsworth and a horrified Nancybeth. Sylvester's heavy silk gown had been slashed by falling glass, and blood was streaming down over her livid face from cuts in her scalp. Her right arm was raised stiffly over her head, where Nancybeth was trying to pull it down to get at the black pistol that Sylvester still held in a steel grip, yelling at her, "Syl, no more, no more..." Meanwhile Farnsworth had Sylvester around the waist and was trying to throw her to the glass-strewn floor; he and Nancybeth had also suffered cuts on the scalp and shoulders. Sylvester's finger tightened on the trigger and an eighth bullet smashed into the riddled stained-glass ceiling, loosing another shower of fragments.

Then Sylvester dropped the pistol, having exhausted the ammunition clip. She relaxed almost luxuriously into the arms of the others, who suddenly found themselves supporting her.

Blake helped them carry her to the side of the room, away from the glass. So much blood was pouring over Sylvester's eyes that she must have been blinded by it—scalp wounds flow copiously, even when they're not serious—but she'd been seeing clearly enough when she sent the first rounds from the illegal weapon into Vincent Darlington's body.

Darlington lay on his back in a spreading pool of crimson, staring open-eyed through the shattered dome at the tops of tall trees on the opposite surface of the central sphere, his body frosted over with powdered glass.

Behind him, safe inside the case that served as a table

for smeared plates and empty glasses, rested the object of Sylvester's passion.

Sparta was inside a kaleidoscope, its broken bits of glass falling with rapid stuttering leaps into new symmetric patterns that repeated themselves endlessly out to the edge of her vision, and beyond. The slowly spinning vortex of jagged colors seemed to be sucking her into infinity. With each shift, a strung-out, whistling explosion echoed through her mind. The scene was dizzying and vivid—

—and part of her consciousness stood to one side watching it with enjoyment. That part was reminded of a cartoon she'd seen on an eye doctor's wall, a car speeding across a desert on a long straight road, passing a sign that read "Vanishing point, ten miles."

She laughed at the memory, and the sound of her own laughter woke her up.

Her blue eyes opened to find Viktor Proboda's brighter, bluer ones, wide in his square pink face, only inches away. "How do you feel?" His blond eyebrows were twitching with concern.

"Like somebody hit me in the head. What was I laughing about?" With his help she sat up. There was a heavy ache in the muscle of her jaw that brought back an old memory, from circa age fourteen, of an abscessed wisdom tooth. Cautiously she touched her cheek. "Oww! I bet that's pretty."

"I don't think the jaw's broken. You'd know."

"Great. Do you always look on the bright side, Viktor?" She pulled herself to her feet with his help.

"We should get you to the clinic. A concussion requires immediate . . ."

"Hold off a minute. Did you pass your friend Sondra Sylvester on your way in here?"

Proboda looked distinctly uncomfortable. "Yes, in the core, just outside the Ishtar gate. I knew something was wrong from her face. She looked at me but she didn't even see me. I was thinking about what that mining robot did on *Star Queen*, and I thought that's why you came here, so I thought I'd better find you."

"Thanks. . . . Dammit." She grabbed at her ear, but her commlink had fallen out. "She knocked it loose. Viktor, call in and send a squad to the Hesperian Museum on the double. Call the museum too, try to warn Darlington. I think she went to kill him."

He knew better than to ask for explanations. He keyed the emergency channel, but as soon as he mentioned the Hesperian Museum the squad dispatcher interrupted.

He listened, his jaw sagging, then broke the link. He looked at Sparta. "Too late."

"Is he dead?"

His chin jerked in a nod. "She put four .32 slugs in him. After they grabbed her, she put four more through his glass ceiling. It's lucky she didn't kill somebody on the other side of the station." Still looking on the bright side.

She touched his arm, half urging him to start moving and half comforting the big, sad cop—recognizing that he was sad for Sylvester, whom he'd admired, not for Darlington, that silly leech. "Come on, let's go," she said.

A tall woman was standing in the doorway, Kara Antreen. Rigid and gray, her square-shouldered severity was at odds with the luxury of Sylvester's office. "Viktor, I want you to take immediate charge of the investigation into the shooting of Vincent Darlington."

Proboda halted, perplexed. "Not much of an investigation, Captain. There was a roomful of witnesses..."

"Yes, it shouldn't take long," Antreen said.

"But *Star Queen*..."

"You are relieved of your responsibilities with respect to *Star Queen*," Antreen said flatly. She cocked an eye at Sparta, daring contradiction. "That's a new case, now."

Sparta hesitated, then nodded. "That's right, Viktor. You've been very helpful, and I appreciate it...."

Proboda's unhappy face grew longer.

"The captain and I should be able to wrap things up pretty quickly," Sparta said.

Proboda stepped away stiffly. He'd been impressed by Inspector Ellen Troy and had unbent enough to let her know it. He had even defended her to his boss. Now she'd grabbed the first chance to cut him out of the case. "Whatever you say," he growled. He marched out past Antreen without wasting a backward glance on Sparta.

Alone, the two women watched each other in silence. Antreen was impeccable in her gray wool suit, Sparta was a weary urchin, battered but streetwise. But Sparta no longer felt at a disadvantage. She only felt the need for rest.

"You've repeatedly and ingeniously managed to avoid me, Inspector Troy," Antreen said. "Why the sudden change of attitude?"

"I don't think this is the place to talk, Captain," Sparta said, tilting her chin to indicate the room's invisible bugs and eyes. "Corporations like this one are good at keeping secrets. But it could still be considered a violation of the suspect's chartered rights."

"Yes, certainly." Antreen's eyelids drooped over her

gray eyes—and here was an excellent liar indeed, Sparta saw, who did not betray herself when she had been anticipated, even two moves deep. "Back to headquarters, then?" Antreen suggested.

Sparta walked confidently past her; Antreen fell into step immediately behind. They walked into the spiraling transparent corridor that overlooked the control rooms.

Sparta paused at the rail.

"Something wrong?" Antreen asked.

"Not at all. I didn't really get to see this on the way in. I was too busy. For someone who's never left Earth before, it's an impressive sight."

"I suppose it is."

From ten meters overhead, behind the curving glass, Sparta and Antreen peered down at the men and women of Ishtar at their consoles. Some were alert and hard at work, some were lounging, idly chatting with each other, sipping their coffees and smoking their cigarettes while watching on giant screens as loyal robots sliced and shoveled through the underworld.

Antreen's right hand was in her outside jacket pocket. She leaned in close to Sparta, a movement that an Arab or a Japanese might not have noticed. But she was close enough to make a typical Euro-American nervous.

Sparta turned to her, relaxed, alert. "We can talk here," Sparta whispered. "They left the eyes and ears out of this stretch."

"You're positive?"

"I checked the corridor coming in," Sparta said. "So let's stop playing games."

"What?"

Sparta heard offended dignity, not guilt, overlaying

Antreen's caution—she *was* excellent. Sparta's tone grew exaggerated. "By now you've got the files I ordered from Central, haven't you?" She was playing the tough cop from headquarters, dressing down the locals.

"Yes, of course."

Anger, persuasively laid over confusion, but Sparta laughed in her face. "You don't know what the hell I'm talking about."

Antreen was suddenly prickling with suspicion. She said nothing.

Sparta prodded her hard. "The files on Pavlakis Lines. Get your staff in shape, will you?"—but behind the contemptuous sneer on her bruised and blackened face, Sparta was striving to keep her throbbing consciousness from fractioning again. The broken bits of the kaleidoscope were whirling at the edge of her vision. "If you'd seen the reports you'd know it was that ape Dimitrios, taking it out on young Pavlakis. Revenge. Because the kid ended the forty-year-old insurance con Dimitrios had been running with his dad. Pavlakis played into his hands by hiring Wycherly to protect him—a guy who was already in on the scam, who needed money more than anything and had the added advantage of being a dead man in advance. Got all that?"

"We have that information," Antreen snapped. Anger again, this time laid over smug relief, for Sparta was talking police work after all. "We have Dimitrios's statement, the widow's statement. Pavlakis came to us himself before we could pick him up—before the blowout. He says he suspected it all along, that Dimitrios rigged a phony accident."

"He did?" Sparta grinned, but it was a weird grin coming out of that swollen, seared face. "Then what are you really doing here?"

"I came to tell . . ." But this time Antreen couldn't disguise the shock. ". . . you . . ."

"You came for me. Here I am. Took you forever to get me alone."

"You *know!*" Antreen looked around wildly. They were hardly alone. But they were isolated from the workers below in a glass tube with no ears. Afterward, what would witnesses make of what was about to happen?

Whatever Captain Antreen told them to think.

Antreen jerked her right hand up and out, but she was close—it had been a mistake to move in so close. Sparta's own right hand came across the space between their bodies and seized Antreen's wrist as it cleared her pocket. In a microsecond Antreen was stumbling; Sparta was taking her down sideways along the direction of the resisting arm, using the resistance. Startled, Antreen's left leg tried to move across for balance, but it went nowhere except into Sparta's solidly planted left thigh. Antreen dove, but Sparta did not let her dive; controlling the weapon, Sparta never let go of Antreen's right wrist, and Antreen spun onto her back as she fell. She hit the carpeted floor heavily.

If Sparta had been a little stronger, a little bigger, a little less tired—if she'd been perfect—she might have prevented what happened next. But Antreen was quick and strong and as practiced at unarmed combat as Sparta. With the leverage of her long legs and free arm she rolled, pulling Sparta across her—Sparta brought Antreen's arm up sharply behind her back as she rolled—another half roll and Sparta would lose her grip; Antreen would be on top of her. . . .

Antreen screamed when she drove the spike into her own spine.

It was a crescendo of pain, but she screamed with more than pain. She screamed in the horror of what was happening to her, what was about to happen to her—what would happen quickly, but not quickly enough.

Sparta yanked the thing out of Antreen's back almost instantly. Only then did she see what the weapon was. She knew she was too late—

—for the telescoping needle had already sprung out and was writhing like a hair-fine worm in Antreen's spinal cord, questing for her brain. Although she could no longer feel the fast approaching mind-death, still she screamed.

Sparta tossed the barrel of the empty hypodermic on the mat and sat back, legs splayed, sagging onto her rigid backthrust arms, sucking in great gulps of air. The corridor thundered with booted feet and around its curve a squad of blue-suits appeared, stunguns drawn. They stumbled to a halt in good order, the front rank to their knees, half a dozen gun snouts pointing at Sparta.

Antreen had kept on rolling, onto her back. She was crying now, great sobs of pity for her dwindling awareness.

Viktor Proboda shoved his way through the patrollers and knelt beside her. He reached out his big hands and hesitated, afraid to touch her.

"You can't do anything for her, Viktor," Sparta whispered. "She's not in pain."

"What's happening to her?"

"She's forgetting. She'll forget all this. In a few seconds she'll stop crying, because she won't remember why she's crying."

Proboda looked at Antreen's face, the handsome face

framed in straight gray hair, a face momentarily stretched into the mask of Medusa but where even now the terror was fading and the tears were drying.

"Isn't there anything we can do for her?"

Sparta shook her head. "Not now. Maybe later, if they want to. But they probably won't."

"Who are *they?*"

Sparta waved him off. "Later, Viktor."

Proboda decided he'd wait; Inspector Troy said lots of things that went past him the first time. He stood and shouted at the ceiling. "Where's that stretcher? Let's get moving." He stepped over Antreen to Sparta, holding out his hand. She took it and he pulled her to her feet. "Practically the whole company was watching you. They called us right away."

"I told her it was clean. She was so eager to get me she believed me. What's happening to her is what would have happened to me. . . ."

"How did you know they'd call us?"

"I . . ." She thought better of it. "Lucky guess."

There was a commotion among the police, and the stretcher came through. As the two bearers were kneeling beside Antreen she spoke, calmly and clearly. "Awareness is everything," she said.

"Are my parents alive?" Sparta asked her.

"The secrets of the adepts are not to be shared with the uninitiated," Antreen replied.

"Are my parents adepts?" Sparta asked. "Is Laird an adept?"

"That's not on the white side," said Antreen.

"I remember you now," Sparta said. "I remember the things you did to me."

"Do you have a Q clearance?"

"I remember your home in Maryland. You had a squirrel that slid down a wire."

"Do I remember you?" Antreen asked.

"And I remember what you did to me."

"Do I remember you?" Antreen repeated.

"Does the word SPARTA mean anything to you?" Sparta asked.

Uncertainty creased Antreen's brow. "Is that . . . is that a name?"

Sparta felt her throat tighten, felt tears well in her eyes. "Good-bye, gray lady. You're an innocent again."

Blake Redfield was waiting in the weightless corridor outside the Ishtar Gate, mingling with the floating pack of gawkers and mediahounds who had been trailing the police in eager desperation. Sparta slipped past the yellow tape and sought him out.

When he saw her face he was surprised, then concerned. She let him study her bruises. "I watched my back, like you told me." She tried to grin with swollen lips. "She got me from the front."

When he held out his hand, she took it. Holding his hand, it was easier to ignore the questions the reporters were shouting at them, the curses of those who sounded like they were ready to kill for a quote. But when Kara Antreen was pulled past on a floating stretcher the photogram recorders all swung to follow the procession, and the mediacrowd swam off after them like sharks after chum. Sparta and Blake lingered behind a moment—

"Want to take the short cut?"

—and a few seconds later they had disappeared.

They darted through the darkened tunnels and conduits toward the central sphere, keeping pace with each other.

"Did you know it was Antreen all along?" Blake asked.

"No, but the first sight of her prodded my memory. Something down deep, something I couldn't bring to consciousness made me know it was a good idea to stay out of her way. This just now was her second attempt. She was the one who used the robot on us."

"I thought that was Sylvester!"

"So did I. Anger is the enemy of reason, and I was so mad I wasn't thinking straight. Sondra Sylvester wanted that book more than anything, much more than she wanted Nancybeth, or even to humiliate Darlington. She never would have risked the *real* book, even if she'd overheard us talking and knew she was caught. It was *Antreen* who bugged the ship and heard us."

They flew in silence, then, until they came to their lookout overlooking the central gardens and went to ground. Perfectly alone in the swinging cage of light, they found themselves suddenly, unaccountably shy.

Sparta forced herself to go on. "Antreen went aboard *Star Queen* and fueled the robot, while I was staging my show-and-tell lecture about sabotage. Setting a trap for the wrong people." She laughed wearily. "She got the opportunity she wanted before she was ready for it. She sure didn't expect to deal with *you*. When the robot didn't do the job I think she realized how hard it was going to be to kill me outright, at least in a way that wouldn't bring suspicion on herself. So she went for my memory. After all, it worked once before. She'd have been after you, next."

"Did you learn anything about your parents?" he asked, quietly and urgently. "About the rest of them?"

Sparta shook her head. "Too late," she said sadly. "Antreen couldn't tell us anything now if she wanted to." This time she reached out to him and gently took his hand.

He covered her hand with his, then reached to cup her chin. "Then we'll have to do it alone, I guess. The two of us. Find them. If you're ready to let me play this game."

His spicy aroma was especially delicious when he was only inches away. "I should have let you before." She leaned weightlessly forward and let her bruised lips rest on his.

Epilogue

McNeil told the rest of the untold truth without further hedging, the next time she confronted him. He had moved out of the clinic and rented a room in transient crew quarters, but he spent most of his time in his favorite French restaurant, on the concourse opposite the poplars of Samarrand. Recorded meadowlarks sang sweetly among the nearby trees.

"I knew you'd be back," he said. "Will you have some of this excellent St. Emilion?"

She declined. She told him what she knew, and he filled in the rest. "And if I cooperate fully, how much time do you think they'll give me for it?" he challenged her.

"Well, since the property was recovered . . ."

"Don't forget, you'd have a hard time proving intent, if my lawyer was to be wise enough to keep me off the stand," he said cheerfully.

"Slim chance. At any rate, we'd get you for the wine bottles."

"Alas, the owner of all the commodities in question is since deceased."

Sparta knew the cause of justice would not be served if she laughed out loud, so she nodded solemnly. "McNeil, you'll be cooling your heels in a cell for at least four to six months."

"Pity. Almost the length of a quick trip to the Mainbelt. Always tried to avoid those."

"Perhaps I will have a glass of that," she said. He poured and she sipped. She thanked him. McNeil grew serious. "One thing you may be overlooking, Inspector. That is a *magnificent* book, not merely an object. It deserved to be owned by someone who could appreciate its contents. As well as its binding."

"Are you suggesting you were motivated by more than greed, Mr. McNeil?"

"I've never told you a lie, Inspector. I admired Mrs. Sylvester. I'm sorry to see her come to ruin."

"I believe you, McNeil. I always did."

McNeil could take care of himself. Blake Redfield needed help. The investigation of Kara Antreen's inexplicable pathological behavior would no doubt continue for months, if not years; it was with fleeting regret that Sparta laid sins at her door that she had not committed. Blake was never suspected of having blown a hatch, of having cut power, assaulted workers, broken into and burgled impounded government property. Instead, he faded into Sparta's shadow. . . .

Viktor Proboda was there at the docking bay to see them off with a bouquet of hydroponic asters. Accompanied by a chorus of mediafolk, Blake and Sparta were about to board the *Helios*, the first step in the long return trip to Earth.

"It was a pleasure, Viktor. If there's any justice, it won't be long until we . . ." Her commlink softly chimed. "One sec."

She cocked her head and listened to the breathless dispatcher: "Inspector Troy! Inspector Troy! New orders from Earth Central! Your trip is canceled—you're to report to headquarters right away."

"What's this about?" She looked up to see a squad of blue-suits already swimming toward them—her escort to unit headquarters.

A few seconds later, when she found time to answer Blake's and Proboda's insistent questions, all she could say was, "I'll have to catch up with you later, Blake. I can't tell you what's happened. And you wouldn't believe me if I did."

Through the many-layered scandal that had absorbed their attention for the past weeks—through the burials and depositions and hearings and trials—the inhabitants of Port Hesperus had never ceased or even slowed their work. Five of Ishtar's huge new robots had gone to the surface immediately after the *Star Queen* impoundment was lifted. The sixth was released to Ishtar and followed its fellows after forensic teams had lifted the last molecule of evidence from it and the ship it had ravaged.

The new robot corps was sent to explore a promising syncline on the glacis of the huge Lakshmi Plateau, in an area previously only lightly surveyed by surface rovers. Among the ore samples gathered on these prospecting expeditions was one odd fragment now residing in the Hes-

perian Museum—a fossil, one among only a dozen
Venusian fossils.

It was not unexpected that when serious mining began
in the region another fossil or two might appear. The operators on Port Hesperus had been asked to keep a close
eye on their screens for just such an event.

The atmosphere of Venus is so dense at the surface and
the light of the sun so diffuse that operating one of the
glowing robots in many ways resembled operating a nod-
ule miner on the bottom of Earth's oceans. It was not always easy for an operator to know what he was seeing on
the big screens. They showed him a bowl-shaped world
with close horizons tilting sharply up on every side, the
sere rock everywhere glowing a dark orange. Looking at
such a screen was like looking at the world through the
bottom of a thick ashtray of orange glass. To drive an
immense robot up a narrow canyon and under the over-
hang of an arching stratified canyon, sampling rock outcrops every few yards, could be both strenuous and
disorienting.

So the operator of the Rolls-Royce HDVM, alert as he
was, may be forgiven for not immediately recognizing that
the creature's slashing proboscis had broken into a cavern
that was not, as it first appeared, a natural hollow in the
cliff. So bizarre were the forms suddenly illuminated by
the glare of the white-hot radiators that the operator had
only moments to react—moments dangerously extended
by the radio delay of the remote signal—to prevent the
destruction of the lines upon lines of carved inscriptions
and the gaunt, monstrous representations that loomed up
suddenly on his screen.

Afterword

by PAUL PREUSS

A glance at the copyright page will show when the first of the six novels that make up the *Venus Prime* series was published. All six incorporate superb stories by Arthur C. Clarke, with the first volume based on Arthur's novella "Breaking Strain." My version of "Breaking Strain" had an earlier genesis, however, in a rather different form.

In the late 1980s, computer text games of the Adventure type—"You are standing in a small room painted white. In front of you is a door. In the ceiling there's a trap door to the attic. On the floor lies a bloody axe," and so on—had spawned a literary genre that would become known as hypertext. While the games were often Agatha-Christie-style mysteries, the sheer novelty of branching interactive text engaged many impressive talents; one, Robert Pinsky, was to become America's poet laureate.

Interactive text was fun, and the serious stuff certainly raised intriguing issues concerning the pact between writer and reader, but animated graphics swiftly overwhelmed text on most personal computer screens. "Breaking Strain, The Game" never made it to diskette.

A few months earlier, when Byron Preiss had proposed the project and invited me to choose among Arthur's stories one with the milieu and the maguffin to make a science-fiction mystery, I accepted happily. Clarke had been my favorite hard-science fiction writer since long before *2001, A Space Odyssey*, and the chance to study how the master did it line by line, the chance to play in the same universe—at once both rational and humanistic—was appealing. In the movie business, they call it *homage*; in science fiction, the terms were to be less polite, but all that came later.

As for mystery material, "Breaking Strain" leaped out at me, a classic life-boat tale of the lone survivor, and sure enough, the maguffin was right there on *Star Queen*'s cargo manifest—that first-edition *Seven Pillars of Wisdom*, which Arthur was later surprised to find was not my invention but his own.

By the time the game died, I had gotten deeply involved. I had a couple of hundred pages of script and flow charts that laid out everything which could be allowed to happen interactively (given personal-computer speed and memory of the time) from the moment *Star Queen* docked at Port Hesperus. I had made crude sketches of the ship and the station and the mining robots; artist Darrell Anderson had already transformed some of these into spare, elegant graphics, using programs of his own that were ahead of their time. I had a long list of all the things the bionic Sparta could do. Sparta's tool kit even contained a Swiss Army knife for when things got really complicated.

There was one significant lack. As a character, Sparta was a hollow shell, a nobody. Or rather an *anybody*—anybody who might sit down at the keyboard to play the game, any "you" who found himself or herself in the airlock of Port Hesperus, challenged with this mystery. Any "you" at all, really, but assumed to be young, and of unspecified sex. For a computer game that was okay and, like Darrell's graphics, maybe even a little ahead of its time.

A novel, however, depends crucially on such details as the age, sex, and history of its protagonist. When Byron asked me if I'd be interested in transmuting the canceled game into the first of a series of novels, I was eager to do so, not least because Sparta, conceived as a computerized nonentity, weighed heavily upon my storyteller's conscience.

I agonized over whether Sparta was male or female for all of about ten minutes. Of course she was a young woman—the whole point of not specifying Sparta's sex in the game was to invite girl players to identify with "you."

And I had no trouble finding the foundations of her superhero status. My appreciation of psychologist Howard Gardner's theory of multiple intelligences is more explicitly acknowledged in the second volume of the series, but in fact I had earlier taken up the notion that monolithic IQ is a sham—that there are several different kinds of intelligence, and that they are more or less incommensurable. Sparta was someone in whom multiple intelligences had been fostered from birth.

But the perversion of her talents, their bionic enhancement? Her mysterious and fragmented past? For that impulse, although I suppose I have to acknowledge several parts mass-media influence and wishful thinking, I have no easy explanation. I'm not much for conspiracy theories. Like the CIA man in John Le Carre's *The Honourable Schoolboy*, when things go spectacularly wrong I tend to favor the screw-up theory.

So in rereading the first chapter of this book, I'm a little taken aback to see how urgently the need to recover an erased identity springs to the fore: "Does the word

Sparta mean anything to you? . . . The word Sparta, what does that mean to you?" Indeed, Sparta's search for her identity, her determination to recover her history and personal integrity, became the plot drivers of the entire series.

I remember calling up Byron and excitedly reading him passages from the first chapter over the phone. Her memory starts to come back! She makes a daring escape in a helicopter! He was bemused, I think, but he encouraged me to carry on. Perhaps he sensed that Sparta had become real to me, a lost soul possessed of immense potential—and that I had internalized her.

Having decided that Sparta was the victim of a conspiracy, I had to decide who was conspiring about what. Again the answer came easily. What to do about the aliens is a question that figures in a number of Arthur's works; he's had fun at the expense of those who would try to manipulate hidden knowledge of alien visitation to their own ends ("Dave, this mission is just too important. . . .").

So there would be aliens in the works—truly Clarkeian aliens, not pallid little humanoids—and there would be shadowy characters trying to keep the rest of us in the dark (although not a cigarette addict among them). On the trail of the aliens, eluding the conspirators, I would begin Sparta's grand tour on Venus in the inner solar system and move outward, through fits and starts, to Earth's moon, to Mars, to Jupiter and its moons, and finally into interstellar space.

The vehicle for the journey was Arthur's incomparable imagination, as expressed in a handful of chosen stories, each a favorite of mine for a different reason. After "Breaking Strain" came "Maelstrom II," a thrilling adventure that uses orbital mechanics to spring a shocking surprise, while "Hide and Seek" is another neat twist on

Newtonian mechanics. "A Meeting with Medusa," on the other hand, is epic in its scope and majesty, and "Jupiter V" isn't far behind, broaching the theme Arthur later made famous in his *Rama* novels. Finally, "The Shining Ones" is an alien vision of rare beauty and mystery.

In Arthur's exemplary science fiction, the dilemma or resolution of every story depends on some physical principle, some fact of nature, but nothing he wrote ever failed to give his characters their due—even as he put them in their place, human sparks against the backdrop of an infinite cosmos, a cosmos inhabited in unimaginable variety. Sparta and her pyrotechnically inclined sidekick Blake are intended to embody just such striving, mostly rational, mostly optimistic Clarkeian beings. At times desperate or discouraged, at times fatally mistaken, at times fragile to the point of collapse, Sparta, who started as a bionic cipher, ended by being as human as I could write her. In Arthur's honor, it was the least I could do.

–Paul Preuss
Sausalito, California
March 1999

Infopak
Technical
Blueprints

Blueprint art by Darrel Anderson

On the following pages are computer-generated diagrams representing some of the structures and engineering found in *Venus Prime:*

Pages 314–317:   *Star Queen* Interplanetary freighter–2 perspective views; wireframe and cut-away views of crew module; main engines; fuel tanks.

Pages 318–320:   *Port Hesperus* Venus-orbiting space station–2 cut-away perspective views; axial components.

Pages 321–323:   *Mining Robot* Mechanism for analysis and processing of Venusian surface elements–2 full-figure side views; individual mining components.

Page 324:   *Visual Feedback Enhancement* A geological analysis of the Venus surface as seen by mining robot.

Pages 325–329:   *Sparta* Neuronal implant schematics–visual components; auditiory components; olfactory components; tactile components.

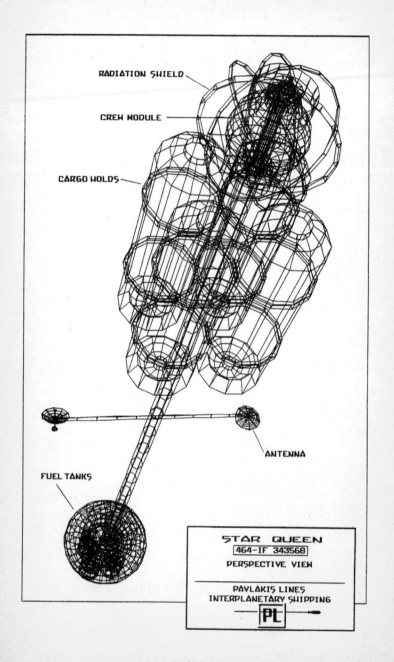

RADIATION SHIELD

CREW MODULE

CARGO HOLDS

ANTENNA

FUEL TANKS

STAR QUEEN
464-IF 343568
PERSPECTIVE VIEW

PAVLAKIS LINES
INTERPLANETARY SHIPPING
PL

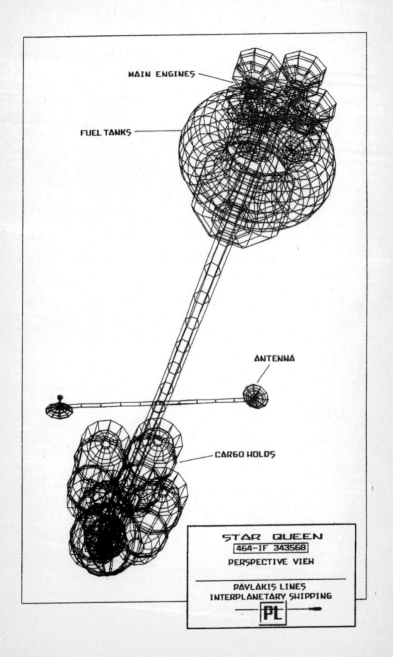

MAIN ENGINES

FUEL TANKS

ANTENNA

CARGO HOLDS

STAR QUEEN
464-IF 343568
PERSPECTIVE VIEW

PAVLAKIS LINES
INTERPLANETARY SHIPPING
PL

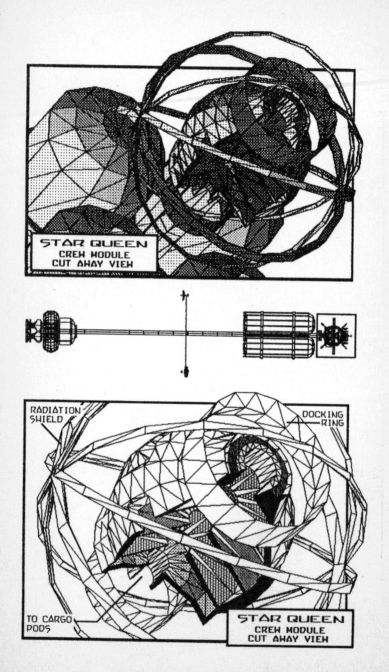

STAR QUEEN
CREW MODULE
CUT AWAY VIEW

RADIATION
SHIELD

DOCKING
RING

TO CARGO
PODS

STAR QUEEN
CREW MODULE
CUT AWAY VIEW

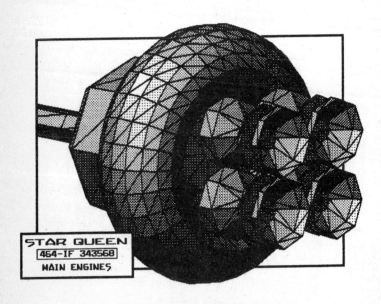

STAR QUEEN
464-IF 343568
MAIN ENGINES

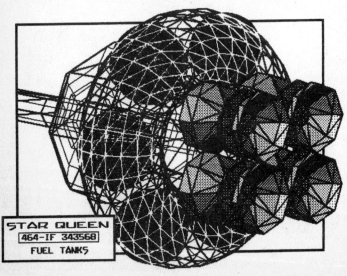

STAR QUEEN
464-IF 343568
FUEL TANKS

PORT HESPERUS

90° CUT—AWAY PERSPECTIVE VIEW.

DOCKING HUB

LOW-G RING

MAIN RING A

GARDEN SPHERE

MAIN RING B

SHUTTLE PORT

PORT HESPERUS

90° CUT-AWAY PERSPECTIVE VIEW.

319

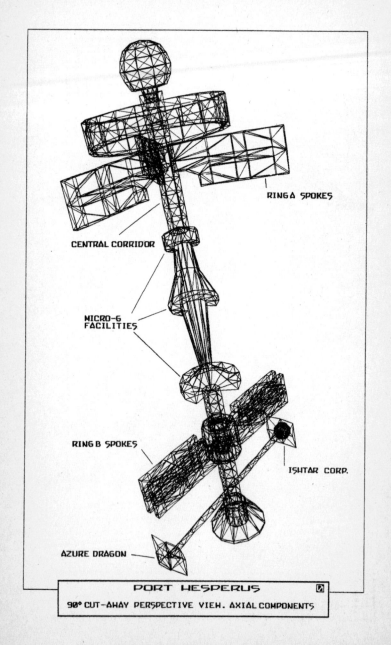

RING A SPOKES

CENTRAL CORRIDOR

MICRO-G
FACILITIES

RING B SPOKES

ISHTAR CORP.

AZURE DRAGON

PORT HESPERUS

90° CUT-AWAY PERSPECTIVE VIEW. AXIAL COMPONENTS

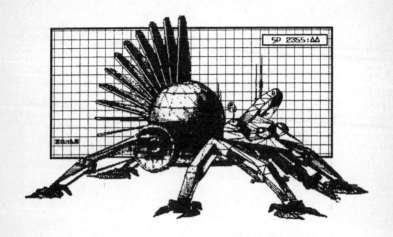

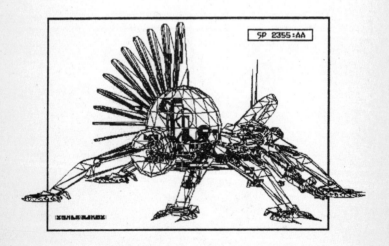

RRC
CUSTOM
ROBOTICS
DIVISION

SP 2355:AA
MINING ROBOT

CLIENT: ISHTAR CORPORATION

I.A. PAT. PEND. 237-22
238-22
244-22
245-23

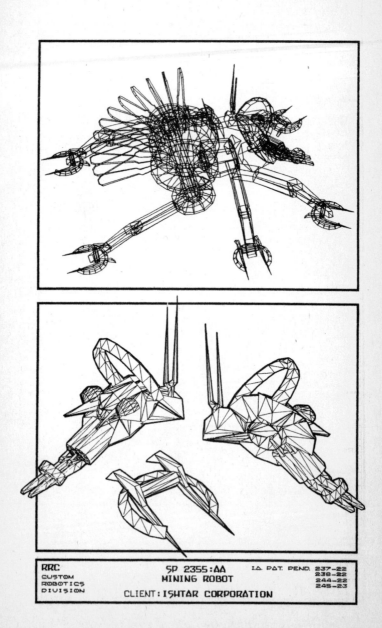

RRC
CUSTOM
ROBOTICS
DIVISION

SP 2355:AA
MINING ROBOT

CLIENT: ISHTAR CORPORATION

I.A. PAT. PEND. 237-22
238-22
244-22
245-23

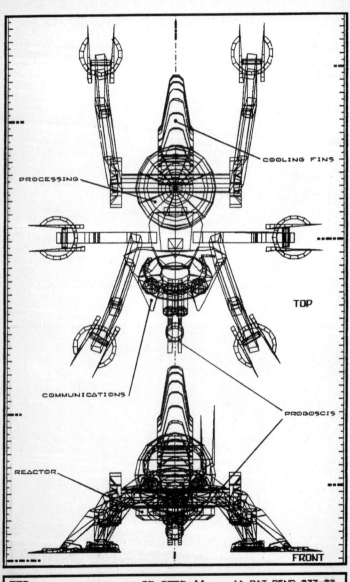

COOLING FINS

PROCESSING

TOP

COMMUNICATIONS

PROBOSCIS

REACTOR

FRONT

RRC
CUSTOM
ROBOTICS
DIVISION

SP 2355:AA
MINING ROBOT

I.D. PAT. PEND. 237-22
238-22
244-22
245-23

CLIENT: ISHTAR CORPORATION

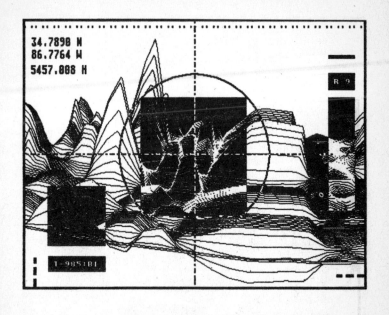

34.7890 N
86.7764 W
5457.008 H

R 9

T-985:B1

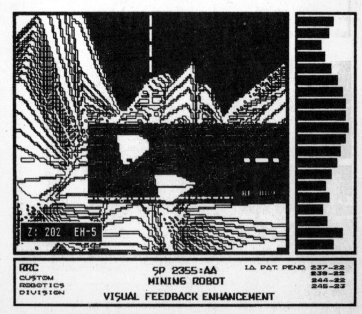

Z: 202   EH-5

RRC
CUSTOM
ROBOTICS
DIVISION

SP 2355:AA
MINING ROBOT

VISUAL FEEDBACK ENHANCEMENT

I.A. PAT. PEND. 237-22
238-22
244-22
245-23

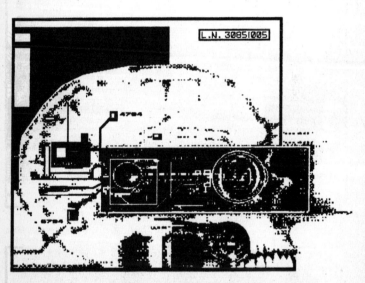

L.N. 30851005

4794

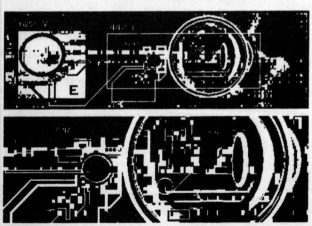

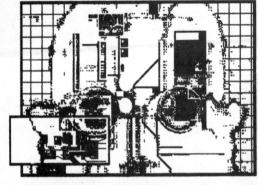

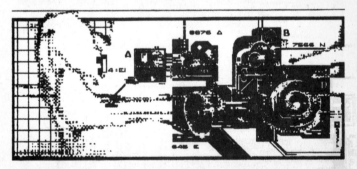

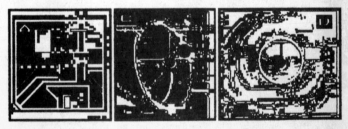

SPARTA

L.N. 30851005

SHEET 2 OF 4
INNER EAR COMPONENTS

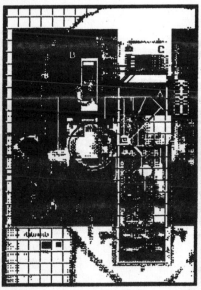
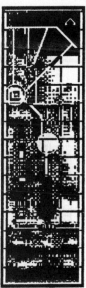
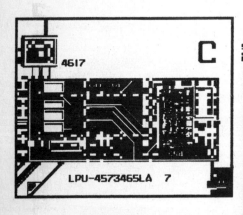
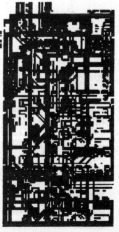

4617

C

LPU-4573465LA 7

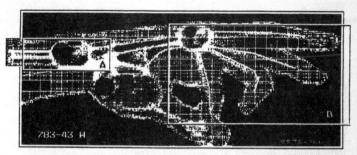

783-43 W

6S-LK

MPU-3428-L

△

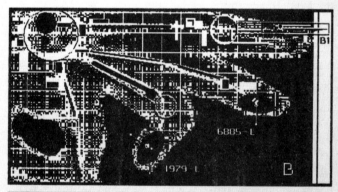

B1

6885-L

1979-L

B

B1

SPARTA

L.N. 30851005

SHEET 4 OF 4
TACTILE SYSTEMS
ELECTROMAGNETIC/INTERFACE

An Open Letter to Our Valued Readers

What do Raymond Chandler, Arthur C. Clarke, Isaac Asimov, Irving Wallace, Ben Bova, Stuart Kaminsky and over a dozen other authors have in common? They are all part of an exciting new line of **ibooks** distributed by Simon and Schuster.

 ibooks represent the best of the future and the best of the past...a voyage into the future of books that unites traditional printed books with the excitement of the web.

Please join us in developing the first new publishing imprint of the 21st century.

We're planning terrific offers for ibooks readers...virtual reading groups where you can chat on-line about ibooks authors...message boards where you can communicate with fellow readers...downloadable free chapters of ibooks for your reading pleasure...free readers services such as a directory of where to find electronic books on the web... special discounts on books and other items of interest to readers...

The evolution of the book is www.ibooksinc.com.